PRAISE FOR THE

'Alexis's latest project is a five-pa... describes as a "quincunx." Beginni... continuing through *Fifteen Dogs* (2015) and *The Hidden Keys* (2016), each book has attempted to resuscitate a forgotten or neglected genre: the pastoral, the apologue, the quest narrative. But while his work deals in paradoxes and tropes borrowed from long-dead thinkers, Alexis has time and again proven himself to be a provocative and modern thinker; his work feels ever current, even as it delivers all the humor and warmth of a well-told tale.'
— Windham Campbell Prize Citation

PASTORAL

'This novel's pleasures indeed include a rich sense of place, but that sense comes without sentimentality, and that place is something one might just as easily flee from as call home. Pastoral beauty is certainly on offer, but Alexis' fluid, evocative descriptions of the rural wonders that surround Barrow are much more than nostalgia for a childhood idyll or mere reverie for reverie's sake — they constitute the very heart of *Pastoral*'s unresolved/ unresolvable crisis of faith.'   — *The National Post*

'It's been clear since his debut novel, *Childhood*, that Alexis is one of our most distinctive and exacting prose stylists, and at its highest pitch, as in the breathtaking final paragraph, these are sentences that attain the level of the best music.'
— *Montreal Gazette*

FIFTEEN DOGS

'What does it mean to be alive? To think, to feel, to love and to envy? André Alexis explores all of this and more in the extraordinary *Fifteen Dogs*, an insightful and philosophical meditation on the nature of consciousness. It's a novel filled with balancing acts: humour juxtaposed with savagery, solitude with the desperate need to be part of a pack, perceptive prose interspersed with playful poetry. A wonderful and original piece of writing that challenges the reader to examine their own existence and recall the age old question, what's the meaning of life?'

— 2015 Giller Prize Jury Citation

'A novel about a pack of talking dogs, you say? The very idea will most likely breed thoughts of insufferable whimsy, like those paintings of mutts playing poker, or of more or less effective satire, in the vein of *Animal Farm*. It's a grand thing, then, that this spry novel by Canadian André Alexis spends its 160 pages repeatedly defying expectations ... I'm far from being a dog person, but as a book person I loved this smart, exuberant fantasy from start to finish.'

— Jonathan Gibbs, *The Guardian*

'Alexis manages to encapsulate an astonishing range of metaphysical questions in a simple tale about dogs that came to know too much. The result is a delightful juxtaposition of the human and canine conditions, and a narrative that, like just one of the dogs, delights in the twists and turns of the gods' linguistic gift.'

— *Publishers Weekly* (starred review)

'Over the course of this novel, slim yet epic in scope, Alexis chronicles the fates of these strangely afflicted beasts, shifting from thought experiment to comic parable to something more delicate, laden with detail, discovery and emotional nuance.'

— *The Globe and Mail*

THE HIDDEN KEYS

'This gorgeously written, funny adventure tale will keep readers up finishing it while also quietly breaking their hearts with Alexis's keen observations of people, kindness, and cruelty.'

— *Publishers Weekly* (starred review)

'The mystery itself does not disappoint, though the events that lead up to the reveal are as much of a gift as the endpoint itself. This unique adventure is a joyful and intelligent undertaking.'
                                                    — *Foreword Reviews*

'[An] intellectual adventure yarn ... Great fun.'
                                                    — *Wall Street Journal*

'Even though the book is an old-fashioned quest yarn, Alexis's immense talent gives it an archetypal patina, glossing characters with shades of honor and subtlety that might have been missed in lesser hands.'   — *Kirkus Reviews*

DAYS BY MOONLIGHT

'With the dream-like touch of a magical realist, Alexis carries us away on a profound and hilarious drive through small-town Ontario as it's never been seen before in search of a mysterious poet named Skennen. It's a journey where the spiritual meets the commonplace and the bizarre, the underworld comes up for air when you least expect it, and the Divine patiently watches over all. *Days by Moonlight* is a funny, moving, and wholly original take on the quest narrative that liberates the imagination with a loud whoop of joy.'
                        — 2019 Rogers Writers' Trust Fiction Prize Jury Citation

'A mash-up that is part fabulism, part faux biography, and part satire, *Days by Moonlight* conveys the experience of grief, managing to transform its inarticulable and symbolic weight into a finely wrought literary work.'   — *Quill & Quire*

'A great novel doesn't try to answer questions, but, like *Days by Moonlight*, complicates them. It's for the reader to puzzle over. An exasperated character asks, "Who knows what the writer believes?"'   — *The Globe and Mail*

Ring

ANDRÉ ALEXIS

COACH HOUSE BOOKS, TORONTO

Canadä

Published with the generous assistance of the Canada Council for the Arts and the Ontario Arts Council. Coach House Books also gratefully acknowledges the support of the Government of Canada, and the Government of Ontario through the Ontario Book Publishing Tax Credit and the Ontario Book Fund.

LIBRARY AND ARCHIVES CANADA CATALOGUING IN PUBLICATION

Title: Ring / André Alexis.
Names: Alexis, André, author.
Identifiers: Canadiana (print) 20210238712 | Canadiana (ebook) 20210238720 | ISBN 9781552454305 (softcover) | ISBN 9781770566842 (EPUB) | ISBN 9781770566859 (PDF)
Classification: LCC PS8551.L474 R56 2021 | DDC C813/.54—dc23

Ring is available as an ebook: ISBN 978 1 77056 684 2 (EPUB), 978 1 77056 685 9 (PDF)

Purchase of the print version of this book entitles you to a free digital copy. To claim your ebook of this title, please email sales@chbooks.com with proof of purchase or visit chbooks.com/digital. (Coach House Books reserves the right to terminate the free digital download offer at any time.)

for Elaine Stasiulis

The violins' mourning voices
sing above the spreading smoke:
'Give thanks to heaven,
You are alone with your love for the first time'

Anna Akhmatova, 'In the Evening'

1

AN ENGAGEMENT AND A MARRIAGE

Gwenhwyfar Lloyd disliked Tancred Palmieri at first sight. There was something unsettling about the way he observed her: as if he were staring at a blemish on her face. Then, when their eyes met, he turned away, as if he lacked conviction, which made Gwen feel even more self-conscious.

His friend Olivier, in contrast, was charming. He asked if she'd like a glass of wine and, when she said she would, a coupe of Prosecco appeared, as if it had been waiting for her.

– Is this okay? he'd asked.

And when she thanked him, he said

– My name's Olivier. And this is my friend, Tancred.

Tancred had turned to her then and smiled, his demeanour changed. Now he seemed entirely at ease, confident. And why not? The man was tall, broad-shouldered, and handsome. His skin was dark and his eyes were a bright blue.

– It's nice to meet you, he said.

All his attention was hers, briefly, before he turned toward an older woman who'd called his name.

– There you are, Tan! said the woman. We should be going soon. Ten minutes?

The woman – lively and trim – wore a black evening dress. Her red lipstick was too much, but, aside from that, she was discreet, her wealth obvious only if you recognized her accessories: white-gold Buccellati earrings and a Serpent Bohème necklace. As it happened, Gwen recognized neither the accessories nor the woman. This was Simone Azarian-Thomson, one of the inheritors of the Azarian fortune.

They were all on the top floor of the Gardiner Museum at a fundraiser for the Toronto Symphony. Simone, who had not stopped to greet or even acknowledge Gwen, was obviously in her element. She must have attended hundreds of events like this one, whereas Gwen could not help feeling out of place. Even things that should have delighted her made her uneasy. The view of the Royal Ontario Museum, for instance. How wonderful to look over at the still-unmodernized face of the building, a place her father had often taken her. In her twenty-eight years, she'd never seen the museum from quite this angle, and the ROM seemed new, wonderful. But it also felt as if she were looking down on an old friend while in the company of men in suits and women in evening wear, all of them conversing as tidbits were presented to them on silver platters: mac and cheese with truffle oil, tuna tartare on crackers, finger-shaped eggplant-and-Parmesan sandwiches.

Gwen – five feet nine, the daughter of a Welsh-born man and a woman of African descent, a 'country girl,' having grown up near Sarnia – had come to keep her friend, Nadia, company. Nadia had got tickets to the fundraiser when one of the executives in the office where she worked could not attend.

– Is it formal? Nadia had asked.

– No, it's casual, had been the answer.

Apparently, a handful of people had been told the same thing, enough of them that Gwen did not feel out of place in her black pencil skirt and dark blouse, her long, frizzy hair held up and out of her face by a navy hair band. But while there was informal wear to be seen, the fundraiser was only 'casual' the way nonchalant displays of wealth are casual.

Olivier was among those who were not flagrantly wealthy, but he was not casually dressed. There was something European about his appearance – a light growth of beard, deep-set hazel eyes, a strong jaw, his ears almost eccentric, one of them sticking out more than the other, his brown hair luxurious on top but neatly trimmed on the side – and his choice of clothes: dark grey chinos, a light-blue shirt (open at the neck), a blue jacket. And he smelled faintly, pleasingly, of sandalwood, vanilla, and citrus.

– Do you go to the symphony a lot? he asked.

Gwen admitted that she didn't, that she wished she could afford it. After that, they spoke – with an ease she found comforting – about a number of things: about music, about her preference for jazz, about her father, a working jazz pianist, about Olivier's parents, about the death of his mother, who'd been, in her time, a piano teacher, and about his admiration for Tancred, whom he'd known from childhood.

As she spoke to him, Gwenhwyfar felt herself at ease. Her self-consciousness dissipated to the point where she could composedly take in her surroundings. Yes, the fundraiser felt strange to her, the gathering a pretext for displays of wealth and standing, but so what? It was in the service of something she, too, believed in: music, which she'd learned to love through her parents. So the fundraiser was meant for someone like her as much as anyone else. This sudden feeling of 'arrival,' which she credited to Olivier, was so pleasant that she was disappointed when Tancred interrupted them.

– Gwen, he said, I'm sorry to take Ollie away from you, but we've got to go ...

He hesitated, looking into her eyes before turning away to say something to Olivier. He then turned back to her and said

— You're from Sarnia, aren't you?

She didn't want to give him the satisfaction of being right, but his rightness disarmed her.

— How did you know? she asked.

— I'll tell you next time, he said. I look forward to it.

He smiled, held up a hand in farewell, and went off. Olivier, meanwhile, apologized for leaving.

— I've enjoyed talking to you, he said. I hope we can do it again. Can I give you my number?

For the first time that evening, he sounded formal. She attributed this to his 'European' background, however, and handed him her phone. He entered his name, number, and email address and, both of them amused, they shook hands as if they'd come to a significant agreement.

Her disappointment at Olivier's going didn't last long. It didn't have the chance, because his departure left her with Nadia and the fragrant cowboy — who smelled as if a clump of lilacs had lost a round to a raft of limes — trying to pick her up. 'Cowboy' in appearance anyway: white ten-gallon hat, brown brushed-suede shoes, faded blue denim shirt, a bolo tie with a ruby clasp, black jeans, and a leather jacket. You'd have thought he came from somewhere in the American South, but Gwen had heard him say he'd come from Barrow, a small town in southern Ontario. He was in Toronto to sell sod and pigs. His outfit was for his clients, most of whom assumed farmers dressed 'country' and were reassured to find that, at least in this case, they weren't wrong.

So, Nadia had asked, what was he doing at a fundraiser for the symphony?

Well, he had a few days off, and one of his clients had offered to bring him to something 'typically Toronto,' and there you have it. His client had gone, but he'd stayed to soak up the culture, which was better than splashing around in cow shit, as he usually did.

— I thought you sold pigs, said Nadia.

– I do, said the cowboy, but that's kind of a sideline. I sell your top-class, organic grain-fed pigs. Hell, those pigs eat better than my kids. But I help with the sod farm my wife inherited and I breed cattle, too. The difference between cows and pigs is I hate cows. I can't stand the stupid things. And that's why I like coming here. You all eat a lot of beef in this city.

Gwen was immediately wary of the man. He was just the kind of 'farmer with attitude' you'd meet travelling around Lambton County, where some of her father's family lived. She could see Nadia was interested in him, though. In fact, Gwen could have predicted it. He was Nadia's type: early thirties, by the look of him, and you could tell he was in good shape. Good-looking, in a way, but not the way she liked. He was like a Sears catalogue version of the 'rugged man.' On top of that, he was not, on first impression, what you'd call bright. Or, on second thought, he was indeed bright but played at being thick in order to attract women like Nadia who preferred stupid men. Nadia preferred men who were 'slow' because she thought them unpretentious. In Gwen's experience, however, they were usually pretentious in their own ways.

Gwen had never seen her friend with a man who was her intellectual equal. A great shame, she thought. But there was no point to having that conversation with Nadia. Not again. For one thing, Nadia agreed with her. She knew herself well enough to identify her own weakness. For another, Nadia knew Gwen well enough to bring up *her* predilections: tall, sensitive, cultured. Now there was a discussion that Gwen, who'd been through a painful breakup a year and change before, did not want to have. Her ex, Roland, had been all the things Gwen found attractive. What he had failed to be was honest, considerate, or faithful. Worse, he'd acted as if it were *her* fault he slept with other women. And she'd forgiven him, and forgiven him again. She might have gone on forgiving him, but mercifully (as she now thought) he'd moved to Vancouver to be with the 'love of his life,' a conniving woman he'd been seeing while he was with her.

Nadia had seen her through the worst of all that, months and months of grief and humiliation that still seemed recent, though it was going on two years. The least she could do was support Nadia, whomever Nadia decided to be with. So it was easier to accept that men like this 'Robbie' would come and go in Nadia's life until Nadia found a man who met enough of her needs to last.

Robbie, married on top of everything else, would not last. Gwen was sure of this, but, for Nadia's sake, she smiled when he happened to look her way and feigned interest in his words.

– You know, he said, you remind me of someone. Where're you from?

– I'm from Bright's Grove, she answered.

– Oh, hell yeah! That's pretty much Sarnia. Had a friend who grew up there. Bet you were glad to get away.

He wasn't wrong, but Gwen didn't want to encourage him.

– Not really, she said.

– What do you mean? said Nadia. You couldn't wait to get out of Buzzard's Grove.

– My parents are there, said Gwen. I miss it. Besides, it's where my placenta's buried. So I've got a connection to it.

– Well, there you go, said Robbie. We've all got to come from somewhere. I'm from Barrow, born and raised. Got a wife and kids there. I can't see the good of bad-talking it. But I don't mind getting away every once in a while. Especially when I get to meet pretty women, like you two.

Under normal circumstances – that is, if she'd been alone with him – Gwen would have cringed at these words. The man had no idea how ridiculous he sounded. But Nadia was interested in him and, if she'd caught Gwen rolling her eyes, would have felt she needed to defend him, and that would have drawn the two closer. So Gwen again smiled politely.

– What do you say we go somewhere for a drink? Robbie asked.

– That's a good idea, said Nadia. Don't you think so, Gwen?

The question was delivered in a tone that left no doubt that the right answer was 'yes.' But, for her own reasons, Gwen actually did think it a good idea. She'd seen enough of the fundraiser, had taken in her share of finger food, had drunk all the Prosecco she wanted, and had spoken to no one, save Nadia and Robbie, since Olivier had gone. She'd have been happy to call it a day. But, as it seemed Nadia wasn't quite ready to be alone with the married cowboy, Gwen agreed to accompany them for a drink. She'd stay until she could plead tiredness without feeling like she'd abandoned her friend.

They walked along Bloor Street toward Brunswick. Robbie had suggested they go to the bar at the Kimpton Saint George, where he had a room. The hotel was not far from the Gardiner Museum, but neither Gwen nor Nadia wanted to drink anywhere 'fancy.' Nadia proposed instead 'one of the bars between Brunswick and Bathurst.' So Gwen found herself walking with her roommate and a man in a ten-gallon hat along a street she liked (Bloor) in a city that had pulled her into its orbit, a place that was, in her mind, the necessary opposite of Bright's Grove.

It was the kind of night that made Gwen nostalgic, bringing as it did a hint of the Toronto she'd held in her imagination in her early teens. Back then, when she visited the city with her father, Toronto seemed dangerous, fast, and thrilling. It wasn't any of those things to her now. But neither was it entirely home. She missed, for instance, the clear skies and dark night of Bright's Grove by the lake, a sky raw enough for her to make out the Big Dipper, say: Ursa Major, once a bear in someone's imagination. In contrast, the night sky above Toronto was poisoned by light, washed out.

As they passed the old school building just before Spadina, Robbie said

— That's what I like about this place: the nice old buildings. By the time anything gets this old, where I'm from, they tear it down and make a shopping mall.

(Gwen tried to picture a building in Barrow grand enough to mourn, but none came to mind.)

They went to Pauper's Pub, having passed a number of bars and taverns, all of which had appealed to Robbie. He'd have been happy, Gwen thought, anywhere there was beer and enough light by which to see it. On the other hand, she'd been amused when Nadia casually asked if Pauper's would be okay, as if the pub just happened to catch her attention. In fact, Pauper's was Nadia's favourite, a holdover from her high school years when she and her friends from Harbord Collegiate snuck in to drink.

Gwen did not like the place. It was too testosterone for her. She'd seen men drunkenly punching at each other on a number of occasions and she didn't find the tension exciting, as Nadia did. But Gwen was now used to it: the way it smelled, its layout, its menu, the beers it had on offer. She was even willing to accept that it was what Nadia called a 'Toronto establishment.' That said, she would have preferred something quieter, a place that was more, well, urbane.

— This place is nice, said Robbie. Reminds me of a bar in Sarnia. You two ever been to Lizards?

— Remind me where Sarnia is again, said Nadia.

(As if she hadn't been there herself, with Gwen.)

— It's not far from Barrow, he answered. Nice town. I'll have to take you to Lizards someday. You'd love it. It's the same as here but not as many students. Do you know Lizards, Gwen?

— It's a little after my time, she said. I left home when I was nineteen.

— I'll just have to take youse both, said Robbie, next time you're in Sarnia.

Gwen turned away from him. She'd been to Lizards. It was the kind of bar women from Lambton County went to, to meet their lovers. As there was something louche about Robbie, Lizards was just the kind of place he'd take you.

From that moment – and for a number of reasons, not just Robbie – Gwen lost interest in the evening, like letting go of a tow rope. She finished her Sleeman, apologized for being a stick-in-the-mud, and, when Nadia decided to have another round with Robbie, left the two to their own devices.

The walk home – to Palmerston, then half a block north – was unexpectedly fine. The cold air was a lens through which world and pavement were in sharp focus, and much that she liked about Toronto accompanied her: the bustle, the presence of others celebrating, talking, shouting, car horns, the lights along Bloor, the smell from its restaurants. In other words, the accumulation of details that, after nine years, were familiar and brought comfort.

It was strange, then, that her sleep was troubled. Stranger still, it was troubled by a dream of Tancred. The dream began in an erotic way. She was walking up the steps at King and Atlantic. She looked up and saw the words 'Goodlife Fitness' above her. As she looked up, she saw Tancred at the top of the steps, coming down. He was tall, beyond handsome, and, though he was wearing a white shirt, she was embarrassed because she could see his muscular chest through the fabric. In the dream, as in reality, she had only just met him, so she wasn't sure if she should greet him or not. This uncertainty deepened her embarrassment, which, in the perverse way of dreams, heightened her physical pleasure.

She'd decided, despite her embarrassment, to greet him when, in an instant, his face took on a frightening look: a mask of anger. She thought he was angry with her, but then she realized he was staring down at someone behind her. Before she could speak, Tancred had already gone past, pelting down the steps on his way to ...

Gwen never found out, because as she turned to see, she was woken by voices from the living room: laughter. When she returned to sleep, the dream world had gone on without her, taking the steps, and Tancred, with it.

The next morning, Gwen woke to the sound of a man's voice, a voice accompanied by Nadia's stifled giggles and low shushing. Nadia was trying to keep her companion quiet, and Gwen was grateful, but then it occurred to her that the voice might well belong to the man from Barrow, Robert.

She considered staying in bed until he'd gone, but curiosity got the better of her. There was, after all, a chance that Nadia had found someone else.

But it was Robert all right. He sat at the kitchen table with Nadia, his coat on the back of his chair, his ten-gallon hat on the table like a dimpled hillock.

– Gwen! he said. Welcome back to the land of the living.

And invited her to sit at her own kitchen table.

Nadia had made pancakes. A sign: she made breakfast only for men she was really interested in. So Gwen sat at the table with them for a while, accepting a cup of coffee that Robbie – 'Robert makes me sound ancient,' he said – had brewed. He'd used ground eggshells, 'the way cowhands used to,' to take the bitterness from their brew.

– It's good, Gwen said.

And meant it.

– I'm full of surprises, he answered. You just watch me!

He smiled then, and winked at Nadia.

– You can't live in the country without learning a few good tricks, he said.

Nadia looked at him happily, and that was that.

When she'd finished her coffee, Gwen went back to her room, leaving them to themselves, knowing she would hear more about Robbie than she wanted when Nadia was ready.

And that is, more or less, what happened. When Robbie had gone, Nadia knocked at the door to Gwen's bedroom. She couldn't hide her happiness, but she didn't burst into song exactly. That was not her style. Instead she asked if Gwen had thought about what she wanted for lunch. Did she have enough on her for something at one of the Korean places on Bloor?

It took only half an hour to get out of the apartment, Nadia having agreed that, as they would not be gone long, there was no need to dress up. That didn't stop Nadia from looking elegant. She was slender, four or five inches shorter than Gwen, with pale skin, dark eyebrows, brown hair. It was difficult for Gwen to imagine her as anything other than simply and attractively turned out.

They went to Imonay, sitting at a small table at the back while, all around them, people spoke and ate. The noise made conversation difficult. They sometimes had to lean forward to hear each other. Which was just as well because Nadia was, as always, unselfconsciously indiscreet, capable of spilling every detail of her night with a man. In some instances, knowing the bedroom preferences of the men Nadia slept with made it difficult for Gwen to be around them without feeling uncomfortable. Nadia expected Gwen to be just as forthcoming, but Gwen was almost incapable of sharing intimate romantic details, in part because she was not an observer of her sexual moments with men. She usually remembered feelings more than she did particulars. Except, of course, in the case of men she'd truly loved. Then the details came to her whether she wanted them or not: taste, smell, touch, motion. (She could not forget, for instance, what Roland smelled like, all his soaps coming from Penhaligon's in London, England.) But these details she stubbornly guarded, feeling almost instinctively that sharing them would diminish her experience. Not that Nadia was diminished when she was indiscreet. Nadia's indiscretion was as much a part of her personality as her elegance. And it was one of the things Gwen admired about her.

Nadia went into great detail about Robbie. To begin with, he was just plain good in bed: attentive and playful, filled with the kind of enthusiasm that could reignite your longing for pleasure. Then, too, all the work he did on his farm was wonderful for his body: pale, muscular, with dark nipples. She could hardly believe her good luck. She was happy she'd let him seduce her. His only flaw, if you could call it that, was the port-wine stain on his body, visible even in the dim light of Nadia's bedroom: a mottled glow created by the paisley scarf she draped over her bedside lamp. Actually, this birth defect, which Nadia found fascinating, was not a problem, not at all, but ...

— It's just that ...

(Here, thought Gwen, come the qualms.)

— I do have doubts about married men, you know.

— You always say that, said Gwen. Why don't you stop sleeping with married men if it bothers you?

— I don't sleep with married men. They sleep with me. Anyways, I don't sleep with them *because* they're married. I sleep with interesting people.

— You find Robbie interesting?

— He certainly *is* interesting. Anyone that good in bed is always interesting.

They'd been down this road before. In fact, it seemed to Gwen that Nadia's conscience — if it was a matter of conscience — needed this conversation, this exact conversation, as a salve, and it was Gwen's duty as her friend to remember her lines.

— But that's just a matter of technique, said Gwen. He's good at this one thing. Why does that make him interesting anywhere else but in bed?

— It's not like he's a plumber, said Nadia. Just because we say someone's good in bed and pretend it means *one* thing doesn't mean it means only one thing. 'Good in bed' means more things than you can name. It's not just mechanics, you know. It's mysterious, and mystery's always interesting!

— But what's any of that got to do with married men?

– I like to sleep with interesting men, said Nadia. It's not my fault some of them are married. Their wives should take better care of them.

– You know you don't mean that, said Gwen. What would you do if a man you loved and trusted had an affair?

(Here, to Gwen's chagrin, she could recall the look on Roland's face as he told her he'd met the 'love of his life,' as if he'd just met her, though it turned out he'd been sleeping with her as long as he'd been sleeping with Gwen, and as if he expected her to be happy for him.)

– I'd kill him, said Nadia.

Despite herself, Gwen was amused. They'd reached this very point in so many similar conversations that she'd have been surprised if Nadia had answered differently. On the other hand, she was – as always! – secretly delighted by Nadia's words, though it was her role, here, to disapprove.

– You know that's ridiculous, right? she said.

– What's ridiculous? Other women should take better care of their husbands if they don't want them fooling around. But I'm not going to marry any old Joe. I'm not marrying anyone who's not my friend, and there's no way a close friend would betray me.

– And if they did?

– If they did, it'd be proof they weren't my friend. So I'd be killing a stranger.

– But people change! Sometimes they fall out of love.

– It's got nothing to do with love, said Nadia. I wouldn't marry someone just because I love them. What's the point of that? Love's too unpredictable. When I marry someone, it'll be someone I respect who respects me!

As if that ever helped anyone, thought Gwen. People fall out of respect as easily as they fall out of love. Maybe more easily. Because once you live with a person, once you learn their bad habits, you can lose respect before you lose love. How many of their married friends remained with partners who embarrassed them, partners who had terrible habits, partners who repulsed them a little? Yet there they were, still married and, in some cases, just as much 'in love.' The death of respect could certainly corrode a relationship. Then again, did anyone truly marry out of respect? Or was it respect *and* something: respect and love, respect and money, respect and social standing?

It was no use telling Nadia any of this, of course. She wouldn't hear it. Respect, for Nadia, was a higher ideal, and whenever Gwen said anything against the idea, Nadia inevitably told her that she didn't understand. She *couldn't*, if she didn't see how respect for another was a higher virtue than love. It seemed to Gwen, though, after much reflection, that Nadia was trying to turn an irrational feeling (love) into something she could control, something rationally given (respect).

For all her talk about respect, Nadia inevitably defended her bad decisions about men by saying that she had thought she was in love. She spoke of respect. She often said that, up until now, respect had escaped her, that one day she and a man would come to a place of mutual respect and be happy. But as far as Gwen could tell, there was no difference between how Nadia felt about respect and how others felt about love. It seemed a matter of terminology.

– Anyway, said Nadia, Robbie's not really married.

– It's amazing, said Gwen, how many of your married men aren't married.

– You don't *have* to be judgmental, you know.

Nadia had been moved by Robbie's story. She'd heard similar stories, but she could tell when people meant what they said, and Robbie had been genuine. His wife did not love him. He'd tried everything to recapture the love they'd shared. They'd been childhood sweethearts. He'd married for love and, at his wedding, he could not (he said) have imagined himself unfaithful. And yet, for some reason, shortly after he'd married Liz —now, *there* was a name Nadia mistrusted, all the Lizes in her life had been miserable — the woman had turned cold. It had been all he could do, before their children were born, to regain her affection. But after their second boy arrived, she'd turned away from him so completely that they no longer even slept together.

— Why doesn't he leave her, if he's so unhappy?

— He loves his children. He doesn't want to leave them without the influence of a man in their lives. You know, Gwen, Robbie's a good man, even if you can't get past his being married. Yes, technically he's married, but does that mean he has to live without affection?

— You make it sound like you're a social worker! And, anyway, you only heard his side of the story. Do you think his wife would tell the same story he does about their marriage?

— Well, there's no use talking about it if you're going to be closed-minded. And you know what's funny about this? He only said nice things about you. How you're a good person. How he thought you'd be a good friend.

For a moment, despite herself, Gwen was pleased by this second-hand praise.

— You know, she said, it's not really about Robbie. I don't like him or dislike him. I just don't trust him, even if he is good to his kids. I know what you're like after a breakup and I'm concerned for your sake. That's all I'm saying. I don't trust him, and I don't like the 'I'm so friendly' vibe. Not just his — anybody's.

— You didn't mind the friendly vibe from the guy last night! At the Gardiner. What was his name? Olivier?

— That's not the same, said Gwen. He wasn't overly friendly. He was being kind. And he's not married! Anyway, you didn't even talk to him.

— Well, said Nadia, whatever. But I appreciate your advice.

The truth was, of course, more complicated. Nadia appreciated *and* mistrusted Gwen's advice. But she listened to it, as Gwen listened to hers, because each understood and trusted the other.

Though it was not what she'd imagined herself doing in Toronto, Gwen had settled into the job she now held. She was a research associate at Toronto General Hospital, working for three geriatricians – Drs. Bellmar, Lewis, and Montgrove – for whom she prepared grant applications, coordinated the research they oversaw, and maintained their web presence: mostly to do with a website that provided resources for the families of people with Alzheimer's and dementia.

It was honourable work and she was pleased to be part of an endeavour that felt necessary, one that was demonstrably useful. For instance, they devised strategies for getting people with dementia to stop driving. If she'd been asked why she hoped to find something better, she'd have objected to the word *better*. She might even have hesitated to bring up her own aspirations. But the truth was, she'd studied child psychology. She'd written her master's thesis on D. W. Winnicott. She hoped to do research on early-episode psychosis. The work she was doing now brought her no closer to that.

So, for all that she respected her colleagues, Gwen felt out of place. It was like being in a room you loved in a house that wasn't yours: awkward at times. Not that she suffered. She wasn't the kind who brooded. But she was aware of a disconnect between her life and her ambitions, and it felt like she was drifting; drifting in the right direction, but still adrift.

Nadia had once said that Gwen lived as if she were looking for something.

– And you're *not* looking for something? Gwen had asked.

– Of course I am, Nadia answered. But I know what I'm looking for: a man who's my friend, a house in Rosedale, enough money to live the way I want, a Mini Cooper, and my own column in the *Globe and Mail*.

– Nothing higher? asked Gwen. Like something spiritual?

– What do you mean? said Nadia. Having my own column would be spiritual.

Nadia had been joking about the *Globe and Mail*, but Gwen had taken her friend's point: it did feel, even to her, as if she were waiting for something. In fact, she'd had that very feeling from her early childhood. That said, she had lately been feeling as if something were on her horizon: an encounter, a discovery, an event. And it was in this mood that, two days after the fundraiser, she texted Olivier Mallay.

Seeing his name in her phone, the first face she imagined was, in fact, Tancred's. But when she recalled Olivier's good looks and European manner, she texted to ask how his evening after the fundraiser had gone. He responded by inviting her for an evening out, and she agreed to meet him at Café Polonez, a restaurant on Roncesvalles.

Roncesvalles wasn't far, but it wasn't close either: five subway stops and a streetcar. If she'd known him better, Gwen would have suggested somewhere along College, somewhere near the ghost of Bar Italia, say. But Roncesvalles had its good points. The street, from Howard Park to the Queensway, was pleasant, its Polish roots showing here and there: European delicatessens, Polish restaurants, a church dedicated to John Paul II. Then, too, in her mind, the neighbourhood closed down somewhere around ten o'clock at night, and the bars that stayed open late were uninviting exceptions. The street's early shutdown meant that, if things were not going well with Olivier, she'd have reason to call it a night early.

Olivier was tall and athletic in build. He was also tasteful in his dress. Beneath his dark winter coat, he wore a salmon-coloured shirt with a button-down collar. He had on recently pressed dark grey pants, with a belt whose buckle was discreet but interesting: an alpha (α) and an omega (o) separated by a thin sword, all within a small silver circle. His shoes looked as though they'd never been worn. They glimmered.

In a word, there was a precision to him, which was odd because Olivier himself did not feel like the kind of man you'd call precise.

She felt from him both kindness and good humour. His smile, for instance, was lovely, as if mocking himself. So, while his exterior was intimidating, the man himself was not. Gwen found this an interesting – but not exactly pleasing – conflict of impressions. Something about the clash of outward and inward reminded her of her ex and, despite herself, she was uncomfortable. She was not uncomfortable enough to leave, though. In part because he was good company.

Olivier was aware of his feelings and happy to share them. For instance, he was happy to admit his relief that here, in this small restaurant, Gwen was the same as the woman he'd spoken to at the Gardiner Museum. He'd felt immediately at ease on seeing her – as though they were tacitly complicit, as if Gwen was as skeptical about the business of dating as he was.

He also admitted to being practical. He accepted that it was better to observe conventions since, for the most part, their observance was something strangers looked for. It was a convention, for instance, that men dressed well if they wanted to make a good impression. And it was accepted – in certain quarters anyway – that women enjoyed a man who took care of himself, one who was confident, one who could make them laugh. Then again, all of that went out the window if the man was too well dressed, too anxious to make an impression. It needed balance, and Olivier dealt with it by trying to keep his emotions out of the equation for as long as he could. The precision Gwen felt from him – the conflict – was this withdrawal of his emotions in order to get things 'right.'

By contrast, Gwen had dressed well, but not as Nadia had advised her: nothing low-cut or revealing, nothing that spoke of desperation, and no makeup save a light-red lipstick. At the sight of Olivier, and hearing him talk about clothes, she did feel underdressed: blue jeans, long-sleeved black blouse, large hoop earrings. The self-consciousness was not painful, but it was there, and it was like another small barrier between them.

– Do you like Polish food? he asked.

– I kind of do, she equivocated. You don't?

– I do, he lied.

From there the conversation drifted forward, each speaking of things they liked. Gwen told him about her fondness for painting (this was her mother's influence), the music of Cecil Taylor, and the films of Pedro Almodóvar – her favourite being *All about My Mother*. She did not feel awkward telling him these things, because she assumed he was a man who liked the things she did: music, film, and painting.

And she was right.

Olivier claimed that, where art was concerned, he was at a disadvantage. But this was only strategy. He did not like to admit, so early in a relationship, to his wide knowledge of the arts, his almost professional appreciation for them. He'd found that his way of talking about the arts could sometimes intimidate. But hearing that Gwen's father was a musician and that her life had been as full of music as his, Olivier did admit to his knowledge of music. In fact, he unashamedly loved it, admired its closeness to mathematics, appreciated its emotional comforts, took pleasure in its dynamics. He *trusted* music, feeling that he could give himself over to it without suspicions or reservations. It was odd, then, that music triggered the first – and, as it happened, only – acknowledged moment of contention between them. Rather than talk about his feelings for Ravel's *Tombeau de Couperin*, Olivier mentioned that he found it interesting that Ravel was, supposedly, atheist.

– Do you really find that interesting? Gwen asked.

– I really do, he answered. *Le Tombeau de Couperin* is so playful, I wonder if someone who believed in an afterworld and demons could have written it.

– Are you an atheist? she asked. Do you think this is all there is to life?

– What more could there be? asked Olivier. All the afterworlds I've heard of are just continuations of this one. To me, it sounds awful. I mean, the birds are bigger and they talk. And the one in charge is very kind. But, other than that, what is there?

Gwen looked up to see if he were pulling her leg about God.

– You don't have to believe in an afterlife to believe in God, Gwen answered. I don't know what comes after all this, but I hope it's not more of the same *or* nothingness. When my grand-mother died, it felt like there was someone on the other side waiting for me. It didn't make Grammy's death easier, but I've thought about death differently since she died.

– I feel something like that, said Olivier. But for me, it's more that nothing waits for me and I find the idea of this coming nothing comforting. Anyway, this is the only world I'm interested in.

Gwen did not disapprove of his ideas. It was fine by her if atheists thrived. Maybe it was even for the best, any struggle with the divine being holy, even the struggle to be free of divinity. But she did wonder if she could love – really love – anyone who thought life so shadowless. What about all our experience? What about our love and the love of those who love us? Do the feelings we had for those we love die when they do? Did they die with us? Do we take nothing from the dead? Does their love for us perish with them? How pointless love seemed if it were not transcendent, if it were not more than we are, if it were not passed on, like a currency – or perhaps a current – between the living and the dead.

– I don't believe in ghosts and curses, said Gwen, but it's hard to believe there's nothing more to us than our time on earth.

– I get that it brings you comfort, answered Olivier. But the idea of divine generosity disturbs me. I'd rather believe in chance than God.

When Gwen next looked at her phone, it was almost nine o'clock. Still relatively early. They'd been talking for two hours, and the time had passed pleasantly. There was no reason to leave but then again, neither was there reason to stay. She wouldn't have refused to see him again. She wouldn't hurt his feelings.

She could, she thought, be friends with Olivier. Maybe even more, depending on her second impression. He was smart, charming, honest, and he was the kind of handsome that made you wonder if you *should* go further. Nadia would have gone further. In fact, it seemed to her that Nadia and Olivier would be a good match. It would do Nadia good to be with an unmarried man.

– Well, she said, it's getting late. I've got work to do around the house tomorrow.

– Oh! answered Olivier. Can I drive you home?

Handsome, smart, and considerate. Maybe she really *should* reconsider. He seemed to find her attractive and, after so long without it, the thought of touching and being touched was not unwelcome. So why did her desire for Olivier feel so theoretical? It was more like something she ought to feel than something she did. Was it that the ease she felt in his presence was not erotic enough? Or was it that some part of her wanted to wait for someone else?

(Here, Reader, we should note a fleeting thought that came to Gwen as Olivier asked to drive her home: he hadn't exactly been pursuing her. He'd been friendly, charming, considerate, but it had felt as if they were *both* waiting for something or someone.)

– No thanks, she answered. I'll just get on the King car to Dundas West.

– I'll wait with you then, he said.

She tried to pay for her share of the bill, but he put the full amount, plus tip, in the waitress's hand before she could take the money from her purse, and he declined to take it from her.

– Unless it offends you to have me pay, he said.

It didn't offend her. She'd have preferred to pay for herself, but you could see he was being kind.

They were waiting at the stop by Fermanagh – the night cold, the street lights haloed – when Olivier was hailed.

– Ollie!

It was Tancred and, with him, an older gentleman.

At the sight of Tancred, Gwen felt a face-warming embarrassment. Her night-thoughts of him had been so intense that desire made the transit from dream to reality before she could catch herself. It felt as if she'd done something wrong. In defiance of these feelings, she refused to look away from him, smiling politely – or what she hoped was politely – as she took in his face.

To Olivier, Tancred said

– What a surprise! I'm only ever on Roncy to see Alex. You know he's on Glendale now, don't you?

Olivier was pleased at the sight of his friend, and he seemed just as happy to see the man with him.

– I did know, he answered, but I haven't seen the new place yet.

Olivier mock-bowed at the older man.

– Sire! he said.

– It's young master Ollie, said the man. Handsome as Adonis!

Then, addressing Gwen:

– Have you been swooning, young lady? I don't see how you could avoid it in such company.

Now, Olivier to Gwen:

– Tancred you've already met, he said. And this is Alexander von Würfel. Alex, Gwenhwyfar.

– Guinevere is it? said von Würfel. A beautiful name for a lovely young woman.

Gwen recognized the man. Alexander von Würfel was the so-called 'Postmodernist Taxidermist,' an artist whose work she sometimes confused with that of Charles Pachter, having been introduced to their art at the same time and there being large moose in the work of both.

– Alex and I were going to hit Tennessee for a drink, said Tancred. Why don't you two join us?

– I think, said Olivier, Gwen has work tomorrow.

Though Olivier was being thoughtful, Gwen was annoyed with him. It wasn't his place to speak for her. She thought of contradicting him. But then she'd actually have to go out, and she was, frankly, tired and a little overwhelmed: by Tancred, by von Würfel, maybe even by Olivier.

– I'm sorry, she said, I've got things to do tomorrow.

Alexander von Würfel said

– I have a better idea. Why don't you three come to my house. It's just a few streets over, and young Ollie can finally learn how a true gentleman lives.

– The place is a jungle, said Tancred. The paintings are almost falling out the windows.

Then, addressing Gwen:

– You should see it, he said. It's impressive.

Now Gwen was annoyed with herself. She'd said no to carrying on with Olivier. It would, she felt, be rude to suddenly show enthusiasm for someone else's company. So, even though she would have been happy to see von Würfel's work, out of consideration for Olivier's feelings she again declined.

– I can also offer, said von Würfel, a full range of corn chips, both broken and whole.

Well, what could you say after that?

The house on Glendale was spacious. It had recently been gutted and renovated so that the first floor could be an artist's studio, with a small kitchen and small bedroom. As Tancred had told them, it was filled with paintings and other works of art. They were everywhere and in various stages of completion. A number of the older pieces were, as was von Würfel's wont, paintings of animals. But a significant number were portraits of his daughters and his grandchildren. In particular, he seemed intrigued by his youngest grandchild's ear. There were sketches, watercolours, and paintings of the child, all featuring extremely realistic ears.

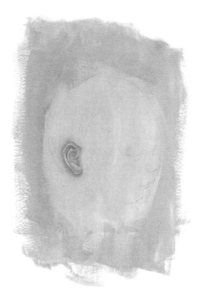

– I'm fixated on Jaakko's ear, he said. The way it sticks out, it's almost exactly like my father's.

The second floor was where von Würfel lived, when he wasn't in his studio. It was almost as spare as the first floor. Von Würfel, clearly, did not much care for furniture or ornamentation. On this floor, too, there were works of art – paintings, sketchbooks, installation pieces. These were not his own, however. Here, where he lived and entertained, von Würfel had works by his friends and contemporaries – from Janice Gurney and AA Bronson to Cathy Daley and Liz Magor. And though Gwen had been impressed by von Würfel's workspace, this second floor was the one that amazed her. In its untidiness and abundance, it left such an impression of vitality.

When they had seen all there was to see, von Würfel brought out four small glasses – not much bigger than shot glasses – and poured each of them a ginger brandy that he had made himself: sweet, tasting of vanilla and ginger. It stung her lips and throat as she sipped it.

Gwen felt entirely at ease. This was like a gathering of her parents' friends – musicians, mostly – who visited them in Bright's Grove and spent hours talking about art and politics. More charming still: von Würfel was an old-school left-winger, one step away from being communist, as a number of her parents' friends had been. To Gwen, this was an invitation to talk back, to argue, which she did. Another surprise: Tancred, who she'd assumed was aloof, was warm and open and clearly loved Alexander von Würfel. Tancred was also well-versed in leftist politics without, it seemed, being leftist himself. He happily bantered with von Würfel over the merits of Justin Trudeau, whom both (in the end) mistrusted, leaving Gwen and Olivier to defend the prime minister.

An entertaining evening with Olivier had become a wonderful one with Olivier, Tancred, and von Würfel. So amusing was it that she was disappointed when, after two hours, von Würfel himself pleaded tiredness and called it a night.

– For someone who was tired, he said to her, you've turned out to be very lively!

He bowed then and kissed her hand as she was leaving.

Feeling revived and stimulated by the company, Gwen decided to walk to Dundas West station. Olivier, his car parked somewhere on Fern, asked if he could drive her to the subway. But she declined, kissing him on the cheek to thank him for a lovely evening. Tancred, who was also going to Dundas West, decided to walk with her, embracing Olivier as they parted.

The Christmas lights, the creche at St. Vincent de Paul, the snow on the ground ... it all made Roncesvalles seem even quainter than usual. For a block or so, Gwen and Tancred were quiet. But then Gwen remembered that Tancred had guessed she was from Sarnia. She asked him how he knew.

– Your accent, said Tancred, is exactly like a woman I went out with, and she was from Sarnia. It was kind of a shock hearing your voice. I didn't know if I should talk to you or not. But then

I thought, 'That means you can't talk to anyone who sounds like they're from Sarnia,' which seemed excessive.

– How many people from Sarnia have you met exactly? asked Gwen.

– Well, two so far, said Tancred, but you never know.

They laughed, less at Tancred's words than at the pleasure of walking together along the quiet street. Gwen was curious about the woman from Sarnia.

– Were you in love with her? she said.

Had she asked Olivier a similar question, he'd have answered in detail, no doubt. But Tancred was not Olivier. She looked up and saw what she thought of as an enigmatic smile. He said yes, without sounding upset or regretful. But he immediately changed the subject, asking her about what she did for a living and then telling her that he himself was between jobs and wasn't sure what he would do when he returned to work.

– I wish I had work like yours, he said. It must be good to know you're helping people.

– What did you do before you stopped working? she asked.

– Me? he answered. Nothing interesting. Odd jobs. Whatever I could find. I'd lost my way, really. If I hadn't got an inheritance, I'd probably still be lost.

He didn't look like a man who'd ever lost his way. There was a calm to him that she associated with arrival and strength, with knowing where you are and what you want. And Gwen found this assumption of arrival very pleasant.

She would have liked to ask him more about his present life, about whether or not he missed working, but instead they talked about Alexander von Würfel, a father figure of Tancred's, and before she knew it they were at Bloor and Dundas West and she still felt like walking with him. But it was now almost midnight. She was tired and happy, and this is why she made what she came to think of as a misstep.

As they sat together in the subway car – she on her way to Bathurst, he to St. George – Tancred asked if she'd enjoyed her date with Olivier. For the reasons mentioned above and because she was caught up in the unexpected pleasure of the night, Gwen answered that she'd had a *wonderful* time with Olivier and that he was great company.

– He's a great catch, she added.

This wasn't untrue, but what she meant was 'He'd be a great catch for someone else.' Nor had she meant to be quite so enthusiastic in her praise. Her words had an immediate effect on Tancred. She could feel him withdraw, as if to make room for his friend. It wasn't unpleasant, because all his affection for Olivier came out in his praise of the man.

– I'm so glad to hear you say that, he said. Ollie really would be a great catch.

He told her then about how they'd met and where and when. And as the train stopped at Bathurst station, he smiled at her and said

– It was really nice seeing you again.

He stood up and chastely hugged her goodbye. The feel and smell of him was intoxicating. Then she was standing on the subway platform, the train pulling out of the station. She thought to wave at him if he looked up as his car passed, but he did not. And she was left with the disorienting feeling that Olivier's interest in her was less than it seemed, while Tancred's lack of interest was more.

The man from Barrow, Robbie Myers, was back in town and, against Gwen's advice, Nadia was seeing him. More than seeing him: Robbie was a few rent payments short of being a roommate, his suitcase poised in their living room, beside the sofa.

Gwen could not decide if it was there to reassure her that Robbie was in transit, or to remind her that, whatever her feelings about it, Robbie had a place in their apartment. In either case, she found the arrangement annoying. She now had to be conscious of what she wore when she left her bedroom, circumspect in her behaviour, like a guest in her own home. She would have complained about the state of affairs — was *about* to complain — but, during the second week he was with them, Gwen and Robbie spoke together, alone.

It was mid-week, a Tuesday evening before Christmas, when Nadia was working late. This was not unusual, as Mr. Wiseman, head of Midori Gold Mining, was both lazy and demanding, while Nadia, his executive assistant, was conscientious and generous. Gwen did not get home until after seven, having treated herself to a falafel plate at Ali Baba's. And she was surprised to discover, on pushing the front door open, that the apartment was dark and quiet.

She felt relief and a sensation she suddenly realized she missed: coming home, knowing that the outside world was, well, outside. The feeling was so pleasant that, as she turned on the lights in the front hall, she allowed herself a defiant belch and, tossing her keys on the kitchen table, imagined the metallic jangle they made as a kind of mechanical birdsong. She'd hung up her coat, placed her boots in the closet, and was unbuttoning her blouse on the way to her bedroom when something gleamed from the living room. The gleaming — from Robbie's cellphone, as it happened — was followed by a sigh. Startled, Gwen turned on the living room lights and there was the man himself, sitting up on the sofa, dressed as if to go out, boots and coat on.

— Why are you sitting in the dark? she asked.

It took him a moment to react, and in that moment Gwen saw that Robbie was in tears. Though it felt unkind, she could not help thinking of a rodeo clown. There were, first, the cowboy boots. Then: his face was pale, save for the blotches of red on his cheeks. Then, too: his leather coat was unzipped, revealing a blue shirt, as if black fruit had been cut to reveal an indigo pith.

– I didn't know it was dark, he said.

Now, what could you say to that? Gwen would have laughed, but he was clearly unhappy.

What's wrong? she asked.

– I'm no good at anything, he said.

Although she heard the distress in his voice, Gwen was still wary. There was so much about the situation that made it difficult for her to sympathize. The man was here, in her apartment, lamenting his life while, as far as she knew, being unfaithful to the mother of his children. She wondered what exactly the poor woman would feel if she heard him complaining. Suddenly annoyed, she almost asked him about his wife. But he mentioned her first.

– I'm a lousy husband. I'm a bad father. I can't do anything right.

She thought: at least he's thinking about his family. So, despite her wariness, she engaged with him.

– Why are you having an affair, she asked, if you care so much about your wife?

– It's not what you think, he answered.

Then, because it almost certainly *was* what she thought, his anguish left and sincerity overtook him.

– It's not like I want this, he said.

What he meant was the usual thing, really: he was unfortunate, he was misunderstood, he was in search of the love he could no longer find at home. The story was the one she'd already heard from Nadia and, despite Robbie's sincerity, it did not move her. But, as she listened, a question – an old question – came to her: how could he treat love, if it truly was love, this way?

– You know, she said at last, it doesn't sound like love, what you're describing. I don't think I could sleep with anyone else if I was in love with someone.

– That's what everyone says, he answered. But it's never been that easy for me. I've been in love with two women at the same time. I felt the same thing with both of them, and I couldn't help wanting them both. Is that because something's wrong with me?

— Why don't you try to work something out with your wife?

— Liz is leaving me, he answered. It took her a long time to get there, but I know her. Once she decides something, it's decided.

For some reason, this thought seemed to comfort him. Sighing, he said

— I guess I should tell Liz I get it, and get on with my life.

— You should do what your heart tells you to do, she said.

Yes, what else were there but rank clichés? She had no guidance to offer and no answers to give. That left nothing but sympathy, a sympathy she didn't feel. What she felt was grateful not to be in Robbie's predicament. Then again, how would she be in Robbie's situation? She was not Roland, not the type to fall in love with more than one person at a time.

— My heart, said Robbie, is the reason I'm in this mess.

The emotion in the man's voice did, finally, touch her. She gave him the benefit of the doubt and accepted that his remorse was genuine. In any case, it is difficult to be wary of someone who's made themself vulnerable.

Yes, but how treacherous the tactics of vulnerability can be! To be vulnerable is a plea for mercy at times, certainly, but isn't it also a weapon of final resort, a kind of charm? Had Robbie opened up because he knew she minded his invasion of the apartment and wanted her sympathy? Honestly, it made you wonder if vulnerability and charm were interchangeable. So, no sooner had her feelings for Robbie softened than she was again wary.

She was going to say something about the heart (its integrity, its resilience, etc.), when Nadia came home: front door closing behind her with a startling clack, keys jangling. And that was the end of Gwen's first meaningful conversation with Robbie. However, the thoughts the conversation provoked were still with her two weeks later, when she came back from Bright's Grove.

It was a Friday in early January.

Gwen had been home for Christmas and her birthday. She had come back to Toronto by bus, the sight of the CN Tower affording her the usual feeling of reconciliation. Whatever her problems and concerns, she almost inevitably felt a kind of optimism on returning to the city. The feeling was tinged with regret at leaving her parents behind, but she had never yet felt the desire to stay home or return there to live. Rather, she wondered if her mother, Helen, would ever leave Bright's Grove. Alun, her father, was the opposite. He travelled the world, playing piano wherever he was invited. More than that, when she was a child, Alun and Gwen would go on the most wonderful excursions around the province: to eat ice cream in Toronto, to a TiCats game in Hamilton, to Storybook Gardens in London. Helen had never joined them, agoraphobic as she was. Or 'agoraphobic' — in quotation marks — as Gwen thought it. Her mother had long ago admitted, after swearing her to secrecy, that she was not agoraphobic — or not exactly — and that, in any case, she had her reasons.

Not that Gwen hated Bright's Grove or southern Ontario. Her father had grown up in the country and was (or pretended to be) enraptured by the smell of cow shit. Gwen enjoyed teasing him about it, but she loved the smell of it, too, and she was enraptured by the land in spring, driving down the small hills on the way to Petrolia, say, the trees pushing forth their first greenery, as if in sympathy with the new grasses, the sky above them a pale, pale blue and, at least in memory, the clouds scarce but white above the world. So why had she dreamed of leaving Bright's Grove years and years before leaving it?

At least part of the answer was there on Dundas Street.

She was walking toward the Eaton Centre, and the smells from the restaurants along Dundas were like exhalations from variously scented worlds. She was on her way to nowhere in particular, led by the vague feeling that Nordstrom's, still new to her, was there to explore, and by the thought that there were post-Christmas sales to be had. That was Dundas in a nutshell, for her twenty-nine-year-old self: a stretch of road, from Spadina to Yonge, that dealt in different tastes and smells and led past the art gallery with its ship-like facade and on to the rush of bodies, voices, and sound as you reached the Eaton Centre. There was nowhere in Sarnia that made her feel this way.

As she reached Yonge, she looked up and was momentarily captivated by the view looking south: the still new vacancy that was Dundas Square, the lights from the Eaton Centre, the restaurants and stores on either side of Yonge, the dark patch to the south that was an intimation of the lake.

It was in this moment of reverie that she heard her name
— Gwen?
and saw Tancred approaching her.

Startled, Gwen's first reaction was alarm. After that, however, there was relief and delight. She suddenly realized how much she'd been thinking of him, even in all the foofaraw of Christmas and New Year's.

— Tancred! she said. What are you doing here?
— I'm on my way to meet Ollie and Simone, he answered. You know, it's funny. I was just wondering how you were doing. I was going to ask Ollie, but here you are and I can ask you myself. Actually, if you're not in the middle of anything, why don't you come to the restaurant with me? Ollie will be happy to see you and you can meet Simone.

Gwen wondered if Olivier really would be happy to see her. They hadn't spoken or texted since their evening with Alexander von Würfel. No doubt because they'd both been busy. But, in any case, she was more interested in how Tancred felt on seeing her.

— I was just thinking about dinner, she said.

(The words were fine. Though she wasn't hungry, they sounded true. Besides, reminded of her walk with Tancred to Dundas West station, she was happy at the thought of spending time with him, and with Olivier, too.)

– But I'm not dressed for anything fancy. Is that okay?

– You look fantastic, he said. There is no issue.

Then, as if he'd said more than he'd meant to, he smiled – caught, but not apologetic.

– It'll be interesting, Tancred continued. It's at one of Simee's favourite restaurants, and the chef's famous. To be honest, I never know what I think about the places Simee likes. They're always over the top, but she and Ollie are great company. I'll just let her know I'm bringing a guest.

After he'd texted Simone, they took an Uber to the corner of King and Portland. She'd have liked to talk to him as they drove, but the driver was proudly French – flags of France were sewn to the headrests in front of them – and blasted his music as they drove. It was music Tancred recognized from his childhood: 'Élégance' by Alain Bashung followed by 'C'est comment qu'on freine.' His mother had been a devoted fan of Bashung's. And Tancred was so obviously pleased to hear the music that Gwen hadn't the heart to ask the driver to turn it down.

As they stood at the corner of King and Portland, it occurred to Gwen that she knew of no 'fancy' restaurants in the vicinity. There was Buca, of course, and the Keg was not far, but neither of them came to mind when you thought 'over the top.' But then, just east of what used to be the Bier Markt, Tancred led her down an alley, then held open the door to a bar named Queen Anne's Corset, a place she'd never heard about.

The bar's exterior was unremarkable, its heavy, rusty door almost indistinguishable from alleyway doors anywhere. It had, however, one salient feature: where a doorknob or handle might have been, there was instead an oversized but lifelike replica of a human hand, in the up-facing palm of which were imprinted two ones and, below them, the name of the place:

11
Queen Anne's Corset

The interior of the bar was stylish but underwhelming. To begin with, once you descended a half-dozen stone steps, you walked through an open door into a space that was some fifteen yards long and ten yards wide: blue-tiled floor, white subway tiles beginning near waist height. To the right of the entrance, along the entire length of the room, there was a hardwood bar behind which there was a bartender: a woman (perhaps) in a white shirt and black pants. There were, on the shelves behind the bartender, hundreds of bottles of spirits. In the bar room, there were three round tables at which three couples sat drinking from glasses in which drinks fizzed. None of them so much as looked up when Gwen and Tancred entered.

The bartender smiled politely and bowed.

— What can I get you? they asked.

It was a mystery, to Gwen, where she and Tancred would sit with their drinks.

— World War I is over, said Tancred. Herbert sent us.

— Did he? asked the bartender. Was he wearing a shirt?

Tancred sighed.

— Yes, he answered. His shirt was blue.

— Forgive us for the charade, said the bartender. Please go up.

The bartender touched a button or, perhaps, flicked a switch behind the bar, and the wall at the other end of the room from the door slid to the right, revealing an elevator.

When she and Tancred had passed through to the elevator and the wall had slid shut behind them, Tancred pushed the elevator button and said, almost beneath his breath

— Christ ...

He turned to her when they were in the elevator.

— Why are people with money so strange? he asked. That business down there is meant to keep the wrong people out, but isn't it ridiculous to go through these rituals just to prove you've got money?

Gwen found the situation amusing: the false bar, the bartender, the ritual, even Tancred's annoyance, which suggested that he was not used to this ... this ...

Before she could finish her thought, the sound of talk and laughter came to them and, as the elevator door opened, swept her thoughts aside. She and Tancred now stood before a large restaurant on the top floor of the building, a bright room filled with people.

As if he'd just coalesced, a young man in a blue suit was beside them and politely said

— Good evening, sir. It's nice to see you again. Will you be joining Ms. Azarian-Thomson?

— Yes, said Tancred. We're with Simone.

Their coats were taken and in exchange they were given numbered chits that looked like miniature white girdles. Then the man in the blue suit led them through the restaurant. Three of the four walls had floor-to-ceiling windows that, it being night, reflected the bright interior and its diners. Gwen's impression of the restaurant was of coloured patches above a plane of white tablecloths, touches of red lipstick as if floating on faces, and light dresses, dark jackets, dark eyeliner. Then, too, there was the aroma: cooked flesh, yes, but delicate, nothing gamey, and the earthy perfume of roasted vegetables and various spices. If she hadn't been hungry before, she was hungry as they approached Simone's table.

Simone Azarian-Thomson smiled up at Tancred — at Tancred alone. She did not stand, instead offering her hand for Tancred to kiss. But Olivier, already at the table, smiled at Gwen and smartly rose to greet her, kissing her in the French manner: slightly warming the air beside her cheeks.

— What a surprise, he said. It's great to see you! I'm sorry I haven't texted you lately. I've been out of town. You look lovely, as usual.

Tancred held the chair for her and she sat facing Simone — Olivier on her right, Tancred on her left.

To Simone, Tancred said

– This is Gwenhwyfar.

Only then did Simone turn her gaze from Tancred.

– Guinevere, she said. What a lovely name. But I hope you don't mind if I call you Gwen. I had a terrible time with Middle English.

Simone's laugh was inviting, not at all derisive. Gwen blushed.

– No, no, she said, Gwen is fine.

She was embarrassed by her own embarrassment. It felt like unintentionally admitting that she was overwhelmed by the restaurant or impressed by Simone Azarian-Thomson. But she was neither. She was, rather, anxious. Something in Simone brought out the anxiety Gwen had felt as a girl, sitting at the dinner table with Grandma Aneira – old, Welsh, and strict – who seemed able to love only those with proper table manners. Or so Gwen had assumed as a girl, but the truth was: Grandma Aneira never could accept the fact that her son had married a woman who was not Welsh. Her insistence on table manners was her way of showing her disapproval of 'foreign habits.'

– You mean she was racist! Gwen had said to her mother, years later.

– No, not really, Helen had answered. She'd have liked me and my manners fine, if I'd been from Wales, Black or not. It was more of a clan thing. And some clan things are important, Gwenhwyfar. Anyway, Aneira's dead, poor cow, and she didn't leave anything to you. So there's no reason for you to worry about her, whatever she was.

Helen Odhiambo Lloyd, Gwen's mother, had been more indignant about the lack of an inheritance than about Grandma Lloyd's obsession with table manners. But when Gwen thought about Grandma Aneira at all, it was inevitably at a dining table. Anxiety about table manners was the only thing she'd inherited from her.

– Would you like something to drink? asked Olivier.

The waiter – Cal by name – a calming presence, leaned toward her and said

– The red at the table is a Nebbiolo. It's like dark cherry and not *too* tannic. The white is a Grüner Veltliner. It's a Smaragd, a late-season harvest. So it's a little more intense, like a nectarine with something herbaceous to it. Both are lovely to drink on their own.

Gwen felt as if her choice might have deeper significance, as if in choosing she would be saying more than she meant to. As casually as she could, she said

– I'll have the white, please.

– Oh, said Simone, I knew we were going to be friends!

The menu was easier to deal with. Simone suggested the chef's tasting menu, and her three *guests* – she insisted on this point – deferred to her. This meant that the table would be served whatever chef Louise Persaud – Michelin starred, as the menu discreetly noted – had managed to create from her winter larder: parsnips, preserves, celeriac, and so on. Each of the fifteen courses – including dessert – would be accompanied by wines that complemented the dishes.

Simone was, as Tancred had suggested, good company: funny and open. So, once past the formalities, Gwen felt relaxed enough to enjoy the conversation. For a time, this centred on the dishes they were served, each presented with such care it felt almost wrong to consume them. Their meal – arranged on bone-white plates or palely varnished circles of wood – was like a fantasia on mushroom, onion, and seafood:

Savory Porcini Beignet with Walnut Cream and
    Warming Spice
Acadian Sturgeon Caviar and Cultured Cream Tartlet
Poached Colville Bay Oyster, Champagne Sabayon
Lightly Pickled Raw Mackerel with Quince Juice and
    Winter Sorrel

Kelp and Oyster Chawanmushi, Dulse, and Grilled
   Winter Radishes
Grilled Foie Gras, Poached Leek and Roasted Hen
   Consommé
Celeriac Gently Roasted over the Coals, McIntosh
   Apple, Black Truffle, and Watercress
Our Bread and Butter, with Flavours of Cedar Smoke
   and Ashes
PEI Handline Cod, Preserved Heritage Tomato, Strawberry
   Kosho, and Dried Scallop Roe
Aged Squab Smoked over Lavender, Dried Red Beetroot,
   Prune, Chestnut, and Sweet Herbs
Grilled Sixty-Day Haldimand County Beef Ribeye Cap,
   Onions Slowly Cooked in their Skins and Sunchoke
Birch Water Ice and Apple Blossom Jelly
Washed Rind Cheese with Koginut Pumpkin and
   Dried Citrus
Salsify Ice Cream, Pear Granite, and Anise Hyssop
Mille-Feuille with Coffee and Rosehip
Mignardises and Sweet Wines

During much of the meal, you could be forgiven, Gwen
thought, for assuming that the four of them made two couples:
she and Olivier, Tancred and Simone. In lulls between group
conversation, Olivier would lean to her and ask what she had
been up to, how work at the hospital was going. He really was
considerate and Gwen was grateful. Tancred, on the other hand,
was circumspect. He was certainly friendly, but whenever she
and Olivier were speaking, he would lean toward Simone, their
interactions seeming like an almost conspiratorial counterpoise.

Feeling, as she now did, that Simone was kind and good-
natured, Gwen was curious about her relationship with Tancred.
She was curious for a number of reasons, but she was held by
the idea of an older woman with a young lover. Why shouldn't

Simone take a young lover, as older men routinely did? But wait, wasn't Simone married? She was wearing a ring. Did that mean Tancred was a distraction from Simone's troubles at home?

Her thoughts were interrupted by the approach of a well-dressed older man who, you could see at once, was related to Simone.

– Good evening, Simee, he said. How nice to see you're keeping up with the younger generation. I'm just on my way out, but when I saw you over here, I couldn't help wondering how your husband is doing.

Simone looked over at Gwen.

– Gwen, she said, this is my older brother, Alton.

Then, turning to Alton:

I'm glad you're here. My husband – whose name is *Gordon*, by the way – was just wondering how you're getting on with the buggering off I suggested last time we spoke.

– Nice language, said Alton, I can hear Tancred's influence.

Witheringly unimpressed by Alton, Tancred asked Simone if she was going to have coffee, as if the taking of coffee were more significant than anything Alton Azarian had said or could ever say. It was a coldness Gwen found unnerving, but also somehow familiar. Something about Tancred, in this moment with Alton, was like the moment in her dream of him when he'd seemed angry. Had her dream been a premonition of this very evening?

Following Tancred's lead, Simone said

– Would you like coffee, Gwen? I'm going to have one.

And not wishing to end the evening, Gwen answered

– That would be great. Thank you.

Alton Azarian turned away, the back of him radiating indig-nation on his way to the elevator.

When their coffees had been ordered, Simone said to Gwen

– You'll have to forgive my brother. He can be very cranky.

When the coffee had come and Simone had convinced Olivier to have a grappa with her, the conversation turned, as it almost inevitably did in these dark days of 2019, to the country south of us and to the decline of civilization. Here, Gwen blushed, because she suddenly wondered if Queen Anne's Corset stood for 'civilization.' She wondered, too, if stunning views and mille feuilles were a bulwark again barbarism or an invitation to it.

– Now, there's a man who hates women, said Simone.

– I'm not sure he *hates* women, said Tancred. It's more that he thinks of them as objects.

– And isn't that hatred? asked Gwen.

– You can only really hate people who are a threat to you, answered Tancred. Do you think he thinks of women as a threat?

– Why else would he attack them the way he does?

– Well, said Olivier, if we judge him by his actions as opposed to what he says, it does feel as if Tan has a point. He insults women, makes fun of the wives of his opponents, and uses women to signal to his followers that he's a strong man. The way he treats women is consistent with someone who views them as pawns, and it's strange to think of a chess player who hates pawns, isn't it?

Simone shook her head, as if marvelling at this delusion.

– Even the best men, she said, will defend the worst, if they think their gender's under fire. First of all, Ollie, there's no contradiction in a man hating the women he treats as pawns. And what does it matter anyway? What difference does it make what his 'true' feelings are? Whether he actually hates us or not, his behaviour is exactly like someone who hates women.

– What I hate, said Gwen, is the way he treats his wife.

For a moment, it seemed to Gwen that she'd said the wrong thing. Simone tilted her head slightly.

– I agree, she said. But fidelity is a complicated thing sometimes.

– How is it complicated? asked Tancred. It's either wrong or right, no?

– Yes, said Simone. It's either wrong or right, but there isn't a universal rule. I used to hate my father, because I knew he was unfaithful to my mother. But thinking back, I wonder if she didn't drive him away. She was very sick and her illness made her difficult, and I'm sure she must have known about his affairs. But I don't think she ever said anything to him. It was a terrible situation for both of them.

– I think I understand, said Olivier, but if you marry someone, don't you owe that person your fidelity, whatever the circumstances?

– What if you fall in love with someone else? asked Gwen. It happens all the time.

– You'd be dangerous to marry, said Tancred.

– Who said I'd marry you? she answered.

And then felt shame, realizing too late that Tancred had said nothing at all about marrying *him*. Olivier and Simone, meanwhile, were both laughing, which only made things worse. And making things worse herself, she said

– I didn't mean I categorically wouldn't marry you. But I'd have to know you first.

– That's a good general rule, said Olivier, knowing someone before you marry them. But what I was saying about fidelity is that there are no good reasons to be unfaithful to the person you married, even if you fall in love with someone else.

– *If* it's the right person, said Simone.

– Are you married to the right person? asked Tancred.

– Yes, I am, she answered. I can't imagine being unfaithful to my husband. We've been close friends for a very long time. The fact that he's sick, that he's not able to enjoy things like restaurants ... it's terrible for both of us, but I meant my vows when I made them, and I still mean them.

Gwen could not tell for whom Simone's words were meant. Was she telling *her* that she and Tancred were not lovers? But why? Gwen was a stranger to Simone, someone she might never see again. Nor could Gwen imagine that the words were meant for Tancred. If they were true, Tancred would know her feelings already. Unless, of course, he knew them to be *un*true, and was indulging Simone's self-deception. But the one who seemed most interested in Simone's words was Olivier.

– Well, there you are, he said. I think you're agreeing with me, aren't you?

To Simone, Tancred said

– You're a strong person. Being faithful's easy for you. I'm not sure I'd *swear* to be faithful to anyone.

Olivier leaned toward Gwen and, in a mock whisper, said

– Tancred hasn't been in love for, what, two years? He's forgetting what it feels like.

Because she'd been drinking and because the conversation now truly interested her, Gwen turned to Olivier and asked

– What about you? Have you been in love recently?

Without hesitation, Olivier answered

– Yes.

– I think he's the most loving person I know, said Tancred. Or the one most likely to fall in love anyway.

– Is that true? asked Simone. How interesting.

– But do you fall *out* of love easily? asked Gwen.

– No, said Olivier. I still love every woman I've ever loved. But Tan's exaggerating. I've only ever been in love four times.

– What about you? Tancred asked Gwen. Do you fall in and out of love easily?

Now Simone, Tancred, and Olivier seemed intent on hearing what she had to say. Suddenly self-conscious, Gwen lied or, perhaps, told a truth complicated enough that it could pass for a lie.

– No, she said, I've never really been in love. I'm beginning to think I don't have the gene for it.

(She certainly thought she had been in love with Roland, but it was no longer possible to think of that long humiliation as love.)

– You're lucky, said Simone. You've got something to look forward to: love! Ollie, Tan, and I are doomed to keep chasing the same feeling.

Now it was Simone who seemed embarrassed.

– I don't mean I'm chasing love, she said. I mean, the surprise is over, once you've been in love and know it.

– I'm not sure about that, said Olivier. Isn't love always a surprise?

– Oh! said Simone. If that's true, you're lucky. But it's something I'll never know. There's only room in my soul for my husband. Anyone else would be superfluous. But then, there are so many beautiful men out there, you don't have to fall in love to enjoy them.

To Gwen, she said

– Ollie would certainly make my heart race, if I weren't old enough to be his mother.

Was she trying to make Olivier blush, Gwen wondered. It didn't work, if so. Olivier considered her words, then said matter-of-factly

– I think I'd be lucky to be find someone as kind and beautiful as you. Why does age matter?

Simone protested that she was almost certainly *not* as thoughtful as he imagined. And Tancred, who clearly found the whole thing amusing, said

– Thank god you're married, Simee! Otherwise Ollie'd be bursting into flames!

As she walked home with Olivier, Gwen wondered if it were possible for a city to know you're in love before you do? This evening, the streets and sidewalks seemed meant for her steps. The buildings looked less precise, more playfully geometric, like Mondrians. The world felt cinematic or false, but its artifice was reassuring, circumventing thought the way clichés will.

She'd had too much to drink, it seemed, though she didn't feel drunk exactly.

Perhaps because he was beside her, she wondered if her thoughts had been provoked by Olivier. He had gallantly volunteered to walk her home, after Tancred and Simone had gone off to talk about business of some sort. And at the corner of Harbord and Bathurst, Gwen looked up at him, as they stood together waiting for the light. Simone was right: he was distractingly hand-some. But Olivier seemed unaware of how handsome he was, while, at the same time, taking very obvious care of himself: his sideburns precisely cut, his hair neat, even in the gusts of winter wind, the passionfruit and alcohol smell of him, his light orange scarf, worn in the European manner, just visible above the collar of his dark blue coat ...

The thought of kissing his lips came to her, and she allowed herself to wonder what kind of kisser he was: forceful, searching, sensual ...

– Are you all right? asked Olivier.

Startled, she answered

– Yes! Why?

The light had changed. It was green.

– Oh! she said.

As they approached her place, Gwen felt butterflies. Would they kiss? She wasn't sure she wanted to. It wasn't Olivier she wanted to kiss, but she wouldn't have minded if he took the lead. Olivier, however, did not lead her anywhere. He said

– You live in a great neighbourhood. I've always loved the Annex.

Then, for the second time that night, he kissed her in the French manner: once on each cheek.

– I had a lovely evening, he said. I hope we can all do it again.

– Yes, she answered. Yes, I hope we can, too.

He left her then, the look on his face unreadable. Had she been inconsiderate? Had he felt her hesitation? Was he waiting for something from her?

– Wait! she said. Would you like to come up for coffee?

But he had turned away and did not hear her or, at least, did not turn around. Which was just as well, because her invitation had not been heartfelt and Olivier's leaving did not disappoint her for long. It was not a moment that stayed with her. The moment that stayed – the *thing* that stayed – was Tancred's look as he asked if she fell easily in or out of love. She'd given a credible answer. But she'd looked up at him and, despite the wine, the surroundings, and the company, she'd had the clear impression he was waiting for a 'no' that did not come.

The memory of her evening at Queen Anne's Corset was on Gwen's mind for days, if only because she finally had something interesting to tell Nadia. She'd kept a copy of the Corset's menu. She described the dishes, spoke of the company, wondered at Alton Azarian's coldness, and praised Olivier's kindness.

– What about Tancred? asked Nadia. I wouldn't say no to two hours with him in a cold bedroom.

– Why does the bedroom have to be cold? asked Gwen.

– God! You're such a virgin! said Nadia. Have you actually had sex or is it just something you read about? I can lend you Robbie, if you need experience.

– No, thank you, Gwen said. And I prefer the room warm, so you don't need the sheets.

– Interesting, said Nadia. But sweat's distracting. I'd rather make my own heat. But that's just details. The real question is: who're you gonna bone? You must know by now. You've spent time with both of them, haven't you?

– I don't know, said Gwen. Maybe neither.

– Okay ... let me make it easier, said Nadia. Who do you *want* to bone?

– Why do I have to choose? said Gwen. Why not both?

– You're impossible! said Nadia. So, let's say there's a curse on you, okay? And you're going to die in an hour, but you get to sleep with one of them first. Only one, before you die. Who's it going to be?

And surprising herself, because she hadn't known the answer before saying it, Gwen said

– Tancred.

For two weeks, it seemed as if Gwen were the only one who'd found the evening at the Corset memorable. She didn't hear from the others, not even from Olivier who, you'd have thought, was the most likely to keep in touch, since he was the one who had her number.

She'd resolved to contact Olivier herself when two significant things happened: Nadia and Robbie broke up and, immediately thereafter, Olivier contacted her to see if she would enjoy spending a weekend with him, Simone, and Tancred at Simone's cottage in Muskoka. The invitation to Muskoka was, of course, a lovely prospect, meaning as it did that she could spend time in company she liked. But the scene between Robbie and Nadia disturbed her and cast its shadow on her days up north.

It had been clear for a while that Nadia and Robbie were not getting along. Robbie was now with them more often – from Thursday evening to Monday morning most weeks. He was going through a painful transition at home, and it felt as if Toronto and Nadia had become his refuge. This was a development that Gwen found irritating, not least because she wasn't asked if she minded having a new roommate. Nadia was, at first, very happy. She and Robbie were successfully playing house. The clouds came on those days when Robbie returned home to visit his children.

– I know I shouldn't mind, but I just don't like it when he goes home, Nadia would say. Or:

– I get that he wants to see his kids, but he sees them more than he sees me!

This problem grew, but Robbie, whose mind was no doubt on other things, seemed unaware of it. He was good-natured, mostly, carefree, you might have said if you didn't know he was leaving his wife. As far as Gwen was concerned, Robbie's lack of awareness was not a problem. Nadia could be generous to a fault, surprising you with gifts, encouragement, attention. But she could just as easily be self-absorbed, vain, unconcerned with the feelings of others. It was good that Robbie ignored the flaws and praised the virtues, wasn't it?

As it happened, it was not.

Robbie's willingness to overlook her flaws seemed to bring out the worst in Nadia, as if his kind nature – kind where she was concerned anyway – gave permission to her worst traits. Her insecurity and jealously were now more often on view. It seemed to Gwen that Nadia, knowing that someone as forgiving as Robbie existed, became more anxious when he was gone. As a result, Nadia allowed herself to wonder what *exactly* Robbie was doing when he wasn't with her.

Gwen did all she could to discourage her friend from speculating about things she couldn't know.

– I could hire a private detective, said Nadia.

As earnestly as she could, Gwen argued against doing anything so sinister. After all, Robbie wasn't even her husband!

Now those words – 'Robbie isn't even your husband!' – seemed to work. Nadia did not mention private detectives again. But Nadia had somehow legitimized the idea that Robbie was a ... well, what would you call it? He'd taken up with Nadia while still married. Was he now taking up with his wife while having a mistress? Was that even infidelity?

More unsettling still: along with Nadia's anxiety about Robbie's fidelity, there were her uninhibited testaments to how wonderful he was in bed. Despite their quarrels, Nadia couldn't keep her hands off him, needing him physically, as if lovemaking were the only thing that brought relief from doubt. It was enough to make your head spin. Gwen could not help wondering if the sex was good because it was therapeutic or therapeutic because it was good.

(It wasn't until sometime later that Gwen began to wonder about Robbie's role in this tormented phase of his and Nadia's relationship. Actually, no: 'tormented' is what it would have been if *Gwen* had been in such a relationship. She could sense, though, that *tormented* was not the right word to describe what Nadia and Robbie lived through. Even at its worst, their relationship must have been satisfying in some way to both of them, a sacrament that both performed, that both enjoyed. Otherwise, how could they have lived through it for so long?)

In any case, on that evening in February, Gwen had come home late from work to an apartment that was nave-quiet, though it felt, as she entered, as if she'd interrupted something. As she went into the kitchen, Robbie was at the table trying to look nonchalant: his coat on, his face red. Her back to Gwen, Nadia was at the stove holding a pot. Gwen could feel the precise emotion coming from her: anger.

– Is everything okay? Gwen asked.

Rather than answer, Nadia turned, the look of her frightening, and without warning threw the pot at Robbie. There was nothing in the pot and, most likely, it would not have killed him had it hit him full on. But Robbie, who must have been anticipating the attack, moved so that the pot – though thrown from not more than ten feet away, glanced off his shoulder.

In an instant, chaos took over. Robbie got up quickly, wordlessly, and hurried to the front door, as Nadia, letting loose a stream of epithets ('you prick! you bastard! you fucking prick!'), grabbed whatever was at hand (a sugar bowl, a spoon, a cup) and launched them in Robbie's direction, the sugar bowl just missing Gwen as it flew by and broke on the floor, the sound of it a brittle thud.

This part of the turmoil – which ended with Nadia screaming incoherently down the stairwell, then throwing some of Robbie's clothes out the living room window – could not have lasted any more than a minute or two, time during which Gwen stood where she was, flinching as the sugar bowl flew by. She'd never seen Nadia quite so angry, nor guessed at her capacity for violence.

Adding to her bewilderment was the fact that Gwen felt admiration for her friend's fury. Yes, the violence was wrong, but

Nadia's anger felt maternal to Gwen. Literally so, as her own mother was the only one she'd ever known to get so irate so quickly – though never at her father.

Almost as bewildering as the blow-up was the end of the evening. Even when Robbie had been gone for hours, anger, regret, and sadness overtook Nadia in turns, as if the emotions themselves paced about before each in turn returned. By two in the morning, the night felt almost granular to Gwen, it was so strange.

Having listened for hours to the jumbled reasons behind Nadia's anger – Robbie was selfish, Robbie didn't love her, Robbie was a liar, Robbie was still sleeping with his wife, Nadia did not love him, Nadia loved him but would not share him, Robbie was unworthy of her love, Nadia was herself unworthy, the world was unloving – and having held Nadia in her arms until exhaustion brought them both something like peace, Gwen checked her phone before falling into bed and discovered that Olivier had texted.

– hey Gwen
– sorry not to get in touch sooner. been out of town. hope yr well.
– Simone wants you and Tancred and me to spend the weekend at her cottage near Gravenhurst,
– would be great if you came.

Had she got his text a week sooner or had she got it before spending the evening consoling Nadia, Gwen would have been excited. She was still gladdened at the prospect of spending time up north, but her spirits had been dampened by Nadia and Robbie. More: under different circumstances she'd have shared the texts with Nadia. Together they'd have parsed its words for buried meanings. Like ... 'sorry not to get in touch sooner'? Was that a real apology? And 'would be great if you came'? That was a little impersonal, wasn't it? Not impolite, but still ...

Gwen stopped herself there. It wasn't fun to speculate on her own and she could not, of course, show the invitation to Nadia while her friend was distraught and exhausted. So, in an act of secret solidarity, she did not answer Olivier's texts until the following afternoon, after she'd told Nadia about them.

There was no question but that she'd accept the invite. Nadia, shuffling through Thursday evening in a kimono Robbie had bought her on a visit to Disney World with his children, summoned the steel to insist that Gwen go.

– If you don't go, said Nadia, I won't know what it's like to be in Muskoka with the super-rich.

Gwen had answered

– Olivier and Tancred aren't rich!

Nadia had only rolled her eyes, stumbling as she did on the too-long kimono.

So, despite feeling defensive about 'hanging with the wealthy,' Gwen arranged to drive to Muskoka with Olivier. Tancred and Simone went on their own.

As they drove together, first along the well-lit 400 and then in the dark quiet of Highway 11, Olivier remembered the first time he'd met Tancred and Daniel Mandelshtam, another friend from childhood. Gwen described meeting Nadia and then recalled her friendship with Rita Sinha. She'd met Rita, one of the few other people of colour her age, in Grade 6, and they'd been close. They were still friends, in principle, and they talked every now and then, but Rita had moved to New York to find work as an actor and they were drifting apart, a sadness Gwen felt comfortable enough to share with Olivier.

How calm and confident Olivier seemed, how unpretentious. There was so much to admire about him: the sound of his voice, his elegant hands on the wheel, his face lit and shadowed by passing lights. Hearing him talk about Tancred – and he did talk about Tancred a lot – suggested a number of questions to Gwen.

For instance, what was it that kept two such different men close? Was it only their childhoods? Or was it that Olivier was more fiery than he seemed, and Tancred more complicated?

— It's nice, she said, that Tan can live for a while without working. I envy him.

— Yes, said Olivier. The inheritance was a complete surprise.

Here, Olivier told her about an Azarian she did not know: Willow. Willow Azarian, Simone's sister, whom Olivier had met and liked, had been the black sheep of the Azarians. She had been a heroin addict, but she and Tancred had been close. In fact, though he did not want to speak for his friend, Olivier doubted Tancred would have had anything to do with the Azarians had it not been for his connection to Willow. As far as Olivier knew — and he knew better than all, save maybe Daniel — Tancred had never in his life been interested in money. He was interested in other things.

— Like what? asked Gwen.

— Like justice, said Olivier, and the difference between strength and power, and how power's used. He gets that from Baruch, Dan's dad. We all do. But just between us: I think Tan struggles with having money. He's still not sure he deserves it. But *deserve* is such a useless word. We all deserve money and none of us do. *Luck* and *chance* are more important words than *deserving*, and I wish he could just accept his luck.

— But Ollie, said Gwen, if Tan believes in justice, it must be hard for him to accept luck and chance, don't you think?

Olivier smiled.

— I do think so, he answered. I think you've got it just right.

By the time they passed Orillia — or, rather, the billboards and businesses on its outskirts — Gwen felt such camaraderie with Olivier that she surprised herself by recounting Nadia and Robbie's breakup, even mentioning her admiration for Nadia.

How different this journey was from their evening at Café Polonez. She even wondered if Olivier wasn't *exactly* the kind of man she needed: gentle, able to talk about all manner of things, modest. But she wondered, too, about the kind of man Tancred was: generous and closed, loving and wary, compelling in a way Olivier was not. The closer they got to Gravenhurst, the stronger was her resolve to ask Tancred the questions Olivier had suggested: what is the difference between strength and power and what does money have to do with it?

But resolutions made while contentedly driving on Highway 11 (at night, with a friend) were easier to make than to keep, especially when faced with the scale of Simone's place on Lake Muskoka.

As it was night, they did not see Simone's home before the GPS told them they'd arrived. The tall, metallic front gate creaked open to admit them to a winding road to the house. Then: there it was, outlined against a moonlit sky. The house was an imposing central structure with two massive, two-storey wings. More like a hotel than a house. There was light from a number of windows, however, and this introduced not warmth exactly, but at least the idea of company.

If this is her cottage, thought Gwen, what must her home be like?

But if the cottage's outward face was intimidating, its insides were not. There was something vulnerable about the foyer, as if an art gallery had been caught putting on its stockings. Near the front entrance, side by side, were two works by Giorgio Morandi: a pencil drawing of seashells, and a watercolour landscape whose reds, pinks, and blues were almost ghostly. Partially obscuring the landscape was a wooden coat rack on which three winter coats were hung.

Gwen's impression of the place was further softened by Simone and Tancred, both of whom had greeted them at the door. Simone was wearing an oversized beige cowl-neck sweater and blue jeans, and she was barefoot. Beside her, Tancred looked almost overdressed in his white shirt and black jeans.

– It's great you two could make it, said Simone. We even managed to save some food for you! Leave your things here. Come to the kitchen!

They reached the kitchen – light blue subway-tile backsplash, wooden cabinetry, platinum appliances – through two tall-ceilinged rooms. The first was a sitting room with plump sofas and armchairs, a fireplace in which firewood sputtered and, on two of the walls, oversized paintings by Betty Goodwin of figures swimming. The second was a wide, chandelier-lit dining room with a rustic table and chairs – 'rustic' meaning they looked like they'd give you splinters – and lithographs by Georges Braque on the walls.

Gwen did not herself recognize the works or their creators, but she asked about them and, as they passed through the rooms, Simone gave accounts of them and pointed out that they'd all been chosen by her husband, Gordon, who collected art and whose knowledge was far beyond hers. Braque, she said, was her husband's favourite painter.

Hearing this, Olivier mentioned that Braque was his favourite painter as well. Because although his parents had been poor, they had collected books about Braque, Olivier's mother being a distant cousin of the artist. That is, books filled with pictures of Braque's work had been a part of his childhood and the sight of them – the sight of this one – made him happy.

– How wonderful! said Simone. I'm so sorry Gordon isn't with us. He'd have loved to hear that, and he'd have talked your ear off about Braque.

Casually taking Olivier by the arm, she continued

– We have some of his paintings at home. You should come see them. It would make Gordon so happy. It would make me happy, too! We have so few visitors these days.

– That would be great, said Olivier. Thank you.

Turning to Gwen, Simone said

– You should come, too. These lithographs are lovely, but the paintings are where you can really see Braque's personality.

Gwen agreed that a visit would be wonderful, but she had the clear impression that she was an afterthought, that Olivier was the one being invited. Nor did Olivier seem to mind the attention. Neither he nor Simone acknowledged her assent to a visit. But Tancred did, and he described Simone's home to her, as Simone and Olivier talked a bit more about Braque.

Of the rest of that first evening, only two other moments left impressions.

First came embarrassment: when Gwen and Olivier had eaten, Simone showed them to their bedroom, an immense space above a brick-and-mortar boathouse. On one side, there were tall windows that overlooked Lake Muskoka. Not that the lake was visible. It was dark with glimmerings on its surface from the lights on the dock. Even so, the lake could be felt and lightly heard, as it struggled in its girdle of ice. The bedroom was both elegant and comfortingly prosaic. There was a full-sized pool table at one end, away from the bed. There were six or seven tall shelves of books, most of the books being monographs devoted to painting and sculpture. There was an en suite bathroom with a wide, claw-footed tub.

Gwen briefly thought about sharing the bed with Olivier – it was wide enough for three at least – before she said

– It's wonderful, but ...

and Olivier added

– I hate to cause trouble, but Gwen and I aren't close enough to share a bed.

at which, Gwen was embarrassed.

– Oh! said Simone. I have just the solution. There's a room in the main house that has almost the same view as this one, but it's smaller. It's beside mine and Tancred's.

Here, Simone immediately corrected herself:

– I mean, it's the room between my bedroom and Tancred's.

The second thing that left an impression was less a moment than a mood: a kind of drifting.

Gwen and Olivier had eaten, and Simone had shown them through the various dens and rooms in the cottage when, because she was tired, Simone suggested they have an early nightcap before going to bed.

The cottage certainly had enough alcohol. A modest room off the kitchen was all silvery shelves and low light. On the shelves were hundreds of bottles of whisky, arranged according to ... well, Simone had no idea. She knew there was order because she knew her husband.

– Does he collect wine, too? asked Gwen.

– Oh, yes, said Simone. But he keeps those at home in a wine cellar. I hardly ever go down there. It's like a church! But I'll say this for Gordie: I don't know anyone more generous. If I asked him for wine, he'd find something ancient and irreplaceable. That's why I never ask him! When we were first married, I said, 'Why don't we drink something special, just for the two of us?' And he went down to the cellar and brought back a bottle that looked like Methuselah had been saving it. The wine was good. I mean, I think it was good. I was twenty-something. What did I know about wine? I was happy my husband loved me enough to sacrifice something special. But when we finished the bottle, he said, 'That was the best hundred thousand I ever spent.' The bottle was a Sauterne from 1831! One of ten bottles left on earth. I was thrilled, but I've felt guilty ever since, because the wine was wasted on me.

Then, as if catching herself, Simone brightened up.

– But I don't have any qualms about whisky! she said. Let's compare a couple of them.

Gwen could hardly tell the difference. Had this been a 'Princess and Pea'-like test of her nobility, she'd have failed. Simone took down a bottle that looked nice but plain. This turned out to be very old whisky. Fifty years old! She then took down a crystalline bottle that had a large **M** on it. This turned out to be just as old. But both tasted like, well, whisky to Gwen, and neither interested her as much as the feeling of being in this place with – it hit her as she drank the **M** whisky – complete strangers.

In other circumstances, at other times in her life, she might have been overwhelmed. That she was neither overwhelmed nor awestruck was testament to ... Simone's kindness? The effects of the whisky? The feel of the cottage itself? Or was it that curiosity about a lifestyle that wasn't hers distracted her?

Tancred and Simone sat on the living room sofa. Above them, one of Goodwin's paintings floated on the wide white wall. Despite being tired, Simone seemed intent on keeping Gwen and Olivier entertained. This is why, as the conversation turned to more interesting things (the weightlessness of Canadian politics, the idea that the good and the inevitable were connected, the strangeness of racism ...), Gwen struggled against sleep and was almost disappointed, the next morning, to find herself in the wide white bed of her room, sunlight illuminating the pool table.

The day was closing and the last of the light was winter blue. It was somewhere around five o'clock. Gwen and Olivier were in one car, following Simone and Tancred, who were in the other, to Bala. They were on their way to the home of Simone's friend Magda von Arnim for a poetry reading.

They'd spent most of the afternoon in pleasant but rootless conversation, the kind of conversation whose words evaporate, leaving only the underlying companionship – the *fact* of conversation – in mind. That said, though Gwen could not recall exactly what the four of them spoke about, she had become increasingly aware that her desire for Tancred was ramifying. She took pleasure in little details about him: his profile as he smiled at something Olivier said, his smile itself, the look on his face whenever he considered a question, the steadiness that seemed an aspect of his being.

But if no words stayed with her from that afternoon, there *was* an indelible moment. At Olivier's behest, Tancred demonstrated his extraordinary skills as a pickpocket, stealing Simone's necklace, wallet, and credit cards while daring her to say when they'd been taken. Simone wasn't the only one who failed to notice when he took her things. Gwen, staring at him as he moved about, could not tell either. The performance, like a great magic trick, was exciting. But it was also disturbing, because she couldn't keep from wondering whence the skill had come. The skill itself did not impress her as much as the devotion it must have taken to acquire it, the attention and time it would have cost him. Then there was the question of its use: had Tancred been a pickpocket? How often had he stolen, if so, and from whom? Gwen did not ask, feeling that the answer would come in its proper time. Besides, he had shown them what he could do as a way to amuse them.

So ...

Magda von Arnim was hosting a poetry reading at her home. She had invited two poets, Lisa Robertson and Roo Borson, neither of whose work Gwen knew well, though she remembered reading one of Borson's poems on a streetcar poster, something about trees and the heart unwinding.

The von Arnims lived in a home that overlooked Bala Bay. Most of its ground floor was taken up by an enormous room — thirty feet long by twenty wide — with a polished wood floor, tall windows, and glass doors that looked out onto the bay. This was where the reading would take place, and there were some fifty chairs facing a dais.

Despite its dimensions, the room felt cozy; it was, in fact, an eccentric shrine to poetry. Immediately on entering, there was, to the left, a life-sized statue of Gwendolyn MacEwen, painted so that she looked alive, save that in the poet's outstretched palm there was a patch of lichen. Then, too, the room's walls were obscured by tall bookcases filled with books of poetry. Between the bookcases and on some of the shelves, there were framed photographs of poets, Canadians mostly, though place was made for others: Eugenio Montale, his profile birdlike; Anna Akhmatova, her eyes looking down and away; Elizabeth Bishop, hair unkempt, fist on cheek; and Wisława Szymborska, smiling as if in sympathy for your situation, whatever it might be.

(Though this room was, as Simone put it, Magda's chapel, the rest of the house was just as devoted to poets and poetry. There were, for instance, drawers filled with small objects: a pen once owned by Emily Dickinson, William Butler Yeats's cufflinks, Gertrude Stein's passport photos, etc. There was a closet filled with the clothes of dead – and living! – poets, and there was a vault, here or in Toronto, to hold the manuscripts she'd bought from poets all over the world. This was Magda's *sanctum sanctorum.*

– Is she a poet herself? Gwen asked.

– No, no, answered Simone. She doesn't even like the *idea* of her writing poetry! And if you ask why, she'll quote one of her great-great-great-grand-something-or-others: '*Die Flasche macht den Wein nicht, aber sie schützt ihn trotzdem,*' the bottle doesn't make the wine, but it guards it just the same.)

They arrived at Magda's in time to catch a sunset that torched the snow-whitened shores along the bay. Simone found Magda, held her friend's hand, and introduced her to Gwen and Olivier. Tancred she'd met already, it seemed. After a while, they went into the 'chapel,' where people stood around talking, quietly staring at the sunset, taking hors d'oeuvres from the platters held out by men and women dressed in white shirts and black pants.

Once Gwen had gotten over her surprise at the lichen-handed likeness of Gwendolyn MacEwen, she looked over the room and wondered if there was any way to tell the poets from the audience. Certainly not by dress. All were more or less casually dressed, except for a handful of teenagers scattered about the room. The teenagers – who were in what looked to be their finest – had won competitions for 'best poetry recital,' held in high schools across the province. This evening was, in effect, the finals, the prize for very best recital being four thousand dollars.

The five finalists were each in turn invited onto the dais, where each recited a poem from memory.

For Gwen, charmed by the venue and the occasion, this part of the evening was unexpectedly absorbing because, as it happened, she, Tancred, and Olivier were near one of the competitors, Lea Kattelus. Lea's mother, Genovaite, was beside her, as was her grandmother, Leah Toini: all three wearing name tags, all three nervous and excited. In fact, it was difficult to say which of them was most excited or most nervous. Lea, her red hair falling to the middle of her back, was between her grandmother – who furtively touched her granddaughter's hair, as if to keep it from flying up – and her mother – who held her hand.

Gwen applauded as Lea was introduced and applauded again when she'd recited a poem by John Skennen that began

> Ticking tocks
> taking clocks
> before they
> hurt me ...

Feeling empathy for all three women, Gwen had been absorbed by the contest, expressing her disappointment when the prize was won by a young woman from Glencoe who'd recited a poem by Dennis Lee. She'd commiserated then with Genovaite and Toini, sharing their disappointment, affirming what they themselves had expressed: that Lea (daughter, granddaughter) was talented and should be proud.

Gwen would not have minded leaving after the competition, but the poetry readings, too, were absorbing. Part of the pleasure was in the difference between the poets, a difference that was in their words and the ways their words were spoken. The work came from such distinct places that the transit between worlds was itself interesting.

From Robertson – tall, grey-haired, her green glasses a part of her performance

> A gate made of a brick.
>
> You are the silence they exchanged.
>
> A gate made of a plinth.
>
> It was a wide and empty Pacific place in too-strong light ...

to Borson – her presence milder, her accent unplaceable

> Each spring
> mirrors the one before,
> pre-owned by those now gone from here,
> but this was late summer, full-fledged, fully formed ...

Then, too, beyond this 'transit' there was the amusing idea – amusing to Gwen, as it occurred to her – that Poetry itself was the great mother from which all poems sprang and to which all poems return. She smiled at this will of the wisp. Honestly, she really did miss her mother! So much so that she resolved to call her that night.

When the readings were done, the poets were applauded, a handful of books were sold and autographed, and Gwen found herself beside Tancred, waiting as people milled about drinking coffee. It was now so dark outside that when you looked at the windows, you could see only a reflection of the interior: the backs of people's heads, their faces, the statue of Gwendolyn MacEwen.

Gwen hadn't eaten any of the finger food from earlier, so she was hungry.

– So am I, said Tancred. Let's find Ollie and Simone.

As they approached a group of people near Simone, Gwen recognized a voice. Not just a voice but a way of speaking. It was Morgan Bruno, one of her parents' oldest friends, her godfather and, formerly, her teacher.

– Well, Professor Bruno was saying, to live poetically is to live in uncertainty, to hesitate between the word and the thing. *That's* how poetry and love are related! Because love comes from uncertainty, too. In fact, love is uncertainty's greatest gift! Always remembering that *Gift* is the German word for poison!

Gwen was immediately pleased to hear the professor's voice. The sound of it was like being transported home. Forgetting that they'd been looking for Simone and Olivier, Gwen touched the professor's arm.

– Ah! My dear Gwenhwyfar! said Professor Bruno. Who could have imagined such a jewel lodged in the golden throat of Muskoka!

The woman next to Professor Bruno – blond, blue-eyed, faintly smiling – tried to move away. But before she could accomplish a step, Professor Bruno touched her arm and said

– Oh, Ms. Wilcox, allow me to introduce you to a girl I've known since she was born! Gwenhwyfar Lloyd. My godchild and one of the best students I've ever had. No exaggeration! Gwenhwyfar, this is Alana Wilcox, Ms. Robertson's publisher.

– Nice to meet you, said Alana. I wish I could stay and talk, but Lisa and I are off for something to eat ...

– Where? asked Professor Bruno. I'd love to tell you more about John Skennen. I've just done a biography and it's genre-bending in the best way! It's a biography but also a mystery and a kind of travel narrative. I offered it to the randy penguins, but it went straight over their heads. It's really just the thing you would love! It's called *Travels with Alfred*, but I could be induced to change the title. I'll come to dinner with you, shall I? It really is an exciting book.

Again, Alana tried to move away. She said

— Yes, well, why don't you send it to me? It sounds interesting.

Professor Bruno followed the publisher off, most of his attention given to her.

— I *will* send it, he said. I'm sure you won't be disappointed.

But, looking back at Gwen, he cried out

— I'm going to visit your parents next week, Gwenwhyfar. Why don't you come with me and Michael? I'll give you a call on Thursday!

The encounter with Professor Bruno had taken not much more than a minute, but Simone was amused.

— Well, she said, that was something.

— I love Professor Bruno, answered Gwen. He's my godfather. Every year he sends me a book on the anniversary of my baptism. This year it was *Yiddish for Pirates* by Gary Barwin.

— Ah, said Simone, that's lovely. Listen, why don't the four of us go for supper? There's a place in Huntsville called Hildegard's. It's been my favourite restaurant up here for years. But why don't we change partners? I'll go with Olivier. I feel like I've barely spoken with him. You don't mind, do you, Gwen?

— No, said Gwen, that's a great idea. I feel like I've barely spoken to Tancred either.

— Don't Ollie and I have a say in this? asked Tancred.

— Oh! answered Simone. I'm sure Ollie longs for the company of an older woman, don't you, Ollie?

— I do! said Olivier.

— Too right! answered Simone. The die is cast! You two can follow us to Hildegard's.

Simone and Olivier were given their coats almost as soon as they asked for them. Simone let Magda know how much of a success the evening had been, then she and Olivier were off, promising to order beer for them when they got to Hildegard's. Tancred's coat, too, came right away, but there was a mix-up with Gwen's. She was given a bulky red overcoat with a hood, and large pockets in which dark mittens were stuffed. It was not hers. It belonged to Roo Borson, one of the poets.

– I'm sorry, said Roo, but I think you have my coat.

Then, when they'd stood around for a bit, wondering where Gwen's coat had gone, Ms. Borson asked her companion if he'd help find the missing coat. Her companion, Kim by name, was just then in conversation with someone who'd bought a copy of Roo's book. He looked up, startled, as if he'd been instructed to stand on his head and whistle.

– But what do you want *me* to do? he asked

the brow over his left eye raised as if it were trying to escape.

By the time Gwen's coat was found, twenty minutes had passed, and very significant minutes they proved to be. Gwen and Tancred, well behind Simone and Olivier, were caught – some twenty-five minutes after they'd started off – in an overwhelming and unforecast storm, unintentionally turning off Highway 25 at Brackenrig, driving away from Huntsville despite the GPS, or maybe because the GPS was as confounded as they were by the entangling whiteness that dissolved distinctions between sky and land, here and there, road and field.

It would all have been romantic, Gwen thought – the silence and the world erased – had they not been stuck in it, which they were when their car – that is, Simone's Flying Spur – tipped into a ditch somewhere along a back road in the middle of nowhere.

Gwen and Tancred had been speaking about the world. He'd been quiet as they drove away from Bala, but then he'd apologized for being quiet and confessed that he sometimes did not know what to think about wealth, about status, about events like this one in Bala where, despite what he knew to be Magda's true love for poetry, the symbols of status were all around.

– I mean, look, he said, we're driving Simone's Bentley. All this metal, rubber, and wood comes to half a million dollars. A part of me just finds it ugly. I find the idea of it ugly. But then, another part of me wants all this. I mean, really wants it, if only to get over wanting it.

– That must make your relationship with Simone tricky, said Gwen.

– No, it doesn't, said Tancred. Simee's always been very kind to me. She's taken my side against some of her own family, even. She's a good person or she tries to be, and that's important to me. I haven't always believed people with money *could* be good. That's why I like to be around her.

– Oh, said Gwen. That's nice. Do you wish you could be a couple?

Tancred seemed not to understand, and then he laughed.

– No, no, he said. It's not like that. Anyway, she really does love Gordon. I'm not sure there's anyone who could even tempt her to be unfaithful. That's another reason I like her so much. I don't believe in astrology, but Simee does, and the way she explains it is: she's a Leo, so she's completely loyal to her partner, but she needs the attention of other people to feel ... alive. That's *her* word. So, like tonight, *of course* she'd want to drive to Huntsville with Ollie. But you don't have to worry about that. Neither of them would do anything to hurt anyone they cared about.

Gwen was not worried, but she was touched by Tancred's effort to reassure her.

– I've known Ollie since we were five, Tancred continued. I wouldn't do anything to hurt him either.

Tancred had not said these words in a pointed way. He was not trying to convey something secret. Still, attentive as she was, Gwen found it interesting that the idea of Olivier being hurt was on his mind. Was he worried about Olivier being with Simone? Or was Tancred telling her that he, Tancred, would do nothing with her that might hurt his friend's feelings?

– I don't think Olivier has any feelings for me, she said.

These words were lightly spoken but they were not lightly meant. She wanted him to know that she was not concerned about her relationship with Olivier. But Gwen almost immediately regretted her words, because Tancred took them the wrong way.

– He really likes you, he said. He's always honest, you know. Ask him anything, he'll tell you the truth. But he doesn't always say what you want to hear, *unless* you ask him. One woman he was going out with said it took him a year to tell her what he felt and by then it was too late. That's his weakness. If you ever really want to know something, just ask him. He'll tell you how he feels about you.

– What about you? asked Gwen. Do you always tell the truth?

– Me? answered Tancred. Yes, when I can. I mean, I don't like to hurt people.

This was the point at which it began to snow – not lightly, not with a gradually increasing number of flakes, but rather as if they'd run into a swan's arse, as Gwen's father might have put it. A sudden, white confusion that, for different reasons, brought calm to them both. In Tancred's case, the idea of distress brought adrenaline, which, counterintuitively, brought a kind of peace. For Gwen, the feeling was akin to nostalgia, as if the years just before she left home were returned to her. Not the boredom or the desperation to leave Bright's Grove but the pleasure of snowfall, all the world quiet and white.

– Well, this is lovely, said Gwen.

They drove on slowly, not able to see even a foot in front of them or to the sides, the Bentley down to fifteen kilometres an hour, occasionally encountering shrouds of light as cars passed on the other side of the road, going in the opposite direction. And then Tancred inadvertently veered off the highway and onto rural roads neither they nor the GPS recognized.

(To be fair to the GPS, its constant efforts to recentre, to recover, to restart, were strangely affecting. To Gwen, its voice – English with an Armenian accent – suggested a European woman lost in the new world, her recalculations testament to a storm that was as confounding to machines as it was to humans. Finding it a distraction, Tancred had turned the voice off just before they veered off 25.)

They'd gone some five klicks along the wrong road before they realized it was the wrong road. Gwen noticed this first, looking down at the GPS, seeing that it was again tracking them and proposing routes to Hildegard's. And she was texting Olivier to let him know their situation, to let him and Simone know that, given the weather, they would not make it to Hildegard's, when, almost as if he were planning it, Tancred gracefully drove the Bentley into a ditch – 'gracefully,' in that there was a gentle decline, the car sliding into the unseen ditch as if sliding into a bed.

– Well, that's all we needed, said Tancred.

But if it was not actually what *they* needed, it seemed to satisfy the storm. Before they had time to decide on a strategy – get out of the car? take stock of what they had to keep them warm? call CAA immediately? turn off the car to save gas? tie a piece of cloth to the Bentley's antenna? – the storm stopped as abruptly as it had started.

Once they'd called CAA and been informed they'd have to wait till morning for help, once Tancred turned the motor off and killed the lights, they saw that they were beside a field, the night bright with stars, the half-moon white, the land around them white, save for the place where a line of trees began. Beyond the trees, there was a driveway that led, presumably, to a house.

The woman who answered the door – Mrs. Atkinson by name – was a deeply Christian soul. She was one who not only read the Bible but also took it as an affirmation of life and our duty to it. It would not have occurred to her, for instance, to do anything but help the two who knocked at her door, odd though it was to find Black people on her porch, there having been so few of them in her life up till then.

Though she was in her home by herself, her husband having gone up to Sudbury for the weekend, she invited them in, insisted on making them tea to warm them up, and, when she heard they hadn't eaten, offered them the potato salad, cold ham, and lime Jell-O that she had in her fridge.

All of this was done with simplicity and self-deprecation.

When they'd eaten, she showed them to the 'guest house,' an outbuilding where her husband's mother had lived: twenty-five feet by twenty-five, a sink, a bathroom, a wood stove (which Mrs. Atkinson lit for them), a table and chair, a bed in which, realistically, no two adults could have comfortably slept without being close.

– I wish I could offer you more, said Mrs. Atkinson, but I wouldn't feel right with strangers sleeping in my house. It would be different if John were home, but I just don't think I could sleep.

– You've been so kind, Gwen said, I wish *we* could do something for you.

– Oh, if it comes to that, said Mrs. Atkinson, if you'll pray with me, I'll consider myself blessed.

With that, she bowed her head, closed her eyes, clasped her hands together, and spoke the Lord's Prayer: '... for thine is the kingdom, the power, and the glory, forever.'

And when she'd finished, she left them.

There are times, of course, when the good feels almost as absurd as the strange, when the good defies the day-to-day. For Gwen and Tancred, this was one. They spent their first moments in the outbuilding bewildered by their host's kindness. Then, too, they talked about Mrs. Atkinson, because it was easier than talking about their suddenly awkward situation: alone together in a bedroom, with one bed for both of them.

As Gwen sat on the edge of the bed, she became increasingly conscious of her surroundings. The room smelled of the maple-wood burning in the stove, but also of dust and age, of their coats hanging beside the door, of lavender from a potpourri left on the table. Tancred sat on the chair, some six feet away from her, but she could smell him, too: his slightly damp clothes, the faintly vanilla soap he'd used, the wet leather of his boots. The light in the room came from a lamp on a table beside the bed. But it was so low, it could not compete with the world-whitening moonlight that came through the window. She was aware of the softness of the bed beneath her. She could still taste the dill and mayonnaise of the potato salad they'd eaten.

All of this was such a sensual onslaught that talk of Christian kindness and how strange the good can be did nothing to stop her wondering how Tancred's lips might feel on hers, or about his chest — the beginning of it just visible above the unbuttoned top button of his shirt. That was not to mention his blue eyes, which, the light being too low, were more a matter of memory and imagination.

She was not, to her own surprise, either embarrassed or ashamed of her imagination. There was no reason for them not to touch. If he had come to her at that moment and leaned down to kiss her, she would have let her curiosity take over and dealt with the consequences later. In fact, she wondered if she should go to him, to touch his face and say 'thank you' — for whatever reason occurred to her when she touched him: for being calm, for getting them to this place, for his company. Maybe she would have, if she'd been certain he was feeling what she did.

– You know, he said, I'm glad you and Ollie met. You're a lovely person.

– What makes you say that? she asked. I might not be as nice as you think.

– I don't know your secrets, he answered. But I trust my instincts about people. Anyway, you can't hide kindness, and you've been very considerate about my getting us lost.

For a moment, she wanted to outrage him, to let him know that kindness and consideration had nothing to do with anything, that she could show him such desire as would change his mind about her. But, in the end, she *was* considerate. She was not one who would think seriously of forcing herself on him. So she smiled and said

— It's nice of you to say that. But, you know, Olivier and I ... we barely know each other.

— Hmm ..., he said

and turned to look out the window.

As if deliberately ignoring her words, he changed the subject or, rather, did not quite change it.

— You know, Ollie's been with some very cruel women. Dan and I are always trying to get him to go out with someone who won't take advantage of him. I don't know how he does it, but he always manages to find women who don't love him or can't love him or whatever. It's like he likes being frustrated.

Tancred smiled as he said these last words — perhaps at a memory — but he then looked at her so seriously that she felt implicated.

— There was one woman who hung around him for a year, because she wanted to go out with Dan. And the thing is: Ollie knew it and he didn't mind. He defended her for years afterwards. He'd say, 'Well, Dan's a great person.' And I'd say, 'Yeah, but he was married, and she knew it!' And he'd go ... 'You can't help irrational feelings, so what's the use treating them like they're rational?'

— Well, Ollie's right, said Gwen. You can't help what you feel.

— Yes, said Tancred, but it's like he's not of this world sometimes. So you can see why his friends want to protect him, can't you?

Gwen looked up at him then, and he was looking at her and she was conscious of her body and her dress and, again, of her senses: salt and dill, moonlight, the potpourri, silence, and the sheets on the mattress beneath her. What a lot of words he'd used to say no, she thought. And who was all this talk about Olivier meant to reassure anyway, himself or her?

— Yes, she said, I get why anyone would want to protect Ollie. But tell me about Daniel?

He smiled then, and it was as if they'd come to an accord or maybe he'd said all he needed to say. Whatever the case, the thought of his friend Daniel brought back a part of his childhood that he didn't mind sharing with her. Daniel's father, Baruch, was a socialist who'd had them read – at fourteen! – Alexander Berkman, Rosa Luxemburg, Friedrich Engel. And Tancred was still grateful for the guidance that had saved him from loneliness, from fatherlessness, from his boredom in a school system he knew to be nothing but 'class and status training.' Then again, it was partly because of Baruch that Tancred had become a thief.

– Is that how you made a living? she asked. Were you really a pickpocket?

– Yes, he answered, when I was younger. Baruch made us read Dickens, and I wanted to be the artful dodger. But that kind of stealing doesn't make you a living. It just gets you addicted to the craft.

Gwen was curious about this, but she didn't press him. The way he spoke of his growing up deepened her feelings for him. But she was also taken by how he listened to her speak, by his interest in her life: what it was like to grow up in Bright's Grove, the strangeness of being Black in such a community, the relief of friendship, the irresistible pull of the city, but also the beauty of the world where she'd grown up, the way she missed it sometimes.

They spoke for so long that it was two in the morning before they knew it, and time to sleep. By then, of course, their relationship had changed. She could not have undressed in front of him otherwise. She'd have asked him to turn around. But she took off her dress, and this act felt oddly like a contradiction. On the one hand, she wanted him to see her. It did something to her to imagine him watching, seeing her in her underclothes, even if it was only for a few moments (by moonlight) as she got into the bed, sliding between the cold sheets. On the other hand: though she liked to imagine him watching her, she trusted Tancred implicitly, entirely. She felt, in the depths of herself, that she was safe with him.

That feeling itself was erotic. When he got on the bed beside her, lying on his side so she had more room than he did, his weight tipping the mattress so that her body moved slightly toward his, his body on top of the quilt, his coat for a cover, she said

– You can get under the covers, Tan. I'm not going to bite you.

He took this good-naturedly, as she'd meant it. And he did get under the covers, taking off his pants and shirt so that she briefly saw his wiry outline by moonlight.

– Good night, he said.

And turned away from her, on his side.

And the last impressions she remembered before she fell asleep were: the intense skin-hunger she felt – the longing to touch and be touched – and the sound of his breathing, regular and deep, the room so lit by moonlight that its white walls looked faintly platinum, the moon itself through the window and above the fields, and the surprising warmth of Tancred's body close to hers.

2

A FAMILY HEIRLOOM

As far as Professor Bruno was concerned, Alun and Helen Lloyd were a perfectly matched couple. Speaking to Gwen from the front seat, he said

— I know, I know! It sounds like an exaggeration, but I've never even *heard* of two people who were better together! I mean, if I were a betting man and if there were a way to judge the suitability of couples, I'd bet my house that your parents would win, *hands down*, the Most Suitable Couple Award for Lambton County. I've never even heard them argue. He talks about her non-stop when she's not around! It's impressive, my dear. It's just impressive. I suppose it's a karmic thing. The stars aligned and they happened to find each other. I mean, these things are mysterious. And you can't just talk about love either. Don't worry, I'm sure your parents love each other, Gwenhwyfar, but the dark secret about married life is that love isn't anywhere near enough for a successful marriage. It takes something more. Let's call it 'soul,' for argument's sake. Your parents are twin souls, my dear girl, and that happens to very few couples. Plato writes about all this, you know. It's in the *Symposium*, a bunch of men sitting around drinking and wondering about love. It's a classic!

– But you have to remember, Morgan, that it was written by a man.

These words were spoken by the professor's friend, Michael, who was doing the driving to Bright's Grove.

– That's true! said Professor Bruno. Undeniably true. But it doesn't invalidate the speculation, you see, because speculate is all anyone can *ever* do about love and death and God and so on. We endlessly speculate. And it's better that way, Michael! All the better. If these conundra were resolved once and for all, the human race would lose a crucial part of its survival mechanism: flexibility of mind. Anyway, all I meant to say was that I adore Gwenhwyfar's parents.

Gwen herself sat in the back seat, only slightly distracted by Professor Bruno's words and the landscape around them: the 403, just past Hamilton, a late winter parade of greys and browns, silver and white. At other times, in other circumstances, she'd have been pleased to hear about her parents, both of whom she loved. But just now, talk of them made her anxious because she had, for the last few days, been wondering what they – her mother in particular – would make of Tancred.

As they approached Brantford, she recalled the feeling of holding Tancred's hand on her breast, her back nestled against the front of him, the two of them spooning unawares, the room having grown colder overnight, the wood stove having almost gone out, her body warm. And how, thinking he'd be embarrassed if he knew they'd held each other this way, she'd gotten up carefully, without disturbing his sleep, put wood on the embers, and then watched him for a time as he slept, the hand she'd held now lying on the bed curled, as if cupping the memory of her breast, his face innocent.

Changing her own subject, warding off desire, Gwen asked

– Where did you two meet, professor?

– Do you mean me and Michael? asked Professor Bruno. We met at a lovely museum where Michael was working. Michael was the best docent I've ever encountered, and knew the museum cold, every detail. Wonderful docent, wonderful person!

– It wasn't under the best of circumstances, though, said Michael.

– No, that's true, said Professor Bruno. Poor Alfred. I still feel guilty about him being bitten.

Michael reached over to touch the professor's leg and it finally occurred to Gwen that the two were more than friends. This idea was intriguing to her, in light of her own thoughts and feelings, but it was also intriguing because Michael seemed much younger than Professor Bruno and, what's more, so different from 'Aunt Barbra,' as Gwen had called the professor's late wife. Yet, at the memory of her aunt, Gwen noticed resemblances between the two: the way Michael's hair was cut like Barbra's (mid-length with bangs), the slightly husky voice, the calm of Michael's demeanour, the fact that Aunt Barbra had also been a knowledgeable person – she'd taught philosophy at University College. Could it be that, despite the disparity in their ages and the fact that Michael was intersex, Professor Bruno could not help responding to the deeper – and more significant – similarities between Michael and the woman he'd loved for thirty years?

This last thought was odd and pleasing in equal measure. Were there, then, aspects of Tancred that she reacted to unconsciously? If so, did that mean there was some part of her that shut off her rational mind when it felt the presence of these nameless aspects? *Consciously*, she thought she preferred men like Olivier. *Consciously*, she sought the ease she felt when she was with Olivier. But, in fact, the longing she felt for Tancred when she was with him was not open for debate, because it was not conscious. This suggested some sort of unseen guidance or 'fate.' Then again, if it was fate, it was fate as the revelation of pleasure.

– I hope you don't mind me asking, Gwen said, but are you two … together?

Immediately, the skin on the back of the professor's neck – the strip where his white hair ended and the top of his blue shirt began – reddened.

– I like your uncle Morgan very much, said Michael. He makes me laugh. But how about you? Are you with someone?

– I'm not sure, said Gwen. But I want to be with him.

(There. She'd said it. And the heavens didn't fall in.)

For the next while – from Brantford to just past London – she and Michael spoke not of love exactly, but of a number of things around it: physical attraction, a sense of humour, beauty, grace, and spiritual connection. Professor Bruno, who was not usually a quiet man, sat quietly, the skin on the back of his neck reddening when certain subjects came up and pinkening at others. He was listening to Gwen and Michael, though. When, for instance, Michael mentioned how much they enjoyed the country-side, Professor Bruno quoted from a poem.

– 'This land like a mirror turns you inward and you become a forest in a furtive lake ...'

It was just before Strathroy that the professor became his usual self again, opening up at the sight of the flat greyness that was Ontario in winter. This wasn't his part of the province; he'd grown up around Nobleton. But the washed-out sky, the wide fields that were brown and grey with, here and there, a faded green that was more like a memory of green ... all of this aroused in Professor Bruno an overwhelming love of the earth. It was, apparently, a love that he shared with Michael, though Michael's feelings about the land were mixed. Being different had caused Michael no end of suffering during a childhood in Hespeler. For Michael, southern Ontario aroused both love and a longing to flee.

Hearing about their ambivalence, Gwen felt even closer to Michael. Though it was late winter and there was little grass to be seen anywhere around them, the image that came to her mind when thinking of what she loved about Ontario was a field by the lake: summer, the grass tall and green, the sky uninhibitedly blue, grasshoppers jumping up unpredictably at times, here and there, one or two, while at other times they sprang up in waves, as if swept up by an invisible hand. In that moment, recalling a field of grasshoppers, Bright's Grove was almost lovable. Gwen even wondered if it wouldn't be better to raise a child somewhere away from the city – if, that is, she were to have a child.

Just past Strathroy, Professor Bruno began talking about nature, a subject that enthralled him without necessarily leading him to novel or even interesting ideas. For instance, Gwen had heard his ruminations on Heidegger often. Professor Bruno began, as always, by protesting that the Latin word *natura* was a corruption of the Greek word it translated, *phusis*. He went on to explain how *phusis*, as it was used by the pre-Socratics, had implicitly to do with being and becoming, how *natura* – from which we got our word *nature* – perverted the Greek word by taking away this *becoming* and making nature an object for human use.

– I adore you, Morgan, said Michael at last, but please stop.

– Why? asked Professor Bruno. Have you heard this before?

– Look, said Michael, if we have to talk about Heidegger, can we at least admit that he misrepresents the nature of words? He starts from Aristotle's various definitions of *phusis* and doesn't draw the proper consequences of these nuances. Words are not static. They're manufacturers of nuance and meaning, even contradictory nuances and meanings. To say that a culture uses a word in '*these* ways' is to deny that it also uses it countless *other* ways at the same time. All Heidegger's investigations into word origins are pleasant for philosophers. But who's to say, Morgan, that a Roman using the word *natura* and a Greek using the word *phusis* don't have exactly the same phenomenon in mind? The way I see it, Morgan, language needs each of us to discover itself. If words could be stopped in their tracks, someone like me wouldn't exist in language. I'd be unnameable.

– Well, I'm not sure Heidegger would disagree with you, said Professor Bruno, but I take your point, my dear, dear Michael. There is always the tragic necessity of being *in* language!

Professor Bruno let his hand linger on Michael's arm.

This touch took place as they drove under a bridge, fifteen minutes from Bright's Grove.

To Gwen, it was remarkable that her mother – a petite whirlwind, interested in everything, knowledgeable about so much – had managed to spend thirty years of her life in Bright's Grove. It was not even a proper town. It was a suburb of Sarnia, which itself was nothing to write home about. How much bad food could you eat on the 'Golden Mile' anyway?

What's more, Helen herself often complained about Bright's Grove.

– I've hidden my light under a bushel, she'd say, whenever she was particularly sad.

Gwen's father would answer

– I couldn't agree more, sweetheart! Why don't we move to Toronto? We'd be able to ...

He never got much further than that, because Helen would change the subject at once. So, although Gwen found it odd that her mother stayed in Bright's Grove, there was no doubt it was her mother who'd chosen Bright's Grove and chose not to leave.

Helen Odhiambo Lloyd. All three names important because, as she put it: one was given to her by her mother, one given by her father, one she'd chosen for herself to express her love for her husband. She would insist on all of them, too, whenever she was introduced to strangers.

It was complicated having such a mother, a woman who stood up for herself and her family whatever the circumstances. It wasn't the standing up that complicated things. It was Gwen's apprehension about the scenes her mother might cause. Gwen had spent part of her childhood dreading encounters with people

– even well-meaning people – who might offend her mother. Some offended her by asking what part of Africa she'd come from, say, or if she'd got used to winter in Canada; others offended in more despicable ways. It seemed to Gwen that her mother was harder on those who were well-meaning. Helen would berate them but engage with them. The ones who suggested she did not belong in Canada she cut out of her life at once and irrevocably. She would not stay in a room with them, whoever they were – and, in Gwen's childhood, these had included schoolteachers, musicians her father knew, even close neighbours.

Though she understood her mother's anger – after all, it was annoying to be asked about Africa when you'd been born in Windsor, Ontario – Gwen did once ask Helen why she raised her voice or yelled at those who'd been unintentionally unkind, while saying nothing to the more blatantly racist.

– There's a difference between thoughtlessness and desecration, Helen answered.

She refused to say anything more about it, leaving Gwen to figure it out for herself.

When Gwen thought back on her childhood, she mostly recalled the admiration she'd felt for her mother – the admiration and, just as importantly, the ways her mother had fought for her, whatever the circumstances. Helen did not spoil her daughter. She'd chastise her, whenever she felt there was reason. But she gave no one else the right to do this. In a word, Gwen was never unsure of her mother's love.

Nor was she now.

But if the thought of seeing her mother was a happiness lightly tinged with apprehension, the thought of being 'home' was pure contradiction. The pleasure of pulling into their driveway on Hamilton Street, the feel of the nearby lake, its muted presence, the houses of people she'd known and grown up with ... all good impressions. But these feelings were met by the onset of an almost instinctive boredom, by the memory of wood-panelled basements that smelled of mildew and of bookshelves filled with leather-bound tomes someone thought they should read. Her visits home were nostalgia mixed with a persistent desire to leave.

This visit with Professor Bruno and Michael, however, was almost immediately different from any other. Yes, Gwen felt the usual pleasure at seeing her mother and father come out of the house, a pleasure heightened by the fact that Professor Bruno had been talking about them. And yes, Helen was pleased at the sight of her daughter. They embraced and Gwen held her mother – five foot two, a hundred and twenty pounds, if that. But as they embraced, Helen almost casually said

– You're in love! I'm so happy for you and there's so much I want to tell you.

There were a number of things that made these words weird. For one, Gwen herself had told no one about the depths of her feeling for Tancred. She'd only just acknowledged them herself. For another, her mother had never before shown interest in her love life. In fact, in the past, she'd dismissed Gwen's relationships: not cruelly, not without feeling, but as if she knew something Gwen did not.

– Mom, how did you know? asked Gwen.

– I've been waiting for this day since you were born, said Helen, and now it's come.

These words were almost as disconcerting as her first had been. Helen put a finger to her own lips and then said

– We'll talk about all this tomorrow. I want to spend some time with Morgan and Michael tonight. Is that okay?

Gwen could not think what to say, but her mother did not give her the time, in any case. Helen turned to Professor Bruno and called out

– Morgan!

going to him, leaving Gwen to greet her father.

Gwen's parents, it seemed, had known and liked Michael for some time. Helen was thrilled by Michael's familiarity with painting, and over supper, the two spoke of Holbein's *Ambassadors*, its hidden signs and symbols.

– I've only ever seen it once, said Helen. On a school trip to London, when I was thirteen, but it's the only painting I've ever dreamed about.

– You should see it again, said Michael. It's brilliant. Everyone talks about the anamorphic skull, but I love the parquet the men are standing on. The design on it is in the form of a quincunx. Holbein copied it from the floor of Westminster Abbey, where Henry VIII had just married Anne Boleyn. The whole painting's so suggestive!

Helen sighed and said

– We don't really travel, Alun and I. We're homebodies.

– That's not true, said Alun. I'm always travelling. But Helen won't set foot outside Bright's Grove. She'd rather read about places than visit them.

– Well, it's a lovely prison, though, isn't it? said Professor Bruno. If you have to have a prison, Bright's Grove's a good one. Anyway, a person can learn everything from books, if they can stand all the reading ...

– She reads even more than you do, Morey!

– Then she's like Immanuel Kant. He spent his life in or around Königsberg, but he read everything, and it was said he knew more about foreign places than people who'd visited them. So, you see, Al, your wife is a genius.

– I agree! said Alun. She's like Beethoven composing when he was deaf. He had music inside him. Helen's got geography.

– Except it's not like that at all, said Helen. I'm not a genius. I'm agoraphobic!

It was here, more or less, that Gwen tuned the conversation out. She'd heard versions of this conversation for years. Besides, her mother's words on greeting her were still very much on her mind. It was even a bit ... *annoying*, knowing she'd have to wait for her mother's elucidations. So she excused herself from the table. It was still early, but she went to her bedroom – kept as she'd left it by her mother, the posters on the walls proof that she was her father's daughter: Cecil Taylor, Marilyn Crispell, Anthony Braxton, Sarah Vaughan.

She looked through her texts, finding one from Nadia, warning her that she and Robbie had made up and Gwen was not to be alarmed if Robbie was in the apartment when she returned. There was also a text from Olivier, asking how she was and wondering if she would care to visit Simone with him and Tancred. The occasion was Simone's birthday, and Gwen would finally be able to meet Simone's husband, Gordon, about whom she'd heard so much.

Olivier's text was the only one she answered, and she laboured over her answer, because it felt as though she owed him a proper response.

> Nice to hear from you. I'd love to celebrate Simone's birthday with Tancred and you! And it would be lovely to meet Gordon. Thank you so much for thinking of me!

> But I'm with my parents, in Bright's Grove. So I won't be going anywhere for the next few days. I hope Tancred and you and Simone are doing well, and that you have a lovely time.

> Please say "Happy Birthday" to Simone for me.

She'd carved those words out from what had been a much longer message, a message in which she'd reminded Olivier of their car ride together, of the questions she'd forgotten to ask Tancred, and about the night she'd spent with Tancred. She'd thought through every word and then erased them and cursed herself for caring so much when it was unlikely Olivier would catch any of the nuances anyway and probably wouldn't care if he did.

She sent the texts off in exasperation.

Then woke up sometime around two in the morning, the lights in her room still on, Anthony Braxton looking over at her while, in her ear, a podcast she'd not chosen droned on about 'no mind,' a Buddhist concept that, it was suggested, could be used to succeed in business. That was all strange enough, but there was also the disorienting surprise of waking in her room, in her parents' home, some small part of her waiting – the child in her waiting – for her mother to come in, as mothers will when their children wake at night.

This feeling, the expectation that her mother would come to her, was so strong that it kept her awake – or seemed to – until she woke for good at seven in the morning, having dreamed that she and Michael were in a vast gallery, standing before Holbein's *Ambassadors*. The painting, which she'd seen on trips to London with her father, had a page number at the bottom of it and, to Gwen's shame, it was being eaten by caterpillars.

The best thing about waking early – the only good thing Gwen could think of – was that it sometimes gave her time alone with her dad. From the year she was fifteen, from the day her mother suggested her father was getting 'hefty,' Gwen went out walking with him if she was up.

In keeping with the general strangeness of this visit, however, this morning was strange, too. For one thing, her mother was up, sitting in the kitchen. This was in itself noteworthy, as Helen was resolutely *not* a morning person. Then, too, Professor Bruno was with her parents, drinking coffee.

Gwen said

– Are you going for a walk, Dad?

– Are you coming with me? answered Alun.

– You should go, said Professor Bruno. Helen and I will keep each other company with talk of literature.

– What? No Heidegger? asked Alun.

– Michael has practically convinced me that Martin Heidegger was a nasty liar, said Professor Bruno. So, you know ...

Looking directly at her daughter, Helen said

– When you come back, Gwenhwyfar, we can talk, just the two of us.

– That sounds mysterious, said Alun. Can I listen in?

– No, said Helen.

If she had not agreed to go walking with her father, Gwen would have insisted that she and Helen begin speaking at once, the 'mystery' now striking her as peremptory and inconsiderate. And, in fact, this unpleasant feeling ate into her time with her dad.

–What she wants to say to you must be serious, he said.

Rather than talk to him about it, Gwen interrupted her father's line of thought. She asked how he was doing. Had he not recently gigged in Vancouver? (*Yes, he had.*) Had he enjoyed playing ... what was the repertoire again? (*Duke Ellington, mostly.*) So had he enjoyed playing 'Caravan' (*her favourite*) for a week as part of a ... was it a trio? (*No, a quintet.*) Yes, he had. He loved the music and always came away from it renewed.

It was, Gwen thought (as she often thought), disappointing that, although he was always busy, her father never received the recognition a musician of his calibre deserved. This lack of grand-scale success did not bother him. He was happiest returning to Bright's Grove to be with his wife, and he often said so. Professor Bruno was right about Helen and Alun being well-matched. But, loving her father as she did, Gwen couldn't help wanting more for him. Just a little more. Enough to show that the world appreciated him as much as he deserved.

On returning from their walk, they found that breakfast had been prepared. The kitchen smelled of onions, bacon, and cooked egg. Morgan, Michael, and Helen had collaborated on a quiche, but it had been Morgan's idea, because quiche reminded him of his late wife, and of their honeymoon in Paris. In fact, as Gwen and her father came into the kitchen, the three were laughing about a time when an obstreperous barman had refused to serve Morgan what he wanted – a café au lait – because his French accent was deemed incomprehensible, though you could tell the bastard – as Morgan termed him – understood every word Morgan spoke.

– Well, said Alun, that could only have happened in Paris.

– Not at all! answered his wife. You'd be surprised where and why people refuse to serve you.

This provoked a discussion about each of their favourite places on earth, a discussion that was for Michael (San Francisco), Morgan (Berlin), and Alun (London) happy and filled with nostalgia, each naming a favourite sight (the bay seen from the Bay Bridge) or neighbourhood (Schöneberg) or place (Sir John Soane's Museum). For Gwen, the matter was more complicated. She hadn't travelled recently. The places she'd visited with her father were now no doubt different from how she imagined them. But if she had to name somewhere, it would be Toronto, for the city, and Glen Stewart Park, for the place.

Helen did not participate in the conversation. After Gwen had spoken, Helen rose from the table, excusing herself and touching her daughter's shoulder.

– Gwenhwyfar, she said, come. Let me show you something I've been working on.

Assuming her mother was referring to a quilt or watercolour, Gwen was pleased to follow her up to the 'eyrie,' the large, two-room attic that was her mother's exclusive domain. Visiting the eyrie was in itself a pleasure. It was where, when Gwen was a child, her mother had fed her, consoled her, rocked her to sleep. As she grew up, the visits had become rare, but she could still remember them. Her father, who had named the eyrie, did not visit it often, as far as Gwen could tell. It was her mother's domain.

The two rooms of the eyrie were spacious and tall-ceilinged, not at all like a typical attic. They had large windows, wooden floors, and they were connected by a heavy sliding door. The rooms were very different in how they looked and felt, though. One was a studio. It was filled with boxes of material, cabinets, and shelves for her finished work. In the centre of this room, there was an ancient treadle sewing machine on a rug, its wrought-iron legs and treadle still as alluring to Gwen now as they'd been when she was a child.

This was the room she knew best, the room she thought of when she imagined her mother in the eyrie. But this was not the room her mother led her to. Instead they went to the 'library', a space filled with books and bookshelves, two wooden trunks, maps of the world on the walls, a large writing desk near the window, a chair, a sofa, a coffee table. If Gwen had ever been in this room, it was too long ago for her to recall. She had glimpsed it, however, once or twice, when the door between rooms was open.

Helen patted the place beside her on the couch and, when Gwen sat down, she said

– Try to remember, Gwenhwyfar. Have I ever lied to you?

The question was amusing. It was one Helen had often asked, when she wanted to reassure her daughter that she was on her side. So the answer did not take thought.

– No, Mom, she said. You've never lied to me.

– I've wanted to, said Helen. At times, I wanted to spare your feelings. But I swore to myself never to lie to you and I never have. It wasn't all heavy going. It was a relief having someone in my life I didn't *have* to lie to. It still is. But the important thing is that you understand I'm not lying to you now. Are you in love, Gwenhwyfar?

Gwen felt calm, relieved even. Some part of her had long been waiting for a moment like this. In fact, when she thought of it later, it seemed clear that her mother had, perhaps unconsciously, prepared her for just this moment. And on hearing the question now, in the eyrie, it felt to Gwen as if her soul were saying 'finally' to something, though she had no idea what.

– Yes, she said, I'm in love. But how did you know?

– I knew it, said Helen, the minute Morgan told us he and Michael were bringing you. It's strange how clear it was. And then, when I saw you, well, there was no question. But what it means is that the box on the coffee table belongs to you now.

Gwen had, of course, noticed the box. She'd ignored it while her mother spoke, but it was unmissable: fifteen inches long, eleven wide, and eleven deep. It was as black as if it had been charred, but also smooth, its edges rounded. Colour-wise, the only irregularities on it were a pale, gold-yellow lock that looked younger than the box itself, and at the very centre of its top, an inlaid white circle whose diameter was about two inches.

– What's in it? asked Gwen.

– Here's the key, answered her mother.

The key was old-style, but it wasn't remarkable. Nor, when she opened the box, was there anything remarkable in it: three books. It was when she took the books out, however, that she saw how unusual the chest and its contents actually were. For one thing, the books were bound in lambskin leather, their bindings flexible and their colour reddish-brown. Each had detailed embossing on its spine: a large bee (1), a beehive (2), and a bear with two cubs (3). The books were not of equal thickness. The first was written in a language Gwen could not read – Greek, as it turned out – and was only forty pages long. The second was some two or three hundred pages, its handwritten text in a variety of inks and languages. The third book was five inches thick, at least a thousand pages long, handwritten and multilingual, but organized in a way Gwen could not understand, the languages following each other without obvious rhythm or pattern.

When the books had been taken from the chest, Gwen saw that there were clusters of pearl-white circles on the wood beneath them: two times two at one end of the chest, two times two at the other:

OO   OO
OO   OO

– When your grandmother gave these things to me, said Helen, she told me what her mother told her: 'Just remember that you're one of many daughters who thought their mothers were loony.'

– But I don't think you're loony, said Gwen.

– Not yet, said Helen.

The inlaid pearl circles were not simply decorative. They were part of a mechanism. Gwen and Helen, each on her side of the box, used two fingers of each hand to push down on all eight circles at once. When this was done, there was a strangely satisfying click, a brief whirr of gears, and, inside the chest, a hinged square pane dropped down to reveal a hidden compartment in which a gold ring was held by two minuscule clasps.

– I can't tell you how often I've imagined this moment, said Helen. But now that it's here, the only thing I can think about is my mother.

Helen did not touch the ring. She directed Gwen to take it and, once Gwen had slipped it from its clasp, closed the hinged piece so that, unless you _knew_ there was a hidden compartment, you would not think of looking for one.

The ring, unremarkable in itself, lay in the palm of Gwen's hand.

– It's fit all of us, said Helen. Let's see if it fits you.

It did: not Gwen's ring finger, but the pinky of her right hand.

– There're a million things I'd like to tell you, said Helen, but most of it's already written somewhere in these books. There are two things I want you to remember, though. First, you mustn't wear this ring or keep it by you after you've settled into your new life. It won't kill you, but it'll bring very bad luck. My great-great-great-grandmother lost two close friends before she took it off. Her name was Magdalene San Giovanni. You can read her daughter's testimony, if you understand Italian. But she's not the only one who wore the ring after settling down. And they all had bad luck. The second thing, the most important thing, is that when the book says this ring will give you three wishes, it's not like in fairy tales. It's more limited. You can change three things about the man you love before you marry him. You can't change anything afterward. The ring comes at a price, and the changes you make *may* have a price, too. That's really all there is to it, except that once you put the ring back between the clasps, you won't be able to reopen the compartment on your own. You'll need two people: you and your daughter.

The absurdity of what her mother had just told her was only slightly undercut by her nonchalant tone. You'd have said Helen was showing her how to work a new toaster. And, in fact, Gwen laughed at the collision of tone and idea. Three wishes? Oh please, pull the other one.

But the fact was: her mother never *had* lied to her. Nor was Helen one for practical jokes. So, after a moment, Gwen found herself more puzzled by what was going on than she was upset by the implications of her mother's obvious delusion.

Taking up the shortest of the books, Gwen opened it to the first pages:

ἤδη γὰρ τότε κάρτα τοσούτους Μάργος ἔδακνε
ὥστ'οὐδεὶς ἄτρωτος ἐπήρχετο δώματα πεζός.
ἡ δὲ θεά κεδνοῦ καὶ ἐσθλοῦ κυνὸς ὄντος ἐρήμη.
καὶ εὐβούλου κεδνοῦ τε θεὰ ἔστενε προστάτις Μάργου
πικρά τ'ἐφώνει· μὴ πάντας γ' ἱκέτους ὑπ'ανάγκης
δάκνεις …

– This is in Greek, isn't it? she asked.

– Yes, said Helen. The whole first book's in ancient Greek. It's why I tried to get you to learn the language: so you could read the original for yourself. The second book – the one with the hive on it – is filled with translations of the first book. So you don't *have* to learn Greek. Of course, there's an argument among our foremothers about translations. Some of them feel it's wrong to read the poem in translation. My mother was disappointed when I wouldn't learn Greek. And now that I *can* read Greek, I see what she meant. I'm sure I'd have liked the poem better in the original. But then, listen: it's not bad luck if you don't read it. It's up to you. It's just that ... the poem is something we share, just us and our foremothers. So I'd read it if you're curious about your heritage.

Still mystified, Gwen said

— Mom, do you actually believe everything you just told me?

— It's important that you remember, Gwenhwyfar, that I was once in your place and my mother was in mine. And I was even younger than you. I fell in love with your father when I was twenty-two. I was angry at my mother at the time, and I didn't want to believe anything she told me. Let's just say I think differently about all this now.

— So you're saying you made three wishes and changed Dad before you married him?

— Gwenhwyfar, you can read as little or as much as you want from the books. You're here for two more days. Before you go back home, I'll answer all the questions I can. I told your father that I'd found letters from my mother that I wanted you to read. And I asked him to keep Morgan and Michael entertained, if ever I have to answer your questions. He knows this is a private matter, and I've asked him not to ask you about it. So no one will be bothering you while you read.

Helen rose from the sofa and swiped at her jeans as if something were on them.

— Can you carry the box by yourself? she asked. Or should we take the books out first?

At the best of times, on her best day, it would have been difficult to accept what Helen had told her. And yes, she did think her mother might be loony. But, resigned to at least looking at the books, Gwen carried the box and its contents — the ring on her finger — down to her bedroom, to her white desk with its *Lion King*–themed lamp.

From the door of the room, her mother looked back with either understanding or amusement. It was hard to tell which, but as soon as the door closed, Gwen began to cry, without realizing she was crying. She was overcome by emotion, and her first thought, though she knew it was childish, was to destroy the books themselves – as if they were the cause of her situation. But, of course, the situation did not stem from inanimate objects. To think that it did was to give books, box, and ring the importance her mother ascribed to them. Besides, she had been raised to revere books. Her mother had often said, in words that held a certain menace

– To burn a book is to burn a soul.

Gwen believed this implicitly. So the idea of damaging the books alarmed her more than it brought comfort. Then, too, the books themselves – their binding, their pages, their illustrations, the writing in their margins – were captivating. They were 'real,' in the sense that they were genuinely old, and they put her in mind of the Gutenberg Bibles she'd seen in the Beinecke library while visiting Yale with her father, before she'd opted to study at the University of Toronto. The Bibles had been under protective glass, of course, but they'd given off the same idea of 'book' as these books did.

Which is to say, there was an almost atavistic reverence in Gwen's response to them.

Book One (The Bee) – Entirely in ancient Greek. With two parts: a poem and a section of prose.

Book Two (The Beehive) – In many languages, with numerous sections. Each section a translation of the Greek poem and prose of Book One.

Book Three (She Bear and Cubs) – In many languages, with even more sections than the second book. From what Gwen could make out, it was made up of commentary on the Greek poem and prose of Book One, as well as including short accounts of the lives of women who had previously owned the books as well as their advice on how to use the ring and how to interpret the poem.

To begin, Gwen took up the shortest of the three, Book One. It was extremely old and incomparably beautiful – 'incomparable' with regard to any of the books she had ever seen, the Gutenberg Bibles included. Realizing again what she held in her hands, Gwen was even more puzzled. Here was a book that was almost certainly centuries old, invaluable, its pages vellum, its ink charcoal black. In the book's wide margins, there were a number of illustrations: a dog, a woman hunting, clouds drifting above mountains, reeds in a pond, strange flowers, a bald man who appeared to be farting, a woman in bed with a man, a ring.

Book One's first section, the poem, was twenty-five pages long, handwritten with the title

δακτύλιος

The second section was an essay. It had an introduction and six numbered parts. Its title was

περὶ χρείας δακτυλίου

In this section, there were some handwritten notes in the margins, notes made in a variety of languages and, judging by the various handwritings, by a number of people. In this part of the book, there was only one illustration, but it was memorable. It was a drawing of what looked to be a large penis, beneath which were the words

προμάθεια
Faites attention!
Ten cuidado!

Vorsicht!
Be careful!

The drawing was memorable for obvious reasons. It was crude and unexpected. But it was affecting, because its crudeness was so unlike anything she associated with her mother. That thought – whether it was right or not – answered a fleeting question that had occurred to her: was this all some sort of ruse? Whatever the intent of the books, it was almost certainly impossible for Helen to have made them herself. The ancient technology, the knowledge of so many languages, the drawings by different stylists – some crude, some refined – the marginalia in different inks, the vellum pages ... all of this would have cost a fortune, *if* you could find the people to do it.

Gwen now turned to the book with the beehive embossed on its spine.

This volume was bound in the same material as the first and of the same dimensions, but its pages were paper, not vellum. It was a few hundred pages long – difficult to tell exactly how long, because a good part of it was left blank, unnumbered. Finally, it had smaller margins and almost no marginalia. Its translations of Book One were in a number of languages, some of which Gwen could read (English, French, Spanish), most of which she could not.

On a closer look, Book Two wasn't quite so straightforward. Yes, there were translations in several languages, but among these were three English translations, two French, two Spanish, etc. These re-translations – or maybe translations of translations – had obviously been made generations apart. The language of the first English translation, for instance, was all 'thee' and 'thou.' On top of that, each translation was signed, and Gwen was moved to see her grandmother's signature – Estelle Homer Odhiambo – at the bottom of the latest translation in English: her grandmother's translation in what she recognized as her grandmother's handwriting. In fact, seeing her grandmother's handwriting, Gwen was almost overcome with emotion. The moment vividly brought the beauty of her grandmother's hands to her mind, as well as how captivated she'd been by them as a child, beguiled by the stump on her right hand where her little finger had been cut off.

Book Three, the one with a bear and two cubs on its spine, was bound in the same material as the other two, lambskin. Its pages were paper. It held countless drawings, some of them quite rude, and its languages were intermingled – pell-mell, it appeared – so that Gwen's impression was of a kind of bazaar where a great many people were talking.

Because Book Three was the record of generations of women who had dealt with the ring, it was the most complex, shameful, and moving of the books. Each entry was like a layer of shale or mica. And Gwen, now beguiled by the book, meticulously counted the layers, identifying each writer by their handwriting. This is how she discovered that fifty-four writers had commented on the poem and prose in Book One, that fifty-four previous writers had left a record of their wishes and described the consequences of their mother's use of the ring. It was in Book Three, for instance, that Gwen discovered her mother had made three wishes about her father before they were married:

1. That he could not be unfaithful to her
2. That he would defer to her in all matters concerning their home
3. That he would never achieve his musical ambitions

It was interesting: all of her foremothers had taken on the task of keeping the ring. All had passed the ring on to their daughters. But not all had used the three wishes. And of those who'd made use of their wishes, not all admitted what they wished for. Her mother had, though, and this outraged her until it occurred to

Gwen that either the ring and its wishes were a fiction, in which case it didn't matter what her mother might have wished, or the whole business was true and, if *that* were the case, the implications went well beyond the relationship of her mother and father.

The books her mother had given her were both a challenge and a gift. The challenge was that it felt to Gwen as if she were now living in a world that looked like hers but that, fundamentally, was not. What's more, she did not want to live in a world of wishes and charmed objects, even if it was her inheritance. As to her foremothers, however: reading their words, Gwen developed an almost immediate affection for some of them. The gift was in their accounts of themselves. It was in the vividness of the writing. If she could, she'd have chosen to meet them on different ground, in a world that was not magical. But, of course, it was as witnesses to the impossible that they'd written in the first place.

Hours passed as Gwen read from Book Three. It was late afternoon before she remembered she hadn't eaten, that she was hungry. She had been absorbed not only by the words of her mother and grandmother but also by those of, among others, her five-times-great-grandmother – Elizabeth Evelyn Umanets – who'd wished her beloved to be 'a foot taller and incapable of loving anyone but her.' It was Elizabeth's daughter who wrote that although her mother's marriage was a good one, her father was insufferably proud of his height – a complete narcissist, but for his devotion to his wife, about whom he bragged almost as often as he did his height.

Wishing to talk to her mother without facing anyone else, Gwen went quietly upstairs, back to the eyrie to see if her mother was there. And so she was, sitting at her desk in the library, drinking tea, the room darkening, the fading light still comprehended in the window, the steam from her tea visible as it drifted up.

How small her mother looked: older, no longer the dark-haired and imposing mother Gwen had in her imagination. There was more grey in Helen's hair and, despite herself, Gwen wished she would dye it. She felt a rush of concern that, perhaps by habit, was expressed as complaint.

– Mom, she said quietly, why are you sitting in the dark?

– Hmm, said Helen. Do you know, Gwenhwyfar, my mother stayed up all night waiting for me after she gave me the books. I think all of us mothers are anxious to know if our daughters experience what we experienced. The first thing I read was Mother's translation of the poem. What about you?

Though there was no reason to, they kept their voices low as Gwen told her mother what she'd read.

– Listen, said Gwen, you don't really believe that you had three wishes and that's why you and Dad have a great relationship, do you?

– The things I wished for all happened, said Helen. They might all have happened anyway. How do I know for sure? But do I believe it? Yes, I do. I believe my mother and my grandmother and my great-grandmother. All of them. The problem is, it's difficult to have proof the ring works unless you wish for some physical change, but all our foremothers who wished for physical changes to the men they married regretted it afterwards. Anyway, I would never have changed your father, physically. There wasn't one inch of that man that didn't work for me.

– But you wished for him *not* to achieve his ambitions, said Gwen. Isn't that worse?

– Yes, it's something I regret. I thought it would change our relationship if he was really famous, and since I was too young to know better, I wished for something I thought would keep us together as we were. I've spent a lot of time wondering about my wish. Anyway, how do I know his ambitions would have been achieved?

– Why did you even write your wishes down in the book? You didn't have to.

– No, I didn't, but when I was twenty-two, I believed in openness. Mother warned me I might be embarrassed by your seeing what I'd wished for, but at the same time she encouraged me to be honest, because she didn't think it would help you if I hid anything. That's why she wrote *her* wishes in the book, so I could take advantage of her mistakes.

– Weren't you embarrassed by what Grammy wrote?

– No, I was more surprised than embarrassed. Your grandmother was straitlaced, very proper. Not the kind of woman you'd think was a witch.

– Who said anything about witches? asked Gwen.

– Well, black books and magic rings. I don't know what else to call it. I didn't believe her when she told me about the ring any more than you believe me now. It's our fate not to believe our mothers and then to have our daughters not believe us. I guess that's every mother's fate, in one way or another. But it's our fate in particular, those of us who know about the ring. And, right now, that's you and me.

Now that they were speaking reasonably about the unreasonable, a thousand questions came to Gwen's mind. Perhaps instinctively, she asked one that she assumed was related to the ring, though she did not understand how.

– I always thought you hated Gram, she said. She came to visit us, but you never came when we visited her. You didn't even go to her funeral. Is it because of something she wrote?

Her mother's regret was almost palpable.

– I don't think you'll appreciate what I'm going to tell you, Gwenhwyfar. Not until you've read 'Rules for Using the Ring.' But I'm going to tell you now, because I want you to keep it in mind. In exchange for the privilege of knowing the sacred, the ring demands a sacrifice. You can choose what you sacrifice or the ring will choose for you. Your grandmother gave up one of her fingers. But I didn't want to do that. So when I used the ring, the thing I chose was to never leave Bright's Grove. I chose what I did because I was sure Bright's Grove had everything I could ever want. And I haven't been able to leave it since. I didn't get the chance to write how much I regret my decision. So the first thing I want you to write, when you write in the book, is how unhappy I've been with my choice. I feel like I gave away much more than I had to. Knowing what I know now, I'd happily give up a finger.

– I'm not saying I believe any of this, said Gwen, but what if I don't want it? Why should I have anything to do with any of it?

– I've had thirty-odd years to think how to answer that question, and I haven't come up with a good answer yet. I don't remember reading any answers to it in the book either. And the reason for that, I think, is that none of us has turned down the ring. Not in all the centuries. I don't say it's the same, but it's a little like Christ asking not to be chosen. Once you accept that the ring is sacred, it's hard not to accept the consequences. But maybe you'll be the first. Then we'll see.

It had been a relief to hear her mother admit she had no idea if the ring had granted her three wishes or not. But then, it had been disconcerting to hear her say that she *believed* in the ring, believed it was sacred or that it brought knowledge of the sacred. It seemed to Gwen that her mother's 'belief' was more like faith, a faith based on the testimony of their foremothers. It wasn't unreasonable per se, but it was odd coming from the one who'd taught her to be skeptical.

That said, what compelling witnesses her foremothers had been! Those she could understand best – those who'd written in English and French – were filled with concern for the daughters who would come after them. And, of course, each one that came after was in turn concerned for her daughter. Each writer had been a reader (or listener), each reader became a writer, all writing for an audience of one, but all aware of the voices that preceded them.

That's not to say that Gwen found the books unproblematic. There was much that was unpleasant in them, because not all her foremothers had lived pleasant lives, despite their good marriages, and much that was crude, because not all had embraced the idea of books and learning. Moreover, it disturbed Gwen that the ring had gone only to women, that all of her foremothers had had daughters. If the ring business turned out to be true, *she* would not hesitate to give the ring to whoever her child might be, irrespective of gender. She was not the only one who'd thought about this, of course. Two of her relatively recent foremothers – from Caen and Port of Spain, respectively – had both expressed concern about having boys. Both of them believed that passing the ring and its three wishes on to a boy would only amount to imposing large breasts on the woman he married. This was not, it seemed to Gwen, unassailably true.

Following her mother's advice and her own curiosity, Gwen spent the rest of the day reading her grandmother's translation of the essay called 'On the Use of the Ring' and her foremothers' various reactions to it.

(An aside: Gwen was not amused to find that, in places, her mother had tried to correct her grandmother's translation of περὶ χρείας δακτυλίου. Gwen found it slightly annoying that, in Book Three, her mother had written 'Rules for Using the Ring is a better translation.' So, making her first marks in the margins of Book Three, Gwen wrote 'Grammy was being faithful to the original,' though she did not know if this was true.)

So, 'On the Use of the Ring,' then ...

The essay was made up of six parts:

1. Origin of the Ring
2. The Ring, Its Rules
3. Suggestions for Use of the Ring
4. Sacrifice
5. Those Who Came before Writing
6. The Ring Protects Itself

The language throughout was clear, either because her grand-mother's translation made it so, or because the original had been. Of course, not all the sections interested her equally. Nor had they been of equal interest to her foremothers. There was relatively little commentary on the 'Introduction' or on 'Those Who Came before Writing,' a list of fifty names that had been memorized by those who'd lived before the teaching of writing. Some of the names may have come before the advent of writing even, when the poem and the rules for the ring's use existed only as legends passed from mother to daughter.

For Gwen, it was fascinating that the ring had its origin beyond the written record. It was intriguing, too, that there had been some animosity among mothers and daughters on the subject of whether or not the rules and the poem ought to have been written down at all. But as far as Gwen was concerned, these were squabbles about unimportant things. Without doubt, without doubt for her anyway, it was best to have things written down, to have them protected from forgetting.

She was not unaware, though, that the writing of the poem must have changed its feel and context and maybe even content. Nor could she imagine anyone numbering the sections of the essay before the written version was made. Clearly, the sense of order that numbers gave made the essay seem more reasonable than it would have otherwise. Though, how reasonable was it?

The parts of the essay that had elicited the most commentary were sections 2, 3, 4, and 6. All who'd gone before her had something to say about the rules, about the kind of wishes to make, about the sacrifices that were best – there was heated debate about which finger or toe to cut off, for instance. There were also many examples of how, exactly, the ring protected itself.

All of that said, the rules for using the ring were, in principle, simple:

1. One was allowed three wishes.
2. These wishes were exclusively to do with the beloved. One could change nothing about oneself.
3. One could, if one chose, change a physical aspect of the beloved. But, in so doing, one forfeited a wish. Nor could one change two physical aspects of the beloved.

You'd have thought these conditions were clear. They seemed clear to Gwen, but each condition had elicited vivid responses and objections. Many struggled with a perceived injustice: if the ring brought three wishes, why should they not *have* three, regardless of what the wishes might be? Why should the sacrifice be the same if, having changed some physical aspect of your beloved, you were allowed only one other wish? Moreover, why should it matter to the goddess – for whose return, according to some, the ring was being kept – if her daughters were granted three wishes, whatever the nature of the wishes?

Then there were questions about the wishes being limited to the beloved. Gwen's French ancestors, two from the seventeenth century in particular, wondered whether it were not better to change *oneself* in order to change the beloved. From which it followed that changing the beloved was, in fact, a way to change oneself. From which it *then* followed that the second of the ring's conditions made no sense. In the centuries that followed, many of Gwen's foremothers thought these objections interesting, though most concluded that they were also irrelevant.

Gwen was not sure how she felt about these ideas from the seventeenth century, the age of 'Scientific Revolution,' but in her second contribution to the books, she rewrote a marginal sentence by her nine- or ten-times-great-grandmother, Marie di Francesca d'Auvergne – '*Au cœur de notre vie, il est un don qui ne se laisse pas connaître*' – and translated it herself ('At the heart of this life is a gift that is unknowable'), adding that she thought it true for people in general. She was later pleased to discover that her grandmother had both translated and commented on the very same sentence, though their translations were slightly different. Her grandmother had translated it 'At the heart of life there is a gift that keeps itself hidden' and beside it had added 'At the heart of life there is guilt.'

Many of the marginal comments in Book Two, the book of translations – or the longest of the comments anyway – were devoted to the third condition, the one about changing a physical aspect of the beloved. None who had changed a physical aspect of their beloved had been satisfied with the results.

It was, of course, in the comments about this rule that Gwen encountered the drawing of the penis in context. The problem for those who'd chosen to alter their beloved's endowments – three in the thirteenth century who'd wished for smaller and two in the twentieth who'd wished for bigger – was not with the penises themselves but rather the effect the change had on the men. In all five cases, the men had become obsessed with their new appendages.

Well, you should have expected this, thought Gwen, and she felt disappointed in her foremothers. But the fact was: *all* those who'd changed a bodily aspect of their partner encountered the same phenomenon. Their men became obsessed with their new height, or greater strength, or longer legs, etc. So it was, in the end, a bad idea to change a man's physique, because it could not be done without changing the man's attitude to himself. More: the physical changes had altered her foremothers' feelings for their beloveds as well. In at least two instances that Gwen discovered, the alterations had somewhat dampened the love a foremother had felt for her beloved.

The third section of the essay, the section called 'Suggestions for Use of the Ring,' was itself a short essay about love. The section was an effort to define 'love.' Its main point, as far as Gwen could tell, was that the life of the beloved is as crucial to the self as the self's own life. The essay offered no actual suggestions for the ring's use. However, the marginalia, filled with suggestions, was almost unreadably dense. As well, hundreds of practical suggestions for uses of the ring were to be found in Book Three.

Not all the suggestions made were helpful. Gwen found some of them eccentric ('Thou shouldst will for a quatch'), some too specific ('Let him learn to fish'), and some she simply found unpleasant. She could not see why, for instance, she should wish for her beloved to be 'pious' or 'God-fearing.' Whatever those words had meant to the ones who'd written them, to Gwen they reeked not of the spiritual but of right-wing business and fools trying to control her body. The useful suggestions were the ones that seemed most straightforward to her: wish him kind, wish him thoughtful, wish him talkative, etc.

If the second and third sections of 'On the Use of the Ring' had elicited riveting, and sometimes moving, testimony from her foremothers, the section entitled 'Sacrifice' brought forth feelings of a different order. 'Sacrifice' was, more or less, an encomium on the idea of compensation: compensation as balance, compensation as justice, compensation as right. It was also where Gwen discovered that, as keeper of the ring, she would have to give up something precious. Being who she was meant that this cup passed to her. She could give something up or something would be taken from her.

Nor was any sacrifice specified. Many of her foremothers had surrendered fingers or toes – hence the debate among them over which one it was easier to lose, finger or toe. But her mother had given up travel, confining herself, like an anchorite, to Bright's Grove. And others had surrendered sight in one eye, hearing in one ear, or even a certain number of teeth.

The idea of this 'sacrifice' was disturbing enough. Gwen felt great pity for the women who'd disfigured themselves in order to pass the ring and its books down to their daughters. But more unnerving still was the assertion that those who did not choose their sacrifice would have one imposed on them: they would lose fingers or toes or find themselves suddenly unable to do things they loved doing.

And what did her foremothers receive in return? Well, if their writings were true, all of their marriages had been loving and happy. All had experience of the magical or the impossible or the sacred – whatever you wished to call that phenomenon beyond human comprehension.

Not surprisingly, the commentary about sacrifice was engrossing. But it was also bewildering to Gwen, because she did not know what to make of her foremothers' belief in magic. It wasn't only the fact of their belief that intrigued her. It was also the slow withdrawal of belief over time. The earliest of her foremothers did not question the existence of magic or the need for sacrifice. But over time, from generation to generation, doubt crept in. Though the ring was kept, questions about the nature of the ring and the sacred were recorded until ... well, until her, Gwenhwyfar Lloyd. In her, she thought, doubt reached its apogee.

Yes, but as to doubt ... perhaps her great foremother, Marie di Francesca d'Auvergne, was right: '*Le doute est et la province et l'avantage de la jeunesse.*' Or, in Gwen's translation, 'Doubt is both the province and prerogative of the young.' Because although questions about the ring and the sacred were more common as the centuries progressed, in every instance the ring swept doubts aside. None of those who had written in the books disbelieved.

And as to compensation ... there was a further, unpredictable wrinkle. For the task of keeping the ring, one sacrificed. But one paid a price for one's wishes, too. It seemed that the ring created or helped to create the domestic space that was a marriage. And the law of that space was equanimity. Marie d'Auvergne, for instance, had approached the wishes as the enlightened person she was. Though initially skeptical of the ring's influence, she wished for things that she would not have minded happening if the ring proved true. She asked only that her beloved always satisfy her sexually and that he be successful in his business endeavours.

It was Marie's daughter, Sophie, who'd written of her mother's conversion to 'outright belief in the ring' and of her mother's revelation that although, for most of her life, she had enjoyed the physical pleasures she'd wished for, the compensation imposed was that she herself could not rise from the marital bed until her beloved was satisfied. As Marie's husband grew older, this became more and more arduous. So that, by the time they were in their sixties, Marie had to calculate whether or not her own pleasure was worth the trouble.

By the time Gwen finished reading about the eccentricities of compensation, she could barely take in the last two sections of 'On the Use of the Ring.' She glanced over them, before deciding to leave the reading of those pages and the commentary they inspired for later.

Nor, it should be noted, did she take in the ominous implications of the essay's final section, 'The Ring Protects Itself.' To be fair, however, 'Part 6' was neither essay nor illustration. It was instead a title

6. The Ring Protects Itself

followed by a blank page.

Avoiding, for the time being, the voluminous commentary on 'Part 6,' – that is, the accounts of how the ring protected itself – Gwen turned instead to the long poem called 'Ring.' She did this out of curiosity, but also in the hopes that it would allow her some respite from the strangeness of what she'd read.

3

RING

In those days Margos had bitten so many
none came to the goddess without wounds.
And though Margos was a faithful dog and good,
the goddess was lonely. And though Margos was
a faithful dog and good counsel, the goddess
spoke bitterly: 'Must you bite all those who come
to our temple?' Margos, immortal and true,
bowed to Aphrodite. 'Would that these creatures
were worthy of your notice! They come grovelling
for favours, but wounds are what they deserve.'
The goddess touched her servant's head where a white
star bloomed on night-black fur. And this was a thing
Margos adored. The goddess spoke and Margos
sat up. 'Is there not one who is worth my while?'
Now Margos to the goddess Aphrodite:
'They are for biting. They die too quickly
for all else.' And Aphrodite to Margos:
'The pleasure of a moment is not lesser
than the pleasure of a moment eternal!'

Find me a mortal worthy of company.'
Aphrodite's wish being law to her servant,
Margos, the good and faithful, sets out at once
in the guise of a mortal dog, his white crest
blackened, his demeanour more frightening still.
How long the hunt! Great mountains subside into
valleys. Valleys sink into lakes. Lakes dry up
and become plains. Plains splinter into mountains.
The world toward which Margos set out was not
like the one from which he returned, returning
with relief, having been so long among mortals
he had begun to take dreams for what is real,
what's real for what is true. Now Aphrodite:
'Have you found one so soon?' Now to the goddess,
her servant: 'I am convinced there is no one
below worthy of a second thought, almost
no one on earth. I have found mostly liars
who know no truth but fantasy, thieves
who know no rights but their own, rapists
who know no law but violence, arsonists
who know no pleasure but in destruction.
I have seen mothers beat their children, fathers
kill their sons. They are merciless and devour
all living things before them. They are a pest!
But there is one who may be different, one
who may divert you for a moment. Mortal
but not simple. Strong but indifferent to power.
Honest and unafraid, proud but unconcerned
with the opinions of those around him, wise
but modest and, best of all, often silent.'
The goddess, now, to her servant: 'A mortal?
Have you not, rather, found some forgotten god?
Bring him to me. Let us see this paragon.'
Margos bows his head at Aphrodite's feet.

'I'd have brought him at once, but he would not come.
I'd have bitten him for refusing but he
bowed and pleaded his own lack of worth!
It is for this that I have come back to ask
what the goddess of love would have me do. Must
Cratinus come to the temple against his will
or Aphrodite go to the soft green hills
where Cratinus tends sheep?' Now the goddess is
surprised. 'You have found me a shepherd, Margos?
Of what shall we speak? Breeding or manure?'
Margos bows lower still, while Aphrodite
considers the words of her faithful servant,
intrigued less by the shepherd than Margos's
faith in him. She had taken any number
of mortals and always appreciated
their care for detail, their eagerness to please,
living through them a version of ecstasy,
a kind of pleasure. But of all her lovers,
mortal or immortal, Margos had approved
of only one: Hephaestus, god of fire,
a husband she loved, but well within reason.
Was this shepherd a shadow of Hephaestus
or something more rare, an immortal within?
For, much as the gods who cannot die behave
as if they could, there are mortals who, though they
perish, hold within themselves a timelessness,
an immortality rare as a blue diamond
caught in quartz, and this Aphrodite would see.
Taking Margos with her, goddess and servant,
appearing as if mortal and doomed, descend
from high Olympus to the low grassy shore
where the sheep of Cratinus graze their fill,
through which a footpath branches, leading here, down
to the sea, and there, up the low, craggy hills

to a scattering of wooden homes sheltered
from the winds and breezes by sea-facing pines.
And they found Cratinus sitting on a rock
a short way from his noisily feasting flock,
his noble profile set against the cloudless
blue of a midday sky, as if painted there.
As when one drinks too much wine and feels light-headed,
so the goddess at the sight of Cratinus.
While Margos, at the sight of Aphrodite,
growls in dismay. For, good though the man may be,
her servant mistrusts the goddess's weakness.
Cratinus to Aphrodite: 'Your faithful
companion senses my flaws and rightly scolds
me for them.' And the goddess to the mortal,
hiding the feelings that blossomed within her:
'My dog, Margos, is thirsty. Is there a well
nearby where we can drink after our long walk?'
'There is,' says the mortal. 'I will bring water
for you both.' And Cratinus rose from his place
and called his sheep, who came bleating at the sound
of his words, as if sheep and Cratinus shared
a tongue. And went up as one, sheep following
shepherd, as schoolchildren follow a teacher.
And in a while came down the hill, sheep leading
shepherd, now like happy children running before the master
back to the fields. Cratinus brought two gleaming
bowls, one made of gold for the goddess and one
of bronze for her dog, both unadorned and smooth
as the sea on windless days. And with this, too,
Aphrodite was charmed, though she did not show
her pleasure. Even Margos, satisfied, sat
at the goddess's feet and seemed to close
his eyes. Now, the goddess and Cratinus spoke
of many things, first among which were the bowls

Cratinus had brought. The goddess, whose husband
was the unrivalled blacksmith, Hephaestus, knew
the art of the forge better than all, save her
husband. And he had made breathtaking gifts for
his wife. A golden cat that licked at its paws
so that fleas jumped from them, while on these golden
fleas smaller fleas jumped. A lily of white gold
that sprouted and opened with the sun and closed
with nightfall. And, most precious, a bowl on which
the face of one whom the goddess had in mind
was engraved, the engraving changing as she
herself changed her mind. And how delightful to catch
one face turning to another and turning
again and again, as changeably as her thoughts!
These bowls made by Cratinus were simple, but
they were of a simplicity that rivalled
the work of Hephaestus, as tantalizing
and smooth as if they'd been made without recourse
to human hands. So, the goddess to Cratinus:
'And have you forged these two bowls yourself, shepherd?
What great skill you possess!' Now speaks Cratinus:
'My father was a smith, as his before him.
What skill I have I owe the gods. It is through
them that our generations have learned the art.'
'And yet here you are, a shepherd. Have you turned
away from the gifts you were given? Forgive
my curiosity.' Now Cratinus smiles
as chastely as one recalling chaste pleasures,
and says, 'There is no need for apology.
It must seem as if I have abandoned my art.
But to learn discipline is to learn freedom
and to know freedom is to enter the realm of Art.
Caring for sheep teaches me about the forge.'
Time, which is nothing to the gods but so much

to mortals, passed. In near darkness, Cratinus
bid the stranger farewell and up the hill led
his sheep, having professed sadness at leaving.
'May I know your name?' he says before he goes.
And the goddess whose names are without number
spoke the first that came to her, Myrtia. That night
Cratinus's face was constant on the face
of the bowl Hephaestus had made for his wife.
It takes no longer for a god to fall
in love than it takes mortals below, and needs
no more reason. Cratinus was as judged,
it seemed, a good man and one true to himself.
But stupid men are loved as often as the wise,
the vicious treasured as often as the kind.
There is love enough for flatterers and thieves,
villains and the vile, the monstrous and the cruel.
Once love takes hold, its grip is hard to loosen.
Thus, surrendering to feelings she indulged,
the goddess of love visited Cratinus
day after day, bringing her wary servant
and counsellor, Margos, with her to the sea,
hills, and woods where the shepherd lived alone and
where there was little to disturb love's journey.
How sweet, too, to feel Cratinus surrender!
In the course of days, of weeks, his confusion
seemed to grow, as he understood that his heart
was no longer his own. Nor was there any
greater pleasure for Aphrodite than this
awkward and off-metred surrender: Cratinus
resisting, resisting again, then falling.
Even for the gods, the love one feels is doubled
when met by love. Now, each detail of the man
seemed to Aphrodite a gift from Gaia.
His brow, his cheek, his arms, his slender fingers,

the curve of his neck, his dark skin, his broad shoulders,
even his sweet breath that smelled always of mint.
She contrived then to stay with him at night,
sharing the pine bed on whose frame Cratinus
had carved graceful and vivid myrtle flowers.
Now, only Margos was watchful and unsure.
To witness surrender and loss of restraint
was, for the faithful servant, like hearing the cry
of peacocks in his mind. What was he to do,
faced with the surrender of Aphrodite?
Faced with the authority of Cratinus?
For as the goddess's feelings grew, so did
the frequency of Cratinus's orders.
His mistress's lover became his master.
Affectionately, respectfully, kindly,
but his master all the same, as the goddess
would not have Cratinus disobeyed. And what
good comes when mortals have dominion over
the divine? So Margos bides his time, wary,
the love between his mistress and Cratinus
falling like silk, softly into disaster.
And Chaos comes at last when Aphrodite,
in a transport of pleasure, admits to her
divinity, revealing her immortal
being to Cratinus, who finds himself now,
at once, with a constellation in his arms.
A reasonable man, but human, it seems,
because he doubts, and in his doubt looks for proof.
Thus, the keeper of sheep to Aphrodite:
'Though I would believe you, my love, how can it
be that a goddess would choose this mortal self,
this frail body, for her pleasure when, among
the immortals, the least is superior
to the poor shepherd that I am?'

Aphrodite, amused, looks on him and smiles.
'What proof can I offer that would convince you?'
And again, Cratinus to Aphrodite:
'A token, a small thing but miraculous.
A ring to grant me three wishes. Only three,
though they be whatever I choose, however extravagant.'
Aphrodite smiles once more. She is charmed
by his doubt about her divinity.
And kissing the chest of Cratinus, she says,
'The ring will be yours, ere I'm next in your bed.'
Which it was, though not easily nor at once.
Made by Hephaestus, after much beseeching.
Made to fit any finger that will wear it.
Charmed by the goddess who has engraved, inside
the white gold band, words in a strange language none
but the gods or immortal souls understand:
e menantu swigafar, ilskedi laut
bahor menanfar, lugesom havita
ø wani sepperti, ana surukai.
And the goddess brings it to her beloved,
as joyfully as if it were meant for her,
this marvellous ring, this gift straight from the forge.
Cratinus is amazed as he takes the ring.
But, putting it on his finger, the man burns
straight to dust. Where Cratinus stood, there is now
a mound of ashes. Both ring and man have gone!
Pity the goddess whose cries of rage and grief
reach distant worlds. The moon itself stops in flight.
Margos comes at once to the goddess's side,
prepared to face what awaits, only to find
the ashes of Cratinus
and Aphrodite's hands and face black, as she
embraces the remains of her beloved.
Rage first, for rage, like Love, is imperious.

What has happened? Who has done this? Who has dared?
Aphrodite's thoughts turn first to Hephaestus,
as her grief turns to a longing for vengeance.
In an instant, she is beside her husband,
abusing him for his betrayal, before
she sees that he knows nothing of her missing
ring nor of any shepherd. Nor can she speak
of Cratinus when her husband asks about
the man. So Aphrodite to Hephaestus:
'He is a worshipper at my temple and
nothing more,' though it hurts the goddess to tell
this lie about Cratinus, her beloved.
Leaving the forge of Hephaestus, the goddess
scours the earth for traces of her lover,
finding nothing, twice nothing, thrice nothing.
Not even Margos, faithful and scrupulous,
who searches the world for his mistress's sake,
can discover where Cratinus is hiding.
What begins in outrage turns quickly
to despair. The grief of Aphrodite brings
hard winter to the soul of Earth. No mortal
creature can know love while the goddess
mourns. Humans mate, but with indifference.
Birds sing, but tunelessly, bees make bitter
honey. Even the clouds, tired of motion, clutter the sky.
And in this hard, loveless season, Zeus himself
must intervene. The goddess of love will not
come to him. It is he who must go to her.
God of hosts, keeper of lightning, he who has
dominion over all, Zeus is yet father
to a daughter in distress and is, before
Aphrodite, as some mere mortal helpless
before a child struck down by an affliction
sent from the gods. He hears her lament and feels

himself her suffering. What can he do, when
she is too distraught to tell him what is wrong?
Zeus calls now for Margos the faithful and learns
of the sea, the sheep, Cratinus, and the ring.
His anger, his rage now fall on the faithful
servant. Thus, Zeus to Margos: 'This is your fault!
What business was it of yours, slave, to find
a mortal for my daughter?' Margos, as one
caught in a sudden storm, hunkers down, ears back,
making himself small against the gusts of rage.
The anger of Zeus is so terrifying,
the immortal servant, Margos, fears not death
but the pain and suffering of deathlessness.
And again, Zeus to Margos: 'What you have done
you will undo. In three days you will bring us
the mortal or the ring. If not, I promise
I'll see to your pain myself.' More than frightened,
Margos, who has scoured the world already
thrice over, flees to the isle of the cyclops
to hide from Zeus and to be beside Brontes,
his own father, greatest of the cyclops, friend
of Hephaestus, maker of lightning, eater
of sheep, and lover of Metis, shape-changing
mother of Margos. But here, too, something is wrong.
Where the noise of the forge usually rings
out with the groans and loud cries of the cyclops,
there is no sound, save for the sound of the sea.
The bellows are unmanned. The fires are low.
The lightning-stuff moves above, in the smithy,
like clusters of maddened wasps set aflame.
In all his timeless time, Margos has never
seen anything like this, nor heard such quiet
here. Nor is his father, nor any other
cyclops, to be seen till, reaching the centre

of the island, Margos comes to a clearing
in the green centre of which Polyphemus,
monstrous, scratching at himself and farting, stands,
while around him other cyclops bow their heads.
This new respect is strange, strange as the quiet,
and to Margos frightening, until he sees
on the finger of Polyphemus a ring,
and recognizes the ring of Cratinus.
The cyclops, held in thrall to Polyphemus,
must all bend to his will. Yes, even Brontes,
Margos's own father, submits, though
of the race of cyclops, Polyphemus is
the laziest, most foul, his smell preceding
him like a servant distinctly announcing
the coming of his lord. What can Margos do?
How many wishes has Polyphemus left?
This he must learn, though there's no doubt at all
that Polyphemus despises him. Indeed
on seeing Margos, Polyphemus cries out:
'Here is the brainless hound of Aphrodite!
Rid me of this four-legged pest, my brethren!'
And Margos to Polyphemus: 'I will leave
at once, if this is what Polyphemus wants.
But I have come bringing my mistress's praise.
I've been sent by Aphrodite who wishes
to say that she would be honoured to receive
Polyphemus, should he consent to visit
her chambers.' And Polyphemus to Margos:
'You lie, you gelded cur! You shit-eating mutt!
Besides, I wouldn't be caught dead in perfumed
chambers.' And Margos: 'I couldn't agree more.
The lowest of cyclops is greater by far
than the greatest Olympian!' The cyclops
laughs. 'Your mistress is the stupidest of them!

She can't tell a doll from a proper mortal!
And neither can you!' So Margos understands
at last that Cratinus was too good to be
human, that the too-good shepherd was fashioned
cleverly from the forges where Zeus's lightning
is made, and the faithful servant inwardly
curses his own mistake, but again flatters
Polyphemus. 'Your brilliance is unrivalled!
Far beyond me! I am only half cyclops.
What hope did I have of seeing through your art?
What hope of seeing through your brilliance?'
These words flatter the cyclops and puff him up.
'You, you mutt, and all the immortals see us
hard at work and never think us capable
of thought. What else have we to do but think,
while we forge lightning for Zeus and trim arrows
for Apollo? Some of my brethren are pleased
with their lot. But I am not. It pleases me
to think up misery for Olympians!'
And so, Polyphemus, his machinations.
On learning that Aphrodite was dredging
the world for worthy mortal company,
the scheming cyclops himself makes the shepherd
from parts littering the forge of Hephaestus.
This creation he imbues with serenity,
with wisdom, making a mirror of the gods,
and controls the shepherd himself from afar.
Patiently waiting for what reward might come,
he leaves Cratinus on a distant island
for Margos to find, setting a trap as
patiently as one who waits without moving
for a fawn or deer to nibble at apples
left in a heap, within range of an arrow.
Were it not for the suffering it brought, one

might have found the cyclops's scheme admirable
for the rightness of its interlocking parts.
And what a prize Polyphemus has taken!
A god-fashioned ring, to make the gods suffer.
But suffering there was beyond the gods, too,
for all who were forced to exist without love.
So Margos to the cyclops: 'Would it not please
Polyphemus to see the goddess of love
caught in the depths of darkness, grief, and despair?'
And Polyphemus to the faithful servant:
'I am pleased as is, but that would not lessen
my pleasure.' Now Margos again: 'How tragic
Polyphemus has no dominion over
Olympus! Would there were some way to subdue
all the gods, beginning with Aphrodite!'
Polyphemus did not deign to answer him.
Touching the ring of Cratinus as he spoke,
the cyclops said, 'May I be more powerful
than all the gods whose home is on Olympus!'
And this wish, too, was granted. Acquiring all
understanding, foresight, empathy, subtlety, and love,
proud Polyphemus dematerialized
in an ecstasy of knowing, and the ring
fell to the ground where Polyphemus had been.
On hearing of the stinking cyclops's fate,
Zeus was troubled. A lord of infinite love
and understanding is a being to fear.
But Margos the faithful had done his duty
and so the god of thunder was obliged
to keep his word, freeing Margos from the threat
of retribution. The goddess's grief, though,
went on unabated and unabating.
Having loved Cratinus, the goddess could not
easily put her feelings by. Though she knew

her beloved had been made by a cyclops,
though she accepted he'd been an illusion,
this changed nothing of her love for Cratinus.
For what is the beloved, if not illusion?
What is love if not longing for what's not there?
And what is it to love a mortal, if not
to love ashes? The goddess could not destroy
the ring, nor yet forget Cratinus, his hands.
In memory of a shepherd who never was,
Aphrodite preserved what Hephaestus had made,
and kept it long after Cratinus's face
faded from the ever-changing wedding bowl.
Should you find the ring, keep it in memory
of the goddess whose names are legion, whose love is eternal,
you who live in an age whence the gods have fled,
who live now as if the gods had never been.

4

A FAMILY HEIRLOOM, CONTINUED

After she'd read some two hundred pages, Gwen's thoughts were so difficult to restrain that she put the books aside and spent the rest of Saturday doing things that allowed her to process what she'd taken in. She talked to her mother about things other than the ring. She played piano with her father. She sat with the others and listened as Professor Bruno sang songs by Arnaut Daniel and other medieval troubadours.

This last was diverting because Professor Bruno could not sing well. When she was younger, Gwen had asked her father how he, a musician, could take pleasure in Professor Bruno's singing. And her father had answered that although 'Morgan is a terrible singer,' there's sometimes beauty in the approximate. That is: though he didn't often like to listen to Professor Bruno's singing, when he was in the mood, he found it affecting, because real striving can sometimes equal – or even surpass – attaining. It was an idea Gwen had found easy to accept in principle but hard to accept where Professor Bruno's singing was concerned. This evening, however, she finally felt what her father had meant:

Professor Bruno's emotion came through, even when not much music did.

That said, she was relieved when he finished singing.

On Sunday morning, mother and daughter were again in the eyrie, alone. Professor Bruno and Michael had gone to Port Huron for breakfast. And Alun was rehearsing for a tribute to Herbie Hancock in Winnipeg.

There was, at first, surprisingly little to talk about. Much of what Helen had meant to say had been said or, she believed, would not mean anything until Gwen came to believe in the ring. Knowing her daughter, Helen could tell that Gwen was still agnostic where the ring was concerned. But each of the women before her had come to believe, so Helen was not anxious.

For her part, Gwen was still 'bracketing' the idea of magic: that is, placing it somewhere in abeyance, rather than dismissing it outright. Helen was right, Gwen did *not* believe, but she'd been influenced by what she'd read in the third book. So they sat together quietly drinking tea – Lapsang Souchong, no milk, honey (for Helen) and Irish Breakfast, evaporated milk, sugar (for Gwen) – until Gwen finally asked

– Mom? Do you think there's a difference between something miraculous and something sacred?

It was a distinction Gwen had been thinking about, because Sophie d'Auvergne had written that her mother, Marie, had been peeved when Sophie referred to the ring as 'miraculous.'

– Now, that, said Helen, is something I haven't thought about for a very long time. I used to think it was a distinction without a difference. The sacred has to do with God and the miraculous is usually attributed to God, so what's the point? But now I think there is a difference. A miracle is something that happens once usually. It's an exception, like a divine caprice. But if a miracle happens regularly, it becomes a kind of law, and laws aren't miraculous. The sacred, though, is something you can feel *through* the miraculous. It's what a miracle connects you to. I think that's where the idea comes from that we've been keeping this ring for generations, until the goddess returns for it.

– I don't know about that, Mom. That doesn't make sense to me. Why, if the goddess exists, would she even need the ring? Anyway, I'm not sure I believe in God. So if this ring business is true, I think it's more like you said: a law that's been passed down to us.

– Well, these are ideas you can knock your head against, over and over. But I've learned to let them be. As I've gotten older, solving these problems has gotten less and less important.

Gwen laughed.

– That's at least one thing I can understand, she said.

They talked then about Tancred: when Gwen had seen him first, how she'd felt, when she'd come to know he was the one – did she know this? – and how he felt – did she know that? Tancred loved her, no? This, Gwen could not say, though she felt it and trusted her feeling. In a word, Helen was ready to meet the father of her granddaughter.

– The father of your granddaughter? said Gwen. I wonder if Tan would be happy to hear that? Anyway, how do you know we'd even *have* children?

Helen looked at her as if she'd said something absurd.

– Gwenhwyfar, every single one of us has had one daughter. Just one. And every single one of our husbands has died before us.

Now it was Gwen who stared at Helen.

– There's always the possibility we'll be different, said Helen. No one can say anything for certain. But my grandfather died before my grandmother, and your grandfather died before my mother. And so on, and so on. I think that's how we pay for the chance to change our husbands. It's a kind of compensation. They get to be spared the grief. I accept this now. But it's hard, some nights, lying beside your father, knowing the night will come when he won't be there.

Helen's tone – the way she'd said these things – was so reasonable that Gwen felt there was nothing to say. Gwen recoiled from it rather, choosing to act as if she hadn't heard. What came to her mind instead was her grandfather, his funeral, and the way her grandmother had changed after his death.

To be fair, Helen had had years to think about what was to come. She'd learned to deal with the idea of her husband's death by, for the most part, ignoring what she knew. She hadn't meant to mention it to Gwen, but, sitting with her daughter, knowing Gwen would come to the knowledge sooner or later, she had spoken of her coming bereavement in the only way that made it bearable. That is, by pretending there was reason behind it, as indeed there may have been, if a god's reason is Reason, or even reasonable.

What Gwen thought about, instead of some possible bereavement, was more prosaic: what would she choose to sacrifice, if ever she came to believe in the ring? Would what she chose be enough? What was enough? How was one to know? And then, too, what would she sacrifice, if it came to that, for Tancred?

It is safe to say that Gwen had passed the strangest weekend she'd ever passed in her parents' home. And Monday morning came almost as a relief.

Gwen placed the dark box with its three books in the trunk of Michael's car, along with her small suitcase, and wore the ring on her little finger. She'd expected the box itself to elicit questions from someone – from her father or Michael or Professor Bruno – but it did not. Her mother was the only one who acknowledged it. That is, as the box was placed in the trunk, Helen grew emotional and looked away.

Whatever else Gwen thought about her inheritance, she believed the books were invaluable historical documents and that the ring – which had the (to her) meaningless message 'e menantu swigafar, ilskedi laut bahor menanfar, lugesom havita ø wani *sepperti, ana surukai*' engraved on its inner band – was a curio. How had anyone managed to engrave so many words in such minuscule script on the narrow band of what was, otherwise, an unremarkable gold ring?

As it was early morning, Professor Bruno elected to sleep in the back seat. Gwen sat in the front with Michael, who drove. She was happy to keep Michael company, at least in part because she was grateful to talk to someone whose perspective was objective. As they got on Egremont Road, Gwen asked Michael if they'd enjoyed the weekend.

– Very much, answered Michael. Your parents are really lovely people. I had a wonderful time talking to Helen. She knows so much about so many things. She and Morgan talked about everything from Innis's *Fur Trade* to Carl Wilson's book about Céline Dion.

– Do you get on well with your parents? asked Gwen.

– No, answered Michael. I haven't seen my parents in thirty years.

– Oh, I'm so sorry, said Gwen.

– Don't be, said Michael. They were happy to see me go, and I was happy to leave.

– Are they still alive?

– I really don't know, but I like to think they are and that they're happy.

Gwen looked over and saw that Michael was unruffled as ever. The subject clearly wasn't painful. It was painful for Gwen, though, to imagine Michael leaving home at fifteen and never looking back.

– I don't miss them, said Michael. I've made a better life for myself without them than I could've if I'd stayed. But what about you? Do you miss your parents?

– I miss my mom, answered Gwen. I see my dad whenever he comes to T.O. But I don't see Mom unless I go to Bright's Grove.

– Morgan says he'd like to go more often, said Michael. You should come with us.

It seemed tragic to Gwen that Michael was cut off from the feeling of family and history.

— I know what you mean about family, said Michael, but it isn't the same for me. My parents hated who I am, and they did a good job of screwing me up. But once I got away from them, I managed to find people to love who love me. I think about my parents sometimes, and the good part is that it doesn't hurt me anymore when I do. Anyway, to me, family isn't something you have. It's something you make. It really should be a verb, like: *I family, you family, we family, they family.*

The two of them laughed at this. Michael said

— You're thinking about family? Does that mean you're thinking about the one you might be in love with?

Gwen welcomed this intimacy and she realized, the moment Michael asked, that she was indeed thinking about Tancred, but not really *about* Tancred. It was more that, for the first time in years, she wondered what it would be like to have a child. The thought of a child brought with it the idea of a father, and that idea included Tancred, though her thoughts about him were more erotic than paternal.

Then again, *family* (the verb) necessarily implied the erotic, didn't it?

It was quarter to eight in the morning when Michael and Professor Bruno, who'd woken up somewhere around Mississauga, dropped Gwen home.

She would have invited them up for coffee, since she hadn't bid Professor Bruno a proper goodbye, but Michael was pressed for time, and besides, on entering the apartment with the box and books in her arms, the first person Gwen saw was Robbie, fully dressed, asleep on the sofa with Nadia's coat over him.

Why was he sleeping on the sofa? Why didn't he have a blanket?

Gwen was plunged into what felt like a previous life. She didn't especially care why Robbie was on the sofa nor why he had his boots on. If she could have avoided the details, she would have. But in opening the door, she must have made some noise because, not long after she came in, Nadia came out to see what was going on.

Then, Nadia and Gwen sitting at the kitchen table, the dull details of Robbie's fate came out: his snoring had been keeping Nadia up, so she'd banished him to the living room where, no doubt, it had gotten cold – thus, the overcoat.

Nadia did not ask Gwen about her time in Bright's Grove, and this lack of curiosity suited Gwen well. She would not have known what to tell Nadia, in any case. More: she did not want to talk about her feelings because she was overwhelmed by them.

The following evening, after a day at work, Gwen came home to find Robbie on the sofa, in the dark, again. He wasn't upset this time. He was sitting in the dark thinking. He admitted this wasn't something he liked to do.

– I guess, he said, it wouldn't surprise you if I said me and Nadia probably aren't good for each other. I know she's not good for me. But, fact is, she reminds me of someone from when I was younger. She's just like her, same temper and all. And I can't help it. I can't stop looking for a woman like the one I was in love with in high school.

– This woman, asked Gwen, is she dead?

– Dead? said Robbie. No. She lives a few blocks from here.

– Why don't you get back together with her then?

– Well, first off, she's married to some guy who wears bow ties and writes about music. And another thing is, she isn't anything like the person I knew. Now she's just another Toronto idiot who thinks they're too good for people from the country. It's funny that people change so much, isn't it? I thought she'd still be at least a little like herself and it turns out she isn't. I guess that's why I keep looking for her.

– So you like the way you and Nadia argue? Is that what you're looking for?

– I guess I kind of am, he said.

Gwen was sympathetic, but her sympathy diminished at the thought that Robbie and Nadia were playing a perverse game in which Nadia was meant to be a 'difficult woman' in order to please Robbie. Moreover, it seemed, they both enjoyed this play-acting. Everything was theatrical: the jealousy, the breaking up, the tears and recriminations, the forgiveness. It was all part of their foreplay.

– *God!* she thought. *How strange relationships are!*

This was followed, in her mind, by a question she knew to be naive:

– *Why can't people just be honest with each other?*

Which was in turn followed by a very difficult question indeed:

– *Why is it so hard to know what one wants?*

This thought led to a moment of clarity: what she wanted, *whom* she wanted, was not something to be figured out. Leaving aside all the business about rings and books, the reason her mother had known she was in love was because she obviously was and had been for a while. Not with Olivier. Imagining herself with Olivier had been her way of avoiding the truth: in Tancred's company she felt something she felt with no one else. She wasn't chasing some illusion from the past either. Her feeling for Tancred was unlike what she'd felt for anyone else. Though accepting this fact made her feel vulnerable, because wanting always makes one vulnerable, it was the first step toward being honest with Tancred.

– Why don't you just tell Nadia all this about your past? she asked Robbie.

– I *have* told her, he answered. She knows how I feel. So now she uses it against me.

Which only added to his pain (thought Gwen) and, thus, to his pleasure.

Following her talk with Robbie, Gwen reflected on the importance of knowing the person one is with. This now seemed to be the whole point of 'Ring,' the poem: Aphrodite did not know Cratinus's nature and, so, suffered. It was also, perhaps, the point of the ring itself, the ring being less an instrument of magic than an implied question: shouldn't you know the beloved before you risk changing them?

A week after her return from Bright's Grove, Gwen decided that it would not be pushy to call Tancred, to ask how he was. So she called him and, after a pause during which she could hear he was waiting for her to speak, she asked if she could see him.

– Of course, he said. Is everything okay?

– Yes, she answered, but I wouldn't mind talking to you about ...

She hesitated, not knowing how to speak her mind, but Tancred filled the silence.

– Olivier? he asked.

– Yes, she said, I wouldn't mind talking about Olivier.

(Which was not a lie, even if it wasn't quite the truth.)

– In that case, we can meet whenever you want, he said. How about tomorrow evening? Do you want to have dinner?

Tuesday evening. She would have to work the following day, so they wouldn't be able to stay out late. She could call in sick on Wednesday morning if she had to, but then again, Gwen hadn't taken a sick day in all the years she'd been working at the hospital. It was a point of honour. If she stayed out late on Tuesday, she would go to work tired rather than miss a day.

So, she said

– It would be wonderful to have dinner, but it's a busy week at the hospital. We've got budget meetings. Can we make it Friday?

– Well, on Friday, said Tancred, I'm supposed to have dinner with Dan. I know he and Fiona would be happy to meet you, since I'm pretty sure Ollie's told them about you. If Ollie wasn't up north with Simone and Gordon, he'd be there, too, on Friday. But if you don't mind having dinner with a few strangers, it'll be good company. And we can talk afterwards.

– That's perfect, said Gwen. What should I bring?

It did sound perfect, but although the extra days allowed her time to prepare for the evening – to decide what she would wear, what she would say, to rehearse in her mind how she'd tell Tancred she wanted him – the days also gave her time to think about what she'd agreed to: an evening with Tancred and one of Tancred's best friends, whom it would be embarrassing to offend. And that was before you considered that Tancred and his friends probably thought she was seeing Olivier.

So, in a stressful moment, Gwen turned to that in which she did not believe: the ring.

There were more reasons for this turn than stress and self-doubt, as there must have been for all the women before her who'd turned to the ring. Chief among these other reasons was the coincidence – but *was* it coincidence? – that her mother had given her the books and the ring just after she'd admitted to herself that she had feelings for Tancred. And so her feelings blended with the words and impressions of her foremothers. That is: the ring suggested itself because it was much on her mind.

Wednesday evening, she touched the ring, thinking to use it.

Yes, but how does one use such a thing, while not believing in it, while half-afraid it might be some dark means to impose her imagination on the world. And how, if the ring were an agent beyond her understanding, to protect Tancred? She did not want to change him, didn't know him well enough to know what to change even if she had wanted. Nor did she want to coerce emotions from him that he did not already have.

What to wish for, though she was unbelieving?

It had to be something trivial, just in case. It had to be something obvious, also in case. It had to be something whose significance she alone would understand. Most importantly, it should be something that would affect the one who loved her and whom she loved. Whatever her feelings for Tancred, she would not pursue a relationship at whose emotional centre she was alone.

So, on Wednesday night, the ring on the small finger of her right hand, Gwen wished that, whatever the circumstances, wherever he was, at the sound of the name *Polyphemus*, the man who was meant to be her husband would say the words inscribed on the inner band of her ring, the words from the poem:

e menantu swigafar, ilskedi laut
bahor menanfar, lugesom havita
ø wani sepperti, ana surukai.

This decision, made though Gwen knew there was little chance the ring could cause anyone to recite gibberish, brought her peace. It felt as if she had at least done something, as if she were being proactive. And with the feeling of having done something, there came release. She found herself drifting off to sleep as soon as she'd finished her 'incantation,' if you could call her wish-making an incantation. She passed an untroubled night, rising near dawn from a dream in which there were sheep eating grass in a field.

That Friday, she wore her favourite jeans (light-blue, mid-waisted), an off-white (oatmeal) cashmere cardigan with an oatmeal cashmere bralette underneath, gold hoops for earrings, a gold necklace (simple, not too long) with a pendant (a copper scallop shell, one inch at its widest) given to her by her mother for high school graduation, and the ring that she accepted was now hers.

Having taken care with how she dressed, she was pleased, as she and Tancred stepped into the front hall of the Mandelshtams' home, to see that Tancred was simply but well dressed: a clean white shirt, unbuttoned to the top of his sternum, recently pressed dark pants, and, when he took off his long coat, the smell of him: subtle, clean, briefly sweet, then gone so that she wanted to lean toward him. He may not have dressed for her, but the fact that he took care of himself was itself pleasing.

And anyway, he hadn't *not* dressed for her.

It was, of course, natural that Gwen should feel uneasy. She had a secret to keep until she and Tancred were alone. Plus: she had to be careful not to show any deep feelings for Tancred, because she was there as 'Ollie's girlfriend.' In fact, much of the evening's early conversation was devoted to how wonderful Olivier was. Each of the others felt obliged, it seemed, to share stories about Ollie, obliged to reassure her about Ollie's absence. To be fair, their stories *did* make Olivier seem lovable.

Gwen wanted to convey good-natured calm, but working against her calm was the business of taking everything in. The house was, relative to anything Simone might own, modest. But it was very close to Gwen's ideal, a narrow Victorian with tall ceilings, a living room with a working fireplace, beside a dining room – brightly lit, with a lightly lacquered rustic table and wooden chairs – through which you got to a small kitchen. All other rooms – bedrooms, bathrooms, offices – were on the two upper floors.

The house was one Gwen would have been happy to live in. On the walls downstairs there were paintings done by one of their 'eccentric' neighbours, a woman whose signature ('Lyla') was big and dark on the bottom right of her paintings. One of the paintings was of a field overrun by rabbits. The other was of a living room overrun by rabbits. The living room rabbits hung above the sofa on which Tancred and Gwen sat.

Of Daniel and Fiona, Gwen had strong first impressions. Daniel and Tancred could have been siblings: same height, same build, same accents, same sense of humour. Both had had African mothers and white fathers, and they'd grown up in the same neighbourhood. But there were differences, too. There was a politesse and stability to Daniel that seemed 'inner,' though he was animated, while Tancred's calm was thoroughgoing, though you could sometimes sense his enthusiasms. Fiona was pale with dark eyebrows and spoke with a British accent. She was maternal in build with long, dark eyelashes, but she was like Daniel, in that there was something steely to her, buried beneath good humour and a mocking intelligence.

Gwen liked both of them almost at once.

For hors d'oeuvres, Daniel had made potato latkes – Tancred's favourite, as they reminded him of Baruch, Daniel's father – and bourekas. To Gwen's disappointment, those were the only hints of Daniel's Jewishness, a subject that, in light of her recent discoveries about her family's past and its influence on the present, she would have liked to discuss. When she asked him if his Jewishness was important to him, Daniel apologized for not knowing much about it, pointing to his father's left-wing atheism as a primary reason for his ignorance and lack of enthusiasm for the subject. At this point in his life – his mid-thirties – the culture of his ancestors (on his father's side) was little more than a vague culinary fact, his father having passed on a love for certain foods. Thanks to his mother, he knew more about his African heritage. That said, the food of the Ashkenazim was something of a tether that kept him just outside the walls of a culture he couldn't quite abandon.

The food was good. By the time they approached the table for dinner, Gwen had eaten enough of the latkes to almost ruin her appetite, and she'd drunk two glasses of the Sauvignon Blanc they'd served. So her guard was lowered.

– I guess I should take these away, said Daniel.

He was referring to two extra place settings on the table.

– Sonja and Seaton were going to come, he said, but they're stuck in Prince Edward County.

As Gwen tried to imagine what a couple with such names might look like, a leaf was taken from the centre of the dining table and she was brought into closer quarters with the others. She sat beside Tancred, facing Fiona and Daniel.

As if sorry for the suddenness of this proximity, both Daniel and Fiona did their best to put her at ease, asking again about her life and her work, about Bright's Grove and geriatrics. Nor were they inquisitorial. Gwen felt, rather, as if she'd been invited to join a relaxed conversation among friends. As a result, she further let down her guard, answering their questions sincerely, even laughing at a bad joke Fiona remembered from work:

– Dog walks into a bar, goes up to the barman, and says, 'I'm looking for the man who shot my paw.'

After that, Gwen began asking questions herself, now feeling as if Tan's friends were hers. So when Fiona mentioned that her first degree had been in classics, Gwen naturally asked

– Where did you study?

– I studied at Cambridge, answered Fiona, but I spent a summer in Athens.

– That must have been wonderful, said Gwen. I've always wanted to go to Athens.

– It was a revelation, said Fiona. My father was an amateur archaeologist, so I grew up knowing classical literature. When I got to Greece, it was like finding out that the world I'd heard such great stories about was real. I remember taking the ferry from Pireus to Chania and wondering which of the islands could have had the cyclops on it. When you're looking back at the islands, you can almost imagine Polyphemus throwing rocks at your ferry.

And just like that, Gwen's life was changed. Because no sooner had Fiona spoken the name Polyphemus than Tancred recited the words on Gwen's ring:

– *E menantu swigafar, ilskedi laut bahor menanfar, lugesom havita ø wani sepperti, ana surukai.*

Fiona and Daniel both looked at him.

– What was *that*? Daniel asked.

Tancred answered, perplexed

– What was what?

– You just said something in a different language.

– I did? asked Tancred.

Gwen tried to change the subject. Turning from Tancred to Fiona, she asked, with an enthusiasm Fiona took as overpolite:

– What made you decide to study medicine after classics?

– Hmm, said Tancred. If I did say anything, it wasn't conscious. I must have been daydreaming.

– Strange daydream, said Daniel. You need to stop with the travel docs on YouTube.

– After my degree in classics, said Fiona, I decided I wanted to do something totally different. And I loved the idea of being a doctor. So ...

The rest of the evening at Fiona and Daniel's seemed uneventful, because Gwen could not take in anything that followed Tancred's recital of words whose significance she alone understood, words whose chief implications were that the ring she wore was unworldly and that Tancred Palmieri was her beloved.

It felt as if she had been drugged, and, as one unaccustomed to a drug whose effects won't let up, Gwen grew increasingly desperate for a former reality that was receding, that was gone. As Daniel was talking about a case of his in which one writer had insulted another, she excused herself and, alone in the bathroom on the second floor, began to weep. Though there should have been at least some joy or wonder in her discovery of the ring's nature, there was only distress until, after a rather long while, she managed to convince herself that what she'd experienced had been a hallucination, something brought on by the wine she'd drunk while tired and nervous.

She returned as meekly to the dining room as she'd left it, thinking to wait out her uncertainties. But, of course, the others noticed the change in her.

– Are you okay? asked Tancred.

– Can I get you something? asked Fiona.

– No, no, said Gwen. It's nothing. I drank a little more than I'm used to and it caught up to me.

– Do you need to go home? asked Tancred.

– No, said Gwen, I don't want to be the one to break up the evening. It's such great company, and you've all been so kind.

– There'll be other times, said Daniel. And next time, Ollie'll be with us. Actually, we'll make it *just* you and Ollie, until Tancred actually learns to commit to someone.

– Let's not go there, answered Tancred.

Though Gwen was unhappy that she was the reason for the evening's conclusion, she was also grateful for it. Company – almost any company – would have been difficult to endure. She wasn't even sure she wanted to be around Tancred. It was one thing to innocently imagine that one's feelings for someone were returned. It was something else entirely to feel that he was hers, that their fates were linked. It felt intimidating and somehow underhanded, as if the power to choose had been taken from her. But Tancred had driven to his friend's home, to keep himself from drinking too much, anticipating that he and Gwen would talk afterwards. And when he offered her a ride home, his voice was so full of concern, she felt it would be churlish to say no. So she accepted and stepped into his car – a blue Prius.

Once inside, once she was in that space beside him, her mood changed again. As he started the car, Gwen put a hand on his arm and said

– I'd like us to go to your place first.

– My place? answered Tancred. Why?

– Because I want to talk to you, and I don't want to do that in a car. And we can't go to my place because my roommate is home with her boyfriend.

He looked at her, as if unsure she were serious. He recovered at once, though.

– Oh, he said. Of course. Yes.

They drove in unforced and, for Gwen, welcome silence, south along Avenue Road, a street she loved, becoming new, as it did, after Upper Canada College, passing old but posh apartment buildings, becoming more obviously wealthy around Yorkville, its name changing south of Bloor, now called Queen's Park, a street in the middle of the University of Toronto curving around the park before changing name and character again at College Street: now suddenly University Avenue, lined by hospitals and office buildings on its way to the opera house at Queen, on its way to the lake, which was completely obscured by tall buildings and, thus, was, in the day, like a coming reward and, at night, like a mysterious notion.

Tancred's home – near Sherbourne Common and Queen's Quay – was in an elegant low-rise, about a hundred yards from the lake. As they took the elevator up, Gwen tried to imagine what his place would look like. She imagined something pleasant – a bachelor pad with black leather couches and, if one of his ex-girlfriends had been pushy, a framed poster of a calla lily by Mapplethorpe or a cow's skull by Georgia O'Keeffe. (Gwen disliked this ex the moment she invented her.) Perhaps, too, a small kitchen, two modest bedrooms and, if the place was really nice, a balcony that looked toward the lake. Knowing that Tancred loved her – the ring had proved it – Gwen couldn't help imagining a home that needed her in some way.

When they stepped out of the elevator on the tenth floor, they were on a clean landing that smelled of lemon – not the industrial scent, but as if someone had had cause, moments before, to squeeze a ripe lemon. Its sour freshness was still in the air. The landing was dimly lit, all straight lines, with a marble floor and double doors to either side of the elevator. The doors themselves were plain, almost crude: lightly stained wood on the left-hand side, darkly stained wood on the right.

They entered an apartment through the dark doors and she saw at once that the place was not close to what she'd imagined, not close to her idea of Tancred, nor yet close to what she might, in her wildest surmise, have foreseen. The apartment was almost monstrously extravagant and, at the same time, severe and ascetic.

It was extravagant because Tancred owned the two top floors — the tenth and the eleventh — of the building, and the first thing one saw on entering was a wide staircase — dark railing and wooden steps — that led to the upper floor.

– I'm sorry, said Tancred. I know it's overwhelming.

As if he were aware of the 'too-muchness' and had tried to mitigate it, there was an almost minimalist feel to the rooms, with little to disturb the straight lines and white walls. To the left of the entrance, past a closet that was not much smaller than Gwen's bedroom, they came to a living room in which there was a concert grand piano and a black leather couch. On one of the walls, there was a self-portrait by Jean-Michel Basquiat, whose one, ferocious red square was the most colourful thing in the apartment.

– Do you play piano? she asked.

– Not really, he said. I bought it because my mother wanted me to learn an instrument and I'm still trying.

This was a lie — a lie about himself, not his mother. Tancred had spent years intensely practising the piano, but he disliked playing for others, playing only, in fact, for Olivier, whose mother had taught piano and who was himself an excellent pianist. Despite Tancred's lie, the piano had emotional resonance for Gwen. Both of her parents played well. Her father was brilliant at it and pianos were an iconic element of her childhood. She, too, played, and it made her happy to see one in Tancred's home.

– Would you like to see the rest of the place? he asked.

He politely held out his arm and she touched it. But though she paid attention as they walked about the first floor of the dark-doored side of his home, and though she was struck by the grand scale of everything, Gwen couldn't take it in. When they returned to the living room, she'd had time to think about what was happening and she was as confounded by her own thoughts and feelings as she was by this revelation of the extent of Tancred's wealth.

(Was it wrong of her to feel intimidated by his wealth? It was too late to change her feelings, if so.)

– You wanted to talk about Ollie? said Tancred.

– Polyphemus, she answered.

And once again, at the sound of the cyclops's name, Tancred recited the words inscribed on the ring her mother had passed on to her. As before, he seemed not to realize that he'd spoken. As much to herself as to him, Gwen said

– I wonder what we're going to do about all this.

– What do you mean? he asked.

– You're in love with me, she said.

Tancred looked at her then, with what seemed to be amusement.

– Where did you get that idea? he asked.

– I'm in love with you, too, she answered.

Tancred moved the bench from under the piano and sat on it.

– I don't see where all this is coming from, he said. I'm not saying it's true, but let's say I love you. My feelings are irrelevant. You're going out with my best friend. I feel like I've done something wrong.

– You haven't done anything wrong, she said. But you're assuming things, aren't you? I'm not going out with Olivier. I'm not in a relationship with Olivier, and even if I was, I don't belong to Olivier.

– I'm not saying you belong to anyone. But if Ollie has feelings for you and if we start seeing each other, it would change a friendship I've had since I was six years old. What kind of person would I be if I didn't think about that?

Tancred spoke these words calmly, as if he were working out a problem in trigonometry. His words were reasonable, but they still felt like a rebuke. For a moment, Gwen wondered if she should care more about Olivier's feelings. But although it was true that she did not want to be with a man who cared only about himself, it was also true that she resented Olivier's presence between them. She'd done nothing to lead Olivier on, nor had Olivier given any sign that he had feelings for her.

– You didn't say if you love me, she said.

And now Tancred to her:

— How does it help us if I do?

— I'd like to hear you say it, she said. Just so we know where we stand.

Again, Tancred seemed amused. Gwen felt like saying 'Polyphemus' over and over, just to be sure, a little more sure, surer still. But then he spoke, not playfully, looking directly at her.

— Yes, he said. I haven't stopped thinking about you from the first moment I saw you. I can't stop thinking about you. People assume it's wonderful to love someone at first sight. And maybe if what I'd felt was love, I'd have thought it was wonderful, too. But what I felt the first time I saw you wasn't just love. It was more. I felt like I was seeing my wife for the first time, and I didn't know what to say. What if I was wrong and you didn't feel the same? But what if I was right and you did? It was easier being around you when I thought you and Ollie were seeing each other. I was jealous, but I could talk to you like one of Ollie's girlfriends, even if I couldn't understand why you weren't coming home with me. You know, when we were walking along Roncesvalles, it was hard *not* to say, 'Gwen, let's go just home.' It felt wrong *not* saying it. Then, in that farmhouse, with you beside me all night, I don't know how I kept from holding you. I had to pretend to sleep until I passed out in the morning. I've never wanted to be with anyone more than I want to be with you. Yes, I love you, Gwen. But I don't know what to do about it, because I've never felt like this before. It doesn't feel wrong, but it doesn't feel normal either.

Gwen rose from the sofa and crossed the space between them. Tancred stood to meet her. He was still in his overcoat, so she slid her hands into it, like parting curtains, feeling the warmth of his body and taking in the way he smelled as she embraced him. She could feel the muscled wiriness of him and wondered if she should lift his shirt to touch his skin.

He put his arms around her then, returning her embrace and, to her surprise — because, before this moment, he'd hid his longing well – kissing her neck, then her lips, in a kiss that went on for God knows how long, neither of them wanting it to end. That they went no further was not her choice. In fact, this too was a surprise, as there was absolutely no doubt about his desire for her or hers for him.

Moments after they'd stopped touching, Gwen could not recall why they'd stopped or who had withdrawn from whom. Perhaps it was because there was something that needed addressing, the question of Olivier. Yes, there was (for Tancred) the question of Olivier, and Gwen was surprised, given the state of him, that Tancred had managed to think of anything at all. Certainly, they'd reached the point where it would have been cruel to touch without going further.

Once they stopped touching, they did not – maybe *could* not – talk about anything important, about Olivier, for instance. Rather, they returned to themselves and, thereafter, said insignificant things as they left his apartment. They had not surrendered to desire. They surrendered, instead, to the improbable end of an impossible evening. Tancred drove her home, the silence between them charged, erotic, and slightly unkind.

It was unkind because Gwen did not know the implications of his having held himself from her. She had, she realized, assumed that, being her beloved, Tancred could not help but want her as she wanted him – emotionally, physically. This chastity of his, however noble, threw into question the inevitability of their union, however slightly.

Gwen was fortunate to have discovered Tancred's feelings for her on a Friday, because the weekend that followed was spent recovering from her evening with him, rereading the writings of her foremothers, and thinking about the consequences of what had happened with the ring.

She read Book Three, now with something more intense than the bewilderment she'd felt while reading from it in Bright's

Grove. She read it now with a need to hear from the women who'd gone through what she was going through. Her certainty that their stories were true brought with it an acquiescence: she would have to give up something significant or allow the ring to take something from her.

She was drawn first to her mother's writings. Reading Helen's words to her, she began to understand the depths of feeling her mother had had before her daughter's birth – a love by anticipation, a sympathy for the pain she knew her daughter would experience. Gwen then went on to the writings and translations of her grandmother. She was comforted by these as well, recalling as she did the touch of her grandmother's hands (dry, but smelling of coconut oil) and the feeling of lying in bed beside an old woman – old, that is, to Gwen's five-year-old self – whose love for her was unassailable.

The voice that brought her most comfort, however, was that of Marie di Francesca d'Auvergne, especially in the letters to her daughter, Sophie, letters faithfully copied into Book Three by Sophie herself, one so devoted to her mother that she was virtually absent from the books or present in the way of echoes.

(Here, Reader, let us note, in passing, that Gwen was troubled by the extent of Sophie's devotion to her mother, a devotion that could be taken for admiration *or* (in extremis) self-dislike. But as Gwen admired Marie d'Auvergne, it – that is, Sophie's self-negation – did not trouble her until she began to write her own thoughts in Book Three.)

It was surprising to Gwen that she should draw more comfort from someone who lived so long before her than from many of those closer to her in time. But as it is with families, so it is in Time: this child preferring that uncle, this grandmother indifferent to her eldest grandchild but besotted with the youngest, and so on. Why *shouldn't* sympathies in Time be as unpredictable as those within families? Then again, Gwen's sympathy came from the simple fact that Marie di Francesca d'Auvergne was preoccupied with the same ideas that preoccupied Gwen, and Marie had thought about them in a style that Gwen admired.

For instance, in a letter that Gwen translated, Marie d'Auvergne wrote to her then two-year-old daughter about the idea of miracles:

To Sophie d'Auvergne
[*Clermont-Ferrand, Monday, January 15, 1657*]

My dearest daughter. To think that you have reached two years of age! I feel it is not frivolous to believe you will live as long or longer than your loving parents. It is with this fervent hope that I begin these letters to you.

I can scarcely think what to write, there being so much to say, but watching you at play this afternoon and hearing you prattle with Margos, as if you believed he could speak, and knowing you would not be surprised if he did, I felt a need to say a few words here about miracles in this world you've come to.

We were but lately at the home of Msgr. and Mdm. Chardin and had occasion to speak with Étienne, your father and I, about the beauty of Msgr. Pascal's arithmetic machine, one of which your father has managed to procure from Msgr. Pascal himself. It was well done and just what one might expect from the hand and mind of Msgr. Pascal. But as we were speaking of it, your father's thoughts turned to the miracles that surround us by God's grace. I, who have had experience of the miraculous, as you will when you come of age, took it upon myself to tell him what I, here, write to you, so you will have it when the time comes.

On the question of whether there are miracles, there can be but two answers: 'yea' or 'nay.' It is my belief, my dear, that they do exist, but that they are not 'miraculous' as people imagine when they say the word *miracle*. As with all that exists, miracles are mundane. They must be accommodated, and the accommodation is itself routine, though sometimes arduous. If, however, miracles do not exist and I am mistaken in my belief, they are not a whit less mundane, being a general aspect of the wishes, thoughts, and dreams of humanity. A sense of the miraculous is as widely distributed as the 'common sense' of which Msgr. Descartes spoke. Thus, whether miracles exist or not, we are still charged with an accommodation of the miraculous.

You will find, my dearest Sophie, that this accommodation will preoccupy you a great deal in future, and concretely. Thus, it is in your interest to abandon any search for a definitive answer to the question of miracles. Look rather to make a place for them in your life and soul, whether you believe they exist or not.

The solace Gwen took from reading the letters of her nth-great-grandmother had little to do with her acceptance of Marie d'Auvergne's ideas. Gwen was not convinced, for instance, that the reality or non-reality of miracles was immaterial. But Marie's pragmatic approach to the ring and, by extension, to all that was 'miraculous,' and Marie's belief that the miraculous can be domesticated: these were what made her letters comforting. Then, too, ever practical, Marie enumerated the kinds of sacrifice she thought would be best for her daughter (the loss of a toe or a little finger) and those she thought unacceptable: self-blinding, say, or the piercing of an eardrum.

Marie herself had given up the small toe of her left foot and Sophie had followed her example.

It was just as well that Gwen took comfort from the thoughts of Mme. d'Auvergne, because the two weeks that followed Tancred's admission that he loved her – weeks that coincided with the coming of spring weather – were not as happy as they should have been. They began and ended with tears: first, tears of empathy, then tears of pain.

Days after being in Tancred's apartment, Gwen called her mother: to apologize for doubting her, to commiserate with her on the sacrifice she had made, to hear her commiseration on the sacrifice Gwen would have to make, and to ask for advice.

They spoke for hours before either of them was aware that any time had passed at all.

— I've been waiting thirty years for this talk, said Helen. Have you used the ring?

Gwen told her what she'd done, and Helen was quiet before laughing.

— Well, she said, you were always a little different, Gwenhwy-far. I don't think any of our foremothers used it that way. If I were you now, I'd wish for his love and understanding.

At her own words, and for no reason Gwen could understand, Helen began to cry. Hearing her, Gwen too began to cry so that, for a moment, neither could speak. After which, they both cry-laughed at their own emotion or at each other's emotions or at emotion in general: hard to say which, in such a melange of feelings.

— I thought, said Helen, I'd be the last of us. People have changed so much since our mothers first received this ring, it feels like a miracle that you believe in it. I wonder if my grand-daughter will believe.

— You know, said Gwen, there's a good chance you'll be there to see for yourself.

— Have you decided what you'll sacrifice?

— Not yet, said Gwen. Whatever I think about sounds horrible. Like: I don't want to lose a toe or a finger.

— Well, that's why some of us have helped our daughters, you know. My mom volunteered to cut a toe off for me! Can you imagine? She'd even bought secateurs for it. I didn't mind the idea of losing a toe or finger, but I really hated the idea of my mother doing it for me. I should have listened to her, though.

Toward the end of their conversation, Gwen asked if Helen would be able to leave Bright's Grove any time soon. The ring was now Gwen's to keep and, when you thought about it, Helen's sacrifice had been a terrible amputation: thirty years of her life without being able to leave her small town.

Helen was pessimistic.

– That would be wonderful, she said. But my idea of Bright's Grove has been shrinking lately. I can barely stand being a few blocks away from home. The panic is terrifying. It really doesn't look like I'm going anywhere.

– I'll visit again soon, said Gwen. I miss you.

The following day, she called Michael and arranged for herself, Michael, and Professor Bruno to surprise her parents with a visit. Professor Bruno and Michael could not leave for a week or so, but this suited Gwen, as it would give her time, she thought, to persuade Tancred to come with them – though this was doubtful – and to work up the resolve to sacrifice some part of herself or her life.

Her longing for Tancred was, of course, constant. It was the kind of longing that makes you wonder how it was that, only a month ago, you barely thought about someone; never mind that, a year ago, you didn't know of their existence. Now here she was trying to picture Tancred in his apartment, trying to imagine what he was doing, then telling herself to *stop* imagining because it only frustrated her.

Tancred called her often. And though he was, admittedly, not one for telephones, his voice was warm and she could hear that he was both holding himself back and failing to hold himself back. He didn't limit himself to these calls either. He sent her pictures from his phone, pictures of places he happened to be when thinking of her: Byng and Danforth, Kingston Road at Glen Stewart Park, Queen East and Glen Manor, Woodbine Station, King and Jameson, an alleyway near Christie and Yarmouth Road ...

On the surface, there was no pattern to the images. No one who saw them on her phone would have taken them for intimate.

In fact, Gwen would have preferred pictures of his face, though she did end up thinking how sweetly erotic it was that the sight of a grey corner in Parkdale — King and Jameson — could make her think about his hands.

Neither wanted to be apart from the other. But both knew that, were they to be alone again, it would be difficult to keep from expressing physically the longing each felt for the other. And this would be, for Tancred at least, a point beyond which he could no longer take Olivier's feelings into consideration. Not that Olivier's feelings, whatever they might be, could stop him from wanting her. But his love for Olivier demanded at least this much: that he wait, in order to confess to Olivier, *in person*, his love for Gwen. This confession, however, could only be made when Olivier returned from Muskoka, where he was spending time with Simone and Gordon.

This last was, more or less, what Tancred answered when Gwen asked if he would come with her to Bright's Grove. She suggested that they would be, in effect, chaperoned and that they could sleep in separate bedrooms. But even she was unconvinced by the suggestion, and his resolve left her caught between admiration and intense physical longing.

Nadia asked Gwen what was wrong, and Gwen, abandoning her usual reticence, admitted that she was in love.

– Well, it's about time! said Nadia. Who is it? Someone you met in Muskoka. Did you sleep with him? Is he rich?

– It's no one you know! Gwen answered.

– Of course it's no one I know, otherwise I'd know who it was, wouldn't I? I'm happy for you. Are we going to meet him?

Robbie, who was sitting at the table with them, said

– Maybe she doesn't want anyone to know.

– Maybe she doesn't want *you* to know, answered Nadia. Why don't you bugger off and let us talk?

But Robbie didn't move. He said

– It's early goings, Gwen. You might as well relax and enjoy it. This is the best part.

– Oh, please, said Nadia, look who's giving romantic advice! You'd be better doing the opposite of what he says!

She said these words with affection, however, and the two of them puckered up across the table from each other. They were getting along, now that Robbie had left his wife and was spending most of his time in Toronto.

Following Nadia's advice, he had ceded control of cows and sod to Liz and her father. His parents' farm he left to his father, much to his father's anger. In principle, Robbie was a Toronto sales rep for both concerns. And he did actually work on their behalf. You could see, though, that Robbie, who had never even considered the possibility of himself as Torontonian, was in fact leaving Barrow behind, casting his fate with Nadia. This was wonderful, as far as Nadia was concerned, but Gwen wondered about Robbie's children and couldn't help feeling a certain discomfort. Was this love, then, that swept away concern for those who needed you?

But what did she know about his concerns?

Robbie's advice was good. So Gwen tried to convince herself that what she was feeling was a kind of pleasure, or would be if only she could flip her feelings over with some sort of emotional jiu-jitsu. It almost worked, too. By that Friday, when she was meant to leave for Bright's Grove, she looked forward to surprising her mother, and looked forward to being with Tancred at last, when Olivier returned and they could speak to him.

She, Michael, and Professor Bruno were meant to leave in the evening, at seven thirty. She put a few things in an overnight bag, leaving the black box and its books beneath her bed, and went down the stairs early, so they could be off as soon as the car arrived.

There was something about the night, though. It felt decisive.

The moon was aggressive, but she was calm as she waited. A dog went by – an Alsatian, dragging its owner along – and looked at her as it passed. She saw Michael's car as it approached, and it occurred to her – out of the blue, really – that the ring had been true to her and that she would be true to the ring. This conviction was not new, but it was like finding something that had long been lost.

What followed was an accident – if one can speak of accidents here – which was followed by deliberate havoc. After Michael, without leaving the car, had opened the trunk for her, Gwen had put her overnight bag in and then accidentally slammed the trunk shut on her own fingers. The pain was excruciating, but she left her little finger where it was and slammed the trunk cover down on it again. This time the trunk locked and she could not move and she cried out.

The minutes that followed were almost dreamlike for Gwen. However many times Michael tried, the trunk could not be opened from the inside, because Gwen's finger was lodged in it. It took both Michael and Professor Bruno to get her finger out and, when they did – Professor Bruno pushing frantically on the button beneath the steering wheel while Michael pried the trunk open – Gwen fell to the pavement in agony, sheltering her left hand.

– Are you all right? asked Michael.

– Jesus, Mary, and Joseph, said Professor Bruno.

Gwen was disoriented, as they helped her up from the pavement. And though she knew what she had done, the reality of it only clarified when she noticed that Professor Bruno, looking puzzled, was staring at something near her waist.

Looking down, Gwen saw that the small finger on her left hand was as if bent in two, a third of it at a right angle to her palm. She felt pain as her mind caught up with her body, and she allowed herself to be helped into the car and taken to Toronto Western: Michael driving, Professor Bruno consoling her from the back seat, she cradling one hand in the other, like holding a small animal.

It should hurt more, she thought.

The surgeon on duty – a doctor from Cornwall who was at the Western on a locum – asked Gwen what had happened to her and then, once the X-rays had come back, showed her the extent of the damage to the little finger. It was broken or fractured in five places, but the doctor felt that she could set the bones so that the finger would function, once it was better, pretty much as it had.

For a moment, Gwen considered if she should let the doctor do her work. It was, admittedly, eccentric to cut a finger off for the sake of an idea whose origin was from millennia past, from a time when people believed god knows what. Her hesitation, however, was brief.

– I don't want to take the chance that my finger will be useless, she said. If you don't mind, would you please amputate it?

The doctor, whose name was Bharath, looked at Gwen as if she'd expressed herself in a strange language. Perplexed, but having weighed the matter – and sensing nothing wrong with Gwen – Dr. Bharath accepted Gwen's request. It was her finger, after all, and thus her decision. Nor was the procedure difficult. Gwen's hand was frozen from the wrist down, a bone shear was used to cut the finger, a scalpel was used to get to healthy tissue, what was left of the finger was sewn into a stump, an appointment was made for the next week, when the stitches would be removed, and Gwen was advised to use an extra-strength acetaminophen should there be any pain.

By the time Gwen left the hospital, it was too late to drive to Bright's Grove. Besides, Michael and Professor Bruno had been somewhat traumatized by what had happened. Nor did Gwen's good humour quell their feelings of guilt. On the contrary, the more Gwen assured them that they had done nothing wrong, the more one or the other felt obliged to apologize.

– It's all right, she told them. I'm fine. My grandmother was missing a finger, too. Why don't we go to Bright's Grove when my stitches come out, next week or the week after?

Michael and Professor Bruno both agreed to this.

– It's the least we can do, said Michael.

– Amen, said Professor Bruno.

In the end, it did not matter to Gwen if the ring were an illusion, or if centuries of her foremothers had been deluded – though she did not think they had been. Nor did the idea that she was keeping the ring for a goddess – for Aphrodite or Oshun, Sekhmet or Ishtar – motivate her. She hadn't sacrificed her finger for any of them. Even the sense of belonging, of being one of the women whose names and impressions were recorded in the black books entrusted to her: even this was more pleasant than crucial. She hadn't sacrificed her finger for any of them either.

As she lay in her bed that night –uncomfortable, careful not to lie on her injured hand – Gwen felt an overwhelming relief. The thing she'd been waiting for, the thing her mother and grand-mother had perhaps unconsciously prepared her for, had arrived, and with it had come Gwenhwyfar Lloyd – no longer waiting, no longer standing on a threshold.

The heirloom she had inherited was not a ring or a box of books. It was this sense of herself as whole, despite the loss of her finger. By making the choice she'd made   rightly or wrongly, deluded or not – she had chosen a road and was confident of the road chosen, despite its consequences: that she could not play the piano as she had, that she would be forever conscious of how her left hand looked, and that she would be constantly reminded of a choice she'd made at age twenty-nine. Against these things she could not do, there was a feeling of adventure, a joy at setting out, and a moving toward a life she wanted.

Before going to sleep, she called Tancred – Tancred first – not wishing to alarm him when next they saw each other.

– I've had a kind of accident, she said. I've lost a finger.

Tancred was – and she could hear it in his voice – upset. Though it was late, he wanted to know if there was anything he could do, anything she needed. Did she need him to buy Tylenol? Did she want to stay with him while she recovered?

(His concern for Olivier's feelings had evaporated, it seemed, in light of her situation. And though she did not point this out, she clocked it, and it made her happy.)

– No, she said, give me a few days. I don't want you to see me like this, with these bandages. The stitches come out in a week. After that … I just hope you don't mind that my hand looks strange.

– It's not your hand I'm after, he said.

Though, of course, in the old sense, it was exactly that.

AN ENGAGEMENT AND A MARRIAGE, CONTINUED

On the night that Gwen and Tancred shared a narrow bed in a farmhouse, Olivier and Simone had eaten at Hildegard's and then spent the night in each other's company. By morning, Olivier found that he was attracted to an older woman who, to all appearances, was attracted to him as well.

Simone was married and was loyal to her husband. There was no question of Olivier and Simone's relationship being anything but platonic. But as they sat with each other talking about music (the *Winterreise* mostly, because of the night) and painting (Lubin Baugin's still lifes) and about the connection between mythology and violence (the subject of Simone's doctorate), something passed between them: a recognition, say, of the feeling they'd been intimates before this intimacy.

Olivier hadn't been physically aroused exactly, but his feelings weren't intellectual.

Speaking now with Tancred, he said
— Well, what does erotic even mean anyway?

– That's something you either know or don't know, isn't it? said Tancred. I don't know if it's something anyone can exactly tell you.

– I'm asking your opinion, answered Olivier. The pleasure of being with another person can be physical, even if you never touch, can't it?

– But is that enough?

– That's the question, said Olivier.

The two were sitting together on the side of Tancred's home Gwen had not seen, the side entered through the lightly stained doors. The windows on this side mostly faced the city or, at least, the barricade of buildings that separated the city from the lake. Its layout was identical to that on the other side, taking up the tenth and eleventh floors, but it was, otherwise, completely different.

In the space that was, on the other side, a living room, there was here a small library devoted to the art of Africa and, to a lesser extent, that of Italy. On the walls there were a number of framed posters from exhibits of African art and a poster of Giorgio de Chirico's *The Enigma of the Hour*. In this space, too, there was a piano, but it was not of the same quality as the other. It was a battered upright that had belonged to Olivier's mother. Olivier had given it to Tancred for safekeeping when his father, as his dementia set in, began to weep uncontrollably at the sight of it. Tancred kept it for his friend, in this place to which Olivier had a key.

Also on this side of Tancred's home, there was a pool table, small ebony statues, totems, masks on walls, a sizable collection of African music, and, in the dining room, a painting of the goddess Oshun given to him by his mother. The kitchen was not quite clean, because it was the one Tancred used, the one at whose table he ate. It smelled of whatever he'd cooked that day or the day before, and there were dishes in the sink.

This was the place where Tancred lived. It commemorated his mother's culture (African) and what little he knew – or cared to know – of his father's (Italian). As well, it brought together the handful of things that were important to him: the painting of Oshun, Olivier's piano, books on anarchy and socialism given to him by Daniel's father, pictures of himself, Daniel, and Olivier when they were boys. Though the other apartment, the one Gwen had seen, was in some ways more impressive, with its clean lines and lake view, this was the side he cherished, and it was known by only a handful of people.

– The thing is, Tan, said Olivier, I love Simone. I don't care if we don't have a physical relationship.

– Have you told Simee how you feel?

– No, said Olivier. I want you to tell her.

– Me?

– Yes. If I tell her, it'll change how we are when we're together. But if you tell her, like you're telling her a secret, she might be flattered and then I wouldn't have to hide my emotions as much. The way it is now, I'm worried about saying the wrong thing.

– I don't understand, said Tancred, why you get this way when you fall in love! It's like you stop being able to think. What if I tell her and she's afraid of hurting Gordon, so she never sees you again?

– But that's the thing! I really like Gordon! The three of us could be like Turgenev with Pauline Viardot and Pauline's husband, Louis.

At Olivier's instigation, Tancred had slogged through a biography of Turgenev, one of Olivier's favourite writers, and he'd been horrified by this love triangle Olivier was talking about, a 'love triangle' in which there might have been love – on Turgenev's side anyway – but almost certainly no lovemaking. Only Ollie, thought Tancred, could envy a ménage à trois whose chief by-product was sexual frustration. The normally straight-thinking, unsentimental Olivier always lost his reason when he fell in love. Worse: he sought out situations that led to frustration. This thing with Simone, thought Tancred, would end as every one of Ollie's relationships had ended: with Ollie heartbroken.

To his own surprise, and against his own interests, Tancred said

– But what about Gwen?

– What about her? asked Olivier.

– Well, you two have been seeing each other …

– Oh please, said Olivier, you've been after her from the first moment you saw her. And I don't blame you. She's perfect for you. Simee thinks so, too. I may not know myself, Tan, but I know *you*. Plus, Gwen has a thing for you, too. I can't believe we're even talking about this. I only 'went out with her' because I knew you'd be more yourself around her if you thought she was with me. I like Gwen. I think she's great. But she's not exactly my type, is she?

Tancred had a mind to contradict him, to refuse to admit that he cared about Gwen, mostly because he found it annoying to be so readable. But then he remembered the place and time: the Gardiner Museum overlooking the ROM, the way Gwen looked slightly out of her element, her skirt, the way her hair was up, the curve of her neck, her eyes as they looked away from him. The memory of it was enough to overwhelm him. Still, he'd assumed he had effectively hidden his feelings, and was annoyed to find that he hadn't. Then again, Ollie knew him as well as he knew Ollie. This was both the benefit and the cost of close friendship.

– Listen, said Tancred. Are you sure you want me to tell Simee how you feel? You'd be better off just letting things go on like they are. You don't care if you sleep together, so being part of her world is probably the best you can get, and you don't need to do anything to get that. You've already got it. I'll do whatever you want me to. You know that. But I think you should reconsider.

– Hmm, said Olivier. I really don't like the feeling of keeping a secret, but I guess I can take it for a while, if I have to.

– I would, said Tancred, if it was me.

For a week, Gwen stayed home, taking days off work. These days off were such a surprise to Dr. Bellmar, the presiding geriatrician, that he expressed as much alarm as he did concern. Was she all right? Should she come to the hospital? Was there anyone to take care of her?

The old Gwen, the one devoted to her colleagues, the one determined to make a life for herself in the city, would have risen from her deathbed to spare Dr. Bellmar's feelings. But the Gwenhwyfar she was now mildly answered 'yes, no, yes,' then put her phone on mute, deliberately ignoring calls from anyone but her mother, Tancred, and Olivier.

This was in part because she needed time to consider what she had done, its implications, its likely effect on her life. She needed the break, in order to give her mind a chance to catch up to her new situation. But it was also because she was now someone without a small finger on her left hand. She was disfigured – the word was strange, when she thought of it in regard to herself. And it felt odd picking things up with her left hand. It was as if her hand were off balance.

For some time, she thought constantly about her little finger, though, to be fair, this was very likely because, when the doctor asked what she wished to do with it, she had elected to keep the finger. It was now in a glass container (filled with alcohol) that stood on the desk beside her bed.

Nadia, of course, could not keep from expressing her pity, nor from giving advice.

– God, Gwen, what are you going to do? You can't go around without a finger! Shouldn't you be wearing gloves when you go out?

It felt now as if *The Chrysalids* were non-fiction.

She'd heard from Tancred about his talk with Olivier. There was no pressing need to talk to Ollie, but she couldn't help wondering how he had known from the beginning that she and Tancred were meant for each other. In this, she was like Tancred:

slightly miffed that others had seen in her what she should have seen for herself. So she arranged to meet Olivier on Roncesvalles, which had become, in her mind, Olivier's neighbourhood, though he lived in Bloor West Village.

This time, they met at an espresso bar and sat in the back. Olivier seemed happy to see her because, knowing she'd spoken to Tancred, he had questions for her. Well, one question: did she, as a woman, think his feelings for Simone were misplaced?

– I'll answer your question, she said, but you have to answer mine first. Why did you think Tan and I would make a good couple?

– That's easy, said Olivier. The first time you met was at the Gardiner, right? And even when Tan was talking to Simone, I could tell he had an eye on you. And you had yours on him.

– I didn't, said Gwen. I didn't even like him.

– I wonder if you really believe that, answered Olivier. People can be so clear about others and so unclear about themselves. I mean, when you two walked into Queen Anne's Corset, you were like this ...

(Here, Olivier crossed the index and middle fingers of his right hand before continuing.)

– You've got similar backgrounds. Your father's a musician. Tan loves music. You're both interested in the arts ... I could go on, you know.

– But Tan thought *we* were going out. It's not impossible we could have been, is it?

– No, not impossible, said Olivier, but that night we were at Polonez, the only time you perked up was when we ran into Tan and Alex von Wurfel. It was pretty much over for us by then, don't you think?

Gwen thought about it before answering. Olivier was right, of course, but it made you wonder if you needed other people so you could be clear about yourself.

– Am I that easy to read? she asked.

– For me, yes, because I've had a lot of experience with failure. I'm sure Tan told you how disastrous my relationships have been. And I admit it. But the benefit is: I know pretty quickly when someone's attracted to me and I can see when they're attracted to someone else, too, because most of my relationships have been with women who want to be with others.

– Why is that? asked Gwen.

– I don't *try* to love people who can't love me. If I had to guess, I'd say I must find something comforting about loss. I'm sure it all goes back to some detail in my childhood. Or maybe there's just so much tension when you're waiting for rejection that the rejection becomes a pleasure. Dan says I've made failure erotic. I'm not sure if he's right, but I don't know if he's wrong either. I guess I'd agree loss is erotic to me. Romantic loss anyway. Failure, not so much.

– I wonder, said Gwen, what would happen if you found someone who wanted to be with you.

– It's never happened, said Olivier, so I don't know.

The strangest thing about their conversation, aside from the fact that he had not mentioned her missing finger, was the good-natured and matter-of-fact way Olivier talked about something that would have been devastating for her. She could not imagine endlessly chasing after men who did not want her. Her unsuccessful relationships had been accidents, accidents that she'd wanted to work. The humiliation she had been through, the awkwardness, the self-blame, the worry that she was unlovable. She could not imagine seeking those things out, and she wasn't sure what to do with the idea that Olivier did. It was perverse, but it was selfish, too, because the other side of the coin, if he really did seek out rejection, was that he didn't give those who might love him a chance. In the end, she agreed with Daniel. Olivier *had* eroticized loss.

And yet he was handsome, kind, thoughtful, and generous.

– So, he said, do you think I'm doomed? With Simee, I mean. I mean, even if I am, it's not like I can help my feelings. But I do wonder.

– If you're doomed, said Gwen, doesn't that mean you'll be happy?

– I suppose it does, he answered.

Accompanied by the sounds of Belle and Sebastian, the smell of freshly ground coffee, the constant chatter around them, they talked about Simone Azarian. As with Tancred when he'd spoken to Olivier, Gwen was concerned about Olivier's feelings for Simone. Simone was married, after all. Then again, something in Gwen *had* changed. Despite her ambivalence about him being involved with a married woman, Gwen wished for Ollie to find happiness with Simone. Love now seemed so mercurial to Gwen, so bound to miracle and mystery, that she was ready to welcome its reign, however anarchic.

She said

– I hope things work out the way you want them to.

– That's possible, too, Olivier answered.

Then his tone changed. He became suddenly solicitous.

– Listen, he said, I didn't want to mention it, Gwen, but what happened to your finger?

As Gwen had taken time off work and as this was unlike her, Nadia and Robbie were both worried about her state of mind. They both felt she was not herself, and Robbie, in particular, wondered if, along with losing her finger, she'd had some neurological event.

He said:

– I've seen this happen to animals, too, you know. They get all quiet and keep to themselves and then they just go off. Like this cow on my friend's farm. Cows are awful creatures and they don't have what you'd call personality, as far as I'm concerned.

So, this one was what you'd call cow-like, but even more. Damn near like a statue of a cow. Then, next thing you know, dead as a doornail. Don't get me wrong. I'm not saying you're like a cow. You know I don't mean *that*. But maybe we're all kind of like cows, 'cause we're animals. So, you see?

Nadia's show of concern was less awkward, but it wasn't more helpful. Gwen's condition – if you could call it a condition – brought out the solicitousness in Nadia, her good side. Whenever she was home from work, she'd knock on Gwen's door, to see if she wanted tea or coffee or anything she could send Robbie out to get. She wanted to help, because she was, at heart, a sensitive person. But Nadia's kindness only made Gwen feel guilty. It made her feel as if *she* should comfort Nadia. So she ended up drinking cups of coconut oolong, Nadia's favourite, and then staying up late, because the tea kept her awake.

Not that she would have slept all that easily anyway. There was, of course, the getting used to missing a finger. She understood now the cruelty of changing a physical aspect of the one you love. She would never have said she was, in any respect, her little finger, that it was an important part of her selfhood. But in the days following her amputation, it did feel as if she'd lost something essential. Then, too, the conversations she had with her mother changed in character. She was not her mother's equal in experience or understanding, but she and Helen were now on the same side of a line, a line that separated those who knew of the ring from those who did not.

Once, briefly unsure she had made the right decision, Gwen said

– Why would anyone take this thing on?

– You've read Book Three, answered her mother. There are as many justifications as there are foremothers. I like to think that, in ancient times, the ring made obvious sense. They had horrible lives back then, very hard. To be able to control your husband would have been a real blessing. If I remember right, in Book Three, doesn't everybody ask 'Why us?' at some point? 'How should I use the ring, and what does it mean?' And as far as I can remember, no one's come close to answering those questions. I spent years asking my mom and she asked hers. There's no answer, except that we *don't* take this on. It's handed to us by those we love most.

— It feels like we're cursed, said Gwen.

— I don't see it as a curse exactly. It binds us, in pain and in sorrow. But it binds us. And all of us have found men we love who love us. I find the best way to think about this is to imagine what the ones before writing thought, how they dealt with this. Somewhere back there, in the past, the first of our mothers wanted this and used it for her own good. Then, too, I imagine the ring is what pushed our foremothers to learn to read and write. And they kept writing, even when that was dangerous for women, because men were afraid of it. I like to think that part of us is still like the ancients, and that we pass our learning on, along with the suffering.

— Part of why this feels weird, Mom, is that I can't tell Tan about it. I hate having to lie about my finger.

— Well, first to begin, you're not lying to him, and second, you *can't* tell him. I mean, it's not possible. You'll see. The thing to remember, Gwenhwyfar, is that the ring protects itself. That's the most important detail in all the books. The ring doesn't want to be known. I tried to tell your father, more than once. I love that man so much, I can't stand not being able to share this with him. But every time I tried, I started speaking gibberish. Like speaking in tongues. And your father thought I was loony. Isn't Book Three filled with warnings about this very thing? By the way, have you noticed any changes in Tancred yet?

— Changes in him? Like what?

— Hard to say. Your grandmother told me that my father started to crave cherries after she used the ring. Your father ... well, your father dresses in black immediately after we make love. Black pants, socks, underwear. It's very strange, like he's in mourning.

(Here, a part of Gwen's childhood was transfigured. She now had an unwanted place to put memories of her father wearing black pyjamas at breakfast.)

— I remember there were other examples in Book Three, said Helen. Some of them funny. Then again, some husbands didn't change at all. I don't know if there's a link between what you wish for and how your husband changes, but my advice is to be careful. Try to be unobtrusive in your wishes. And remember that it's going to influence you, too. You remember my wishes for your father. I wished he could never love anyone but me, and now I can't see an attractive man without feeling physically ill. I can't watch Hollywood movies at all, because the men are too damned attractive. You remember? I threw up when I tried to watch *Dances with Wolves*.

— Jesus, Mother! Why should I use the ring at all? I mean, why should I use it again?

— Well, that's the question, isn't it? I was wilful when I was your age. I felt that if I was going to pay a price for having it, I might as well use it. Anyway, isn't there one of our mothers who didn't use it and *that* brought her bad luck? Or at least she thought it did. The ring is a bit of a curse, I admit, but so is life itself. And anyway, there are worse things than to be acquainted with the sacred.

Despite her mother's reasonable suggestion that there were worse things on earth than this inheritance, the more Gwen read the books, the more glaring the ring's uncanny aspects became.

The fear that the ring might hurt Tancred if she did something to betray its secret was now added to other anxieties. And yet, also thanks in part to the ring, Gwen was more certain than ever that Tancred was the one with whom she wanted to share her life. In fact, Gwen now felt that she could only ever have chosen Tancred. They had not seen each other for two weeks, two weeks that felt like two years.

The day after her stitches came out, Gwen texted Tancred to let him know that she would see him later. And her text – cu later – felt illicit and exciting. This, combined with the relief of getting away from the distractions of Nadia and Robbie, lifted her spirits.

What she thought she'd do, for a few hours before seeing Tancred, was to begin writing her own and her mother's story in Book Three. For this, Gwen decided to find a quiet place downtown. She wasn't sure that she would spend the night with Tancred – or didn't want to presume – but she took along a change of clothes, a toothbrush, and toothpaste, as well as Book Two (to read) and Book Three (to write).

It was a Saturday afternoon, and she walked along a crowded Bloor Street for the pleasure of it.

Just east of Bathurst, she managed to stop worrying about her and Tancred's fate. The day was warm and Bloor was almost back to the Bloor she loved best: its summer self when, during the day, the street is busy and you can imagine going into By the Way for Jerusalem Eggs and sitting at the window, looking out at Brunswick, looking over at Future Bakery – outdoor tables, a Stella Artois sign, a mural that looked like aggressive blue waves staring up at their mistress, a woman carrying a basket of bread – trying to remember when the bookstore at 501 closed, when the Brunswick House closed, and where some of the restaurants she'd once frequented had gone.

As she approached Spadina, she saw someone she recognized walking toward her: one of the poets she'd met at the poetry reading in Muskoka. It took her a moment, but the woman's name came back to her, because it was unusual: Roo. Gwen suddenly wondered about her – greying thin hair, an almost sharp chin, not quite prominent cheekbones, eyes slightly recessed yet lively, the whole of her face looking as if she'd just remembered or just forgotten something, though perhaps not anything important.

Though Roo was walking with another woman – taller, the same kind of chin, long hair swept back in a bun so that her ears (with their minuscule black earrings) were visible – Gwen decided to ask a question that had been on her mind since reading the poem 'Ring.'

– Excuse me, she said, aren't you Roo? We met in Muskoka. You helped me find my coat.

– Oh, said Roo, I remember! How are you?

– I'm fine, answered Gwen, but do you mind if I ask you a question? Do you think poetry is fiction or non-fiction? I mean, it doesn't feel like non-fiction, but it doesn't always feel like fiction either.

Roo turned to the woman with her and laughed.

– This is my friend Jan, she said. I'm laughing because we were just talking about that! It's a hard question.

– We know, said Jan, or we imagine that poetry and philosophy were one and the same in the beginning. So you could say that poetry started off as non-fiction.

They moved away from the middle of the sidewalk and stood by the window of Cobs Bread.

– That's a good answer, said Roo. But my answer's simpler. I think poetry is non-fiction because I can't write it unless I see everything in the poem clearly. I can't invent people or names or stories. So my poetry is non-fiction by default.

– Are there a lot of poets like you? asked Gwen.

Here, Roo and Jan laughed again, but not unkindly.

– A lot? answered Roo. I don't know. I think everybody's probably different.

– Even if we're all different, said Jan, I wouldn't be surprised if a lot of poets agreed with you about seeing clearly ...

Jan and Roo began to talk then, to each other mostly, about whether poets saw more clearly than philosophers, about whether it was possible to use abstractions to reach truth, about whether Edward Thomas, say, was more faithful to the world – to the Earth, to 'all that was the case' – than Wittgenstein.

Gwen found this interesting, but it was also overwhelming. After a respectful few minutes, she thanked the poets for their generosity and continued walking east, turning south at Queen's Park, still thinking about the relationship between seeing clearly and telling the truth. There was enough clarity in 'Ring,' the poem, to make you wonder how much of it was her ancestor describing what she'd actually seen (the sheep going up a hill, maybe) and how much was conventional (the gods, certainly), and how much of the conventional was nevertheless true because it conformed to the thoughts and feelings of she who'd first recited the poem. Her mother had spoken of trying to imagine the earliest of their foremothers. Now Gwen thought about the woman – if there was only one – who'd conceived of 'Ring.' She tried to imagine her desires, beliefs, and needs, tried to imagine what it was like to be at home in a world where a ring could alter a human being's body or change their personality.

But imagining the first singer of 'Ring' was not easy. Nor was it easy to see how the world changed when one accepted that 'magic' was a real aspect of it. Looking south, there in the distance, the CN Tower stood – drab, grey, and tall. Magic or not, it now signified home. Magic or not, the trees along the road put out their lime-green buds and early leaves, leaning away from the too-close buildings to catch more light. Magic or not, the avenue bifurcated after the ROM, and one walked with the buildings of U of T to one's left (or right, depending on the way one had chosen) and the tree-full park with its wintry patches and young grass to one's right (or left, again depending). Magic or not, the street lights turned amber or red or green and cars along the road slowed, stopped, or started accordingly. Magic or not, Queen's Park came together again at College, and, on crossing the street, one found oneself on University Avenue, the broad road with hospitals on either side.

Yes, it would be difficult to pinpoint what exactly changed in the world, once you allowed the miraculous in. Then again, that wasn't the question exactly. The question was how to recover the first singer, how to recover the past. As she walked, it seemed to

Gwen that there were (at least) two roads to the past. Along one of them, one tried to imagine, as clearly as possible, the wide world that no longer existed in fact, though it still lived in minds and books. This way was both playful and ruthless, a substitution of what is for what was: no cars but horses, no stone buildings but wooden huts, no avenues but beaten paths, no towers but in the distance a blue expanse of water that, for all one knew, stretched on to the mouth of the underworld. The other road to the past was just as playful but harder (for Gwen, at least) to stay on. Here, one imagined oneself as ancient and tried to feel, amid the modern, the strangeness of cars, buildings, avenues, traffic lights, and towers. One tried, amid the modern, to grasp the present's otherness. This way, in holding to otherness and wonder, one did not inhabit the past. One was, rather, inhabited by it.

All well and good and tidy. It was, for Gwen, one of those moments when an idea feels sharp and whole. And although its clarity is fleeting, the idea leaves a sense – also fleeting – of accomplishment. As Gwen approached King Street, she realized to her surprise that, while thinking of the past and of poetry, of 'Ring' and of the ring, she had been thinking also of Tancred. He had accompanied her along University. In fact, unbeknownst to her conscious self, she was walking toward Queen's Quay. That is, she had been walking toward Tancred, though she'd intended to find a spot where she could read, before going to him.

At King and University, she called.

– Hi, Gwenhwyfar, he answered

and the sound of his voice excited her.

– I want to sleep with you, she said.

There was a pause.

– Well, he answered, it's … it's a bit early for sleep. Are you far?

– No, I'm at King and University. Can I see you?

– Any time you want, he said. Call me from the lobby. I'll come down and get you.

There was nothing — nor stubble nor birthmark, nor curves nor fingernails — that Gwen would change about Tancred physically. If anything, had she been able, she'd have chosen to stop time so that, ever after, she could make love with this Tancred. That said, it was while making love that Gwen discovered the compensation the ring exacted for granting her first wish. Or, more exactly, it was Tancred who discovered what the ring exacted.

As she walked along Queen's Quay, she felt the butterflies that come with anticipation. But if Tancred was at all nervous, he did not show it. He'd come down to meet her and was waiting for her in the lobby. She could see he was pleased to see her, but he was also calm, introducing her to the concierge, a man who happened to be named Odhiambo, John Odhiambo! Well, thought Gwen, it's a common enough name in Africa. But the coincidence brought on the uncanny feeling one has when the world fusses over the details of one's life, or seems to.

In the elevator up, Tancred asked if she'd eaten.

— I forgot all about it, Gwen answered. I was thinking about something interesting.

— Oh! What was it? he asked.

She was about to tell him about the ring, maybe even show him one of the books, when her palms began to sweat, her spinal column felt as if it would catch fire, and she started to cough, coughing until panic drove all thought of book, ring, and reading from her mind.

Gently rubbing her upper back, Tancred said

— Are you okay?

— I guess I should take better care of myself, she said.

They were on the tenth floor then, and she had turned toward the door she'd previously gone in. But Tancred touched her and said

— Let me show you this side. It's a bit messy, but I feel more at home over here.

Gwen immediately understood why he felt at home, because she felt so, too. This side was a mirror image of the other, but the view from its windows was of the city, not the lake: a curtain of buildings that recalled the image of 'the city' her younger self had when dreaming of escape from Bright's Grove. The apartment's posters and the art – sculptures standing, posters and paintings on the walls – were such as she might have chosen herself. The piano, on this side, was like one of two she'd grown up with, the one in the basement that had been her father's first instrument.

(Here, of course, it was as if her left hand had its own memory and longed for what it missed.)

As if all that weren't enough, there was the music playing as they entered the living room: low but rising, insistent, and thrilling. She recognized it at once. It was music she knew intimately, note for note, having listened to it all her life: 'The Healing Song' by Pharaoh Sanders. And as they came in, the basses were as if happily chasing each other, waiting for the piano's return.

Gwen was moved to hear the music of her childhood, here to greet her.

– Is that your music? she asked. Or is it the radio?

– It's mine, said Tancred. Do you want to change it?

– No, she answered. I love Pharoah Sanders.

It really *was* as if the world – or fate or the gods or chance – were fussing over the details, obviously paving the road for her.

The next two hours passed as if time were a series of discrete impressions. She was hungry, but she asked to see the apartment's other rooms. The bedroom – the room she most wanted to see – was tidy and smelled faintly of the aftershave he wore and of the wide bed, its sheets deep blue and clean. This room, too, looked out on the city and tall buildings, and she wondered if anyone could see them. Not that it mattered. Not at all. She felt a hint of shame as she kept him from leaving the room, standing before him, her head on his chest. And then ... the feel of his warm skin as she pulled up his white shirt, surprising him, the coolness of his belt buckle, the thought of her missing finger, the smell of leather, a flickering light from a distant building, the taste of his tongue, the clean smell of him, and from out of nowhere the thought of summer in Bright's Grove, the smell of a field of weeds, the intrusion of the words *mercury* and *pallor*, the wondering if she smelled all right, the sound of his breathing, the sound of her own, a sigh, the salt taste of him, the feel of him on her tongue and lips, the wondering how she tasted, the chemical whiff of a condom, the sweet feel of taking him in, then holding on, his breath sweet, and then losing track of herself, and a long while after that great pleasure: feeling around for the covers because they'd thrown them off. There were whispered words, whispered for no reason, and how quiet it was, how silky the afternoon shadows, and then the coolness of a glass of water that he'd brought for her, his body momentarily framed by the bathroom door, the warmth of him as he slid again beneath the bedsheets, the way the room now smelled clearer, somehow, because the smell of their bodies beneath the sheets was musky and feral, and then a pun on the words *bush* and *brush* that, in that moment, she found very funny, and they both laughed, before all that was swept away as they began to touch each other again and it occurred to her that she'd been thinking again of summer and Lake St. Clair near home, the sheets now wet beneath her and slightly clinging as she straddled him, and then again losing track ... nothing, all thought fading into a dreamy, unpredictable wash of rhythm and touch, beyond which there was only pleasure.

When they'd stopped trying to arouse each other further, spent, now lying tired in each other's arms, Gwen began to feel hungry at last. She remembered that she hadn't really eaten since morning and this thought made her hungrier still. She didn't want to get up from bed, didn't want their first carnal hours to end, but her hunger was a distraction, so she suggested they get up to eat something, a soup maybe.

Tancred smiled mischievously, and said

– How about something Greek?

Gwen laughed before realizing she wasn't sure if he were suggesting anal sex. This was not something she particularly liked, but in the mood she was in, feeling open as she did, she was prepared to try, for his sake.

– Do you like anal sex? she asked.

Now it was Tancred who laughed uncertainly. They were clearly not on the same page, and it took him a moment to understand why.

– Gwen, if you like it, I like it, he said, but I was only suggesting Greek food, because you were just *speaking* Greek. I mean, you said 'O Zeus,' didn't you?

('O Zeus' – ὦ Ζεῦ – is what Tancred heard and understood, but Gwen had said and excitedly repeated, as she lost herself in pleasure: ὦ Ζεῦ! ὃ παπαῖ! ὡς ἀρεστόν!)

– When did I say that? she asked.

– While we were making love, he answered.

Reacting to her confusion, he held her, a hand on her back, one of his legs held between hers.

– It was great, he said. I could tell you liked what we were doing. And I liked it, too.

She was about to tell him that she didn't speak Greek, *couldn't* speak it, had never learned the language, when it struck her that, just as he did not know the words he spoke when he heard the name Polyphemus, so she was in the dark about this 'speaking' of hers. More, the thought came to mind – 'came to mind' as forcefully as if instilled by a mind other than her own – that it was best to simply accept that, from now on, when she was lost in orgasm, she would speak ancient Greek.

On reflection, this was not a bad thing. There was balance to it. Tancred would know she was in the midst of pleasure when he heard her speak Greek, just as she had known – as she *knew* – that he was hers when he spoke the words on the ring.

So she kissed him and changed the subject

– I love how you touch me, she said. But I really am hungry.

They got up then, she putting on one of his pyjama tops while he wore the bottoms. He had thought to order something, but they foraged in his kitchen and found all they needed for a red beans and rice with salmon. So the two of them, together, made a small meal – he cutting the onions and garlic, opening the tin of tomatoes and beans, then lightly frying the salmon before putting it in the oven; she making the rice and beans in a vegetable stock.

There was, Gwen felt, no question but that they belonged together. For all that the ring was strange or impossible or unworldly, if it were true that this feeling of being in the right place with the right person and at home in the world ... if this was the feeling the first of her mothers had felt, the feeling that all of her foremothers had subsequently known ... if this happiness was what the ring passed down to them, then the 'curse' was worth it.

At this very thought, the ring on her finger grew warm, as if politely making its presence known.

As they sat together in the kitchen, talking first about Simone, and then about Olivier's feelings for Simone, it occurred to Gwen that, rather than deciding for herself if or how to change Tancred, it would be convenient to ask him if there was anything *he* would change about himself. The opportunity came when Tancred mentioned that 'Ollie is always Ollie' – which is what he loved about Olivier – but that he wished him slightly more emotionally self-aware. This was not because he really wanted to see his friend change. It was rather because he hated to see Ollie suffer for love.

– That's really nice, she said. I like how close you two are. But don't you think we all have flaws we're not aware of?

– Yes, said Tancred. I think we do. I know *I* do.

– From where I'm sitting, she said, there's nothing about you I'd change. But if you had the chance ... if you could change one thing about yourself ... what would it be?

Tancred laughed.

– I can't tell you that, he said. That would be cheating. Wouldn't you rather find out for yourself?

– No, she answered. I'd much rather know in advance.

Tancred thought about it.

– What if, he said, the thing I don't like about myself is the thing you *like* about me? I don't like that Ollie gets hurt like he does. But it's what makes him Ollie. So I guess I really don't mind him getting hurt, now that I think about it.

Later, when it was night and they were tired from the intensities of the day, they made their way back to the bedroom where, only half-joking, Gwen claimed the side of the bed with the best view of the city. Not that she saw much of the city that night, because the two of them were face to face and talking as she fell asleep. In fact, her last impression was of Tancred, mock-crying out as her feet touched his beneath the covers.

– Your feet are freezing! he said.

– I know, she answered. That's why I'm putting them on you!

That night, Gwen woke from a deep sleep, somewhere around two in the morning. No longer sleepy and not wanting to wake Tancred, she left their bedroom and, going downstairs, decided to read from Book Three and, if she was clear-minded enough for it, to write about her mother.

She had set herself up in the dining room, when she had an urge to be in the other, lake-facing apartment. Once there, she found an office on the upper floor – desk and window facing the lake – that reminded her of her mother's eyrie. And it was there, in what would become *her* office, that she began to reread the English entries and then, using Google Translate, the French, Italian, and Spanish ones.

She had a pressing question in mind as she read: should she use her last two wishes? And reading in light of the question, she was surprised by the number of suggestions made by those who wrote of what their mothers *wished* they'd wished for. Gwen hadn't quite understood, on first going through Book Three, that at the heart of it there was an inescapable time lag: one was only allowed to read the books – only allowed to *own* them – in the brief time between finding love and 'marrying' one's beloved. As a result, much of what she read was theoretical, the words of women who had made choices they sometimes wondered about, while writing of the regrets (if any) their mothers had. It was all second-guessing, all echoes and re-soundings!

Marrying was not an uncomplicated word in Book Three. It did not necessarily refer to weddings and rituals. The earliest of her foremothers did not 'marry' in that sense. The ring did not seem to care about religion. So, 'marrying' referred to the moment when one committed to one's beloved. Nor did there seem to be any sort of timeline for finding the beloved. Some found them in their teens, some in their twenties, and some even later. Throughout the history of her family, however, there was a constant: mothers knew when their daughters had found love, as Helen had known with Gwen.

It was still moving to reread what her mother had written about her grandmother. Gwen had adored Estelle Homer Odhiambo. And her grandmother had not even tried to hide her adoration of Gwen. From as far back as Gwen could remember, Estelle had spoken to her as an equal, had bought her anything she wanted, so that her mother had to remind Gwen that she was *not* better than other people, *not* entitled to whatever she wanted.

Gwen had loved her grandfather, Raymond Odhiambo, almost as much as she had loved Estelle. He was not as expressive as she had been. He was much more subdued, but he was just as generous, and Gwen had fond memories of excursions with him, shopping for Christmas and birthday presents or simply driving along Lake St. Clair. So it was not surprising to read that Estelle's first wish for her husband had been

1. That he never lose his temper.

Her second wish:

2. That her husband never contradict her.

And her third:

3. That he be impeccably dressed at all times.

All of this accorded well enough with the grandfather Gwen had loved. She had never seen him angry, never heard him so much as raise his voice to her grandmother and, the clinching detail, had never once seen him without an ascot – even on Christmas morning when he was in pyjamas – or been next to him without smelling the aftershave she associated with him: Hai Karate. Her grandmother had made three good and *reasonable* wishes, you'd have thought. But, in fact, Estelle expressed regret about them. Estelle had told her daughter that, after years with a man who *couldn't* argue with her, she had an affair with the next-door neighbour, an ill-tempered and disagreeable town councillor, out of a desperation for conflict.

(Reading again of her grandmother's infidelity, Gwen stopped for a moment. Her grandparents had been so correct, so upright, she could not help wondering if Helen had recorded this affair out of some lingering resentment for her mother. Gwen briefly considered striking out her mother's words as a way to protect her poor grandfather.)

More: when Grandpa Raymond discovered Estelle's affair with the neighbour, he was so reasonable, so agreeable, that Estelle could never get over the guilt she felt. The qualities Estelle had prized when she was young – an even temper, an unwilling-ness to argue, a great sense of dress – pursued her like hungry dogs as she aged. Oh, and there was more. Until Helen herself inherited the ring and, at last, understood what her mother had gone through, she'd resented the (seeming) unkindness her mother had shown her father: the covert rolling of the eyes over what he wore, the secret scorning of his opinions.

You'd have thought that here, at least, was an example of the ring *failing* to create a safe haven for itself. But you'd be mistaken. The marriage of Raymond and Estelle was a very good one, in part because the wishes that Estelle had made were countered by changes in herself.

1. He could not lose his temper.

   1.1 She could do nothing to anger him. (As he was not a jealous man, her affair with the neighbour amused him more than anything else. But she had to deal with [or avoid] the things he could not stand – unmade beds, unwashed dishes, conversation while his favourite program was on television, et cetera.)

2. He could not contradict her.

   2.1 She could say nothing that provoked his contradiction. (Whether or not she agreed with his views of the world or world events, for instance, she found herself unable to correct him or even to suggest he should moderate his beliefs. In other words, she found herself obliged to tolerate his views. And this did, though she sometimes resented it, smooth many things over.)

3. He had to be impeccably dressed.

   3.1 She had to dress in ways that pleased or excited him. (As Raymond had a fondness for black lace stockings, garter belts, and silk underwear, Estelle wore these to bed, almost exclusively, for the fifty years they were married, and informed her daughter that, at first anyway, it was 'damned hard to read a newspaper in silk stockings and a corset.')

At Raymond's death, Estelle was devasted, and her devastation was, in fact, something Gwen remembered. She recalled her grandmother languishing in her own bedroom, refusing to come out. Her terrible grief had frightened Gwen as a child and the idea of it unnerved her still.

The complex mix of love and resentment between mothers and daughters was also on display in Book Three, and it occurred to Gwen that, in her family at least, it could not be otherwise. Their inheritance – as much a shared guilt as a shared gift – complicated matters between the generations. For instance, there were a number of mothers who'd felt crippling guilt at passing the ring on to their daughters. Many of these had, as Estelle had, found release and unconditional love in their relationships with their granddaughters. This caused resentment in their daughters. Then again, there were as many daughters, like Helen – and Gwen herself actually – who sensed and resented a *something* in their mothers that was beyond their reach, a remove, a secret. And this distance dampened their affections until they, in their turn, inherited the ring.

On this night, in the office overlooking the lake, Gwen's reading did not so much answer her pressing question – 'Should I use my final wishes?' – as it focused her attention on two ideas. The first was that she should know Tancred better before wishing any change on him. To do this, she would have to uncover his flaws if she could. But here she'd be working against love itself, which, as pointed out by Marie d'Auvergne, protects itself by blinding one to flaws in the beloved. The other idea – also from Marie d'Auvergne – was that one ought to consider changing the beloved in ways that would be *helpful* rather than simply pleasing or practical. Morally helpful, for instance. On this score, Marie suggested that one should wish the beloved to be morally infallible in his judgment. This was not so that one would be forced to do the right thing – though, of course, doing the right thing is always desirable – but, rather, so that one would always *know* what the right thing is. One could then embrace it or ignore it, as one chose.

This would mean turning the man you loved into a moral compass.

Gwen couldn't help wondering if her sympathy for Marie d'Auvergne's thinking wasn't a kind of longing. Her foremother had lived in a seventeenth century that valued thoughtfulness and believed 'right' and 'wrong' were discoverable, while she was caught in a twenty-first century that mistrusted thinking as 'elitist.' Not that she would have wanted to live in the seventeenth century herself. But it was still shocking to read snipes at Marie from her more recent foremothers, some of whom objected to her 'Reason' as a betrayal of true feeling and of 'reality.'

One of those who most disliked Marie, Alice Lobden Homer, Gwen's great-grandmother, wrote that she'd wanted to 'pull out old Frenchy's pages' because she found them 'dry and stupid.' Alice advised *her* daughter – Gwen's grandmother – to wish for 'an ever-ready prick with a good salary,' as she had done. Moreover, Alice had been scornful of *her* own mother's advice and believed that any problems that arose from her wishes were unlikely to be worse than the kinds of problems life generally threw at a woman. Alice's words to Estelle were: 'Who gives a shit if any of this is real? You're still going to end up doing lots of things you don't want to.'

Estelle, while loving her mother, had found Alice 'vulgar in a showy way' and she had, it seemed, tried to be as unlike her as she could. But Helen had adored every little thing about her Grandma Alice. And, in reading about Alice, Gwen thought she could see the roots of Helen's behaviour: the brashness, the courage of her opinions and feelings.

It was almost perplexing that two such different women – Marie d'Auvergne and Alice Homer – should both be related to her. But then again, as different as they were, both had come to accept that the ring was real, that its power was actual. If Gwen, too, accepted this, was it not simply a matter of using her remaining wishes and getting on with life?

Around four in the morning, with the first inkling of day just beginning to lighten the dark waters of the lake, Gwen wrote in Book Three the first words to a daughter she addressed as 'Clémentine,' a name she had always loved and one that felt right:

Dear Clémentine,
I'm writing these words to you sometime before your birth. It's four in the morning and I'm alone in our home with your father. It's very quiet now, and daylight is coming, though it's still dark.

There is so much to tell you, I'm not sure where to start. But I want to tell you about your grandmother (my mother) and the wishes she made for your grandfather ...

Gwen did not decide to live with Tancred, nor did he invite her to. It was, rather, that they both understood that Tancred's home was now also hers. He said so and there was no question that he meant it, but he did not have to. She joked that she would turn his life upside down.

— That's exciting, he said.

More troublesome for Gwen were the details. In particular, there was the running out on Nadia. How would Nadia pay the rent without her contribution? It did not seem fair to leave without warning.

— If you want, said Tancred, we can pay for a year's rent. Would that give her enough time?

— No, said Gwen, that would mean *you* paying, and that's not fair. I have to deal with this myself. I mean, maybe I can stay with you *and* keep paying my share of the rent.

— If you prefer to do that, I'm fine with it, but ... let me show you something.

They were in the kitchen, having finished breakfast. Tancred stood up and they went to the other side of his home, across the lobby, through the lightly stained doors, and up to the very office where Gwen had been writing in Book Three. From a drawer in the desk, Tancred took a dark blue bank book and handed it to her.

— I know, he said. Nobody uses bank books anymore. But I keep this one in memory of Simone's sister, Willow. I inherited a lot of money from her.

Gwen turned to the book's last page:

$$\$15,011,957.07$$

— Is all this yours? she asked.

— It's part of what I inherited, answered Tancred. I have more in that account, but I've never updated the book, because it reminds me of the first time Willow showed me how rich she was. But that's another story. What's important right now is that you don't have to worry about leaving Nadia in trouble. We can help her out, if you want.

— I think I need a minute to take this in, said Gwen. I mean, I knew you had money. But it's different imagining someone has money and then seeing proof. I've got to be honest, Tan, I've been wondering how you make your money.

— I can imagine, said Tancred. I'd have wondered, too. I'm sorry to do this to you, Gwen, because it's a shock, I know, but I've got a lot more than this. About half a billion dollars. An insane amount.

Gwen looked at him, to see if he was joking.

— A half a *billion?* she asked.

— I'm not a thief anymore, he said, and I don't deal drugs. Nothing illegal. It was a complete surprise when Willow left me her fortune. I couldn't even decide if I wanted to keep it. It's against my own principles to have so much. But giving it away at random makes no sense either. Because you don't want to just pass the problem on to others. People get strange when they're around so much money. I feel like I've gotten strange, too. Honestly, I've been avoiding telling you all this, because I was afraid what it might do. I bought this place because Simone suggested it and because I love the lake. Since then, I pay taxes and I try to help my friends, when they'll let me. But mostly the money is sitting in banks, while I try to figure out what to do with it.

— How long's it been since you got the inheritance? asked Gwen.

— Two years? Three years? I can't remember exactly when Willow died.

Gwen tried to imagine what Tancred had been like before the inheritance. She wondered if he'd changed. The reality of his wealth complicated things, regardless. For one thing, it made the trajectory of her last few months even more odd: meet a man, fall in love, inherit a magic ring, change the man, lose a finger, then find out that the man you love is insanely wealthy. God, what was next?

— I'm glad you told me, she said. It doesn't change the way I feel about you, but I'm going to need time to think about all this. So for now I'd rather not use your money, if that's okay. I've got enough saved to give Nadia a few months' rent. That should be enough time for her to find a new roommate. But are you *sure* you want me to live with you?

— Yes, he said, I'm sure. You can't imagine what a weight is off my shoulders, just telling someone about this money thing. I feel a lot better about living here, imagining you with me.

The ring on Gwen's finger again grew warm, warmer than last time, and it did not take any great insight to see where this was heading. As her life with Tancred began, her time with the ring was coming to an end.

Knowing that Tancred had money changed how Gwen felt about some things — about money, for instance, and how best to use it for others – but she did not allow it to affect her aspirations. She went back to work, leaving from her home by the lakeshore. She had picked up most of her belongings from what was now Nadia's apartment. And she arranged to hang out with Nadia on a Friday evening, to give them a chance to catch up, to properly introduce Tancred to her friend, and to let Nadia know that she'd be leaving.

On the appointed evening, as she and Tancred climbed the steps to the apartment, there was a charivari of weeping, of thumping feet, of Nadia screaming that she hated Robbie, absolutely hated him. Gwen stopped on the staircase, uncertain whether to go on. But Tancred calmly went before her and knocked at the door. And then knocked again, louder, until the noise and screaming stopped.

Without opening the door, Nadia called out

– Who are you and what do you want? We're busy!

To which Gwen answered

– Nadia, it's me. Is everything okay?

Now Nadia came out, dressed only in a bathrobe, and began to cry on Gwen's shoulder.

– He proposed to me, she said in between sobs.

What's more, Nadia had *accepted* Robbie's proposal, but their engagement was complicated by Robbie's behaviour (as per Nadia) as much as it was by Nadia's reaction to it (as per Robbie). Gwen and Tancred had walked in on a bitter moment in their celebrations – bitter, that is, for Nadia. For Robbie, who stood sheepishly at the door – shirtless and bleeding from a scratch above his left nipple – it was painful.

The beginning of Gwen's life with Tancred had coincided with a change in Nadia and Robbie's relationship. Though still volatile, it entered a phase of harmony. This was in part because Robbie was relieved to be away from the atmosphere in Barrow, after his divorce.

He missed his children, of course, but his ex-wife had informed him that his presence was disruptive. So he agreed it might be better for all concerned if he found his own place, rather than staying with them when he was in Barrow. He'd then rented a small apartment in the town centre. And this meant that, for Robbie, coming to Toronto was an escape from three rooms with crooked floors and mice, a place that smelled of mildew and rotten onions.

There was another reason for his gratitude. Needing more money than what he was paid for representing 'pigs, cows, and lawns,' Robbie had managed to find a job in Toronto. Despite having not much of an education, despite having little experience with men's clothes, he was hired as a salesman at Holt Renfrew. Although it was early days, he seemed to be good at it, too. He certainly wasn't style-conscious himself but, for some reason, he could tell what looked good on others. Or, more exactly, he could sense what others *believed* looked good on them. He could read people. So his sales patter had none of the mental thuggee of the overconfident.

Robbie attributed his success at reading people to his wide experience with women. He had learned, he believed, the 'subtle language of pleasure' – the difference between a hand on your cheek, a hand on your ear, a hand on your bicep, a slight move-ment of the hips to left or right, a quickening of breath, a redden-ing of the skin here or there. Each woman he'd slept with had wanted different things of him or wanted the same thing, differ-ently. He had learned to pay attention. And there you have it! All of this, carrying as it did the suggestion that good salespeople were good lovers first, was arguable but interesting. Robbie's mistake was in sharing these thoughts with Nadia shortly after he'd proposed to her.

They'd been lying in bed together, happily. Robbie had had a particularly good day. He'd begun to feel, if not at home in Toronto, at least 'unforeign' to the city. He still reflexively despised it, it being Hogtown and all, but he now felt there was a part of Toronto that was hospitable to him. The source of this hospitality was, of course, Nadia. With Gwen away from the apartment and Robbie committed to her, Nadia was happiness itself.

When they were not arguing – or, since Robbie did not really argue, when Nadia was not berating him – they made plans for a life together. For instance, Nadia wanted to have children. Having seen him with his children, she knew Robbie was a good father: playful and loving. And, unexpectedly, she found herself very attracted to this side of him. It was one of two things – the other being bed – about which she could not fault him. And she told him so, often. Another instance of planning: Robbie wanted to move to a bigger place. He wanted to live with Nadia. This despite (or perhaps because of) the failure of his marriage.

These two desires – hers for children, his for a home together – were connected, in Robbie's mind, to the idea of marriage. And on the night Gwen and Tancred came by, while lying in bed together after a 'quick one,' Robbie bravely broached the subject.

– I think it's just about time we got married, he said.

To Nadia, the impracticality and suddenness of the proposition was appealing, romantic even.

– You're just talking, she said.

– No, I'm not, said Robbie.

He proved this by reaching for his pants – on the floor by his side of the bed – and extracting a small black velvet box from one of its pockets. In the box there was an engagement ring on which two tiny blue zircons were embedded. Sitting up in bed and looking her in the eyes, Robbie opened the box and said

– Nadia McMurtry, will you be my wife?

She was, to understate it, astonished – astonished by the ring above all, because it meant he'd been thinking about her, something she often accused him of failing to do. It was true that she'd been planning to have children with him, but in her plans she'd cast him as *father*, not husband, because she did not enjoy berating him for his untidiness, his inability to convey his feelings, his conservative ideas about men and women. It made her feel as if she were a nag and a scold or, worse, his mother. Strange though it sometimes felt to separate 'father' from 'husband,' it was far easier to think of Robbie as sperm donor than as 'he who'd have to be mothered.'

And yet, though she didn't think of him as husband material, and though she would have preferred to have been proposed to somewhere other than in bed, she was swept up in the moment and, as happens when conflicting emotions compete, she was short-circuited.

— Yes! she said.

This was immediately followed by buyer's regret.

— But shouldn't we be thinking this through? We don't even have our own place.

Which was followed by regret of her buyer's regret.

— But this is so sweet!

And regret of regret of her buyer's regret ...

— But we don't have enough money to get married, do we?

— Well, said Robbie, this is an engagement ring. It's me saying I want us to try to be married. Anyways, we'll have enough money pretty soon. I'm pretty good at what I do, you know ...

This was the last moment at which it would have been possible to avoid an argument. Sadly, the moment passed. It passed when Nadia frowned, a frown that Robbie took for doubt about his abilities as a salesman. To help her see things his way, he patiently explained his theory that his womanizing was a virtual guarantor of his success.

Realizing, a moment too late, that talking about all the women you've had sex with was not a good idea when proposing, Robbie quickly added

— But that was the old me! I haven't slept with anyone but you and my wife for months!

The effects of this last sentence were the cries and tears that Gwen and Tancred heard and witnessed at the door to the apartment.

One could be forgiven for assuming that Robbie and Nadia's relationship had been irreparably damaged by Robbie's tactlessness or that Nadia had thrown her engagement ring back in Robbie's face. But neither of those things happened. Robbie was contrite and apologetic – as he always was after his contretemps with Nadia – and Nadia forgave him, because she was self-aware enough to know that she and Robbie were in the middle of a play, a theatre where she had brief glimpses of herself as if from the audience. You couldn't say she enjoyed the tears (actual) and the hurt (real). But she found the whole thing familiar and perversely reassuring, because it suddenly struck her that the 'theatre' preceded Robbie. She'd had exactly this kind of moment with a dozen men and, in retrospect, she saw herself playing the scold the way some actors play the villain: over the top, with relish. In a moment of insight, crying on Gwen's shoulder, Nadia recognized both her pleasure and her distress.

Distress, first: she was one who wanted love and sought it passionately, but she was desperately afraid of it, too. She was afraid of all the usual things: humiliation, regret, lies, insincerity, etc. Which is why she sought these things out, hypersensitive to the merest trace of a lie or, as on this night, a hint that Robbie regarded her as just one of many women he'd had sex with.

Now, pleasure: suspecting as she did that she was doomed to be cheated on, lied to, humiliated, there came an almost cleansing 'I knew it!' when she sensed she'd been cheated on or lied to. It was confirmation that the world was as hateful as she imagined, and, although her psyche tried to hide this triumph from her by burying it among painful emotions, it was hard to say which was the more intense: distress or vindication.

Then again, Robbie had proposed to her and, though she wasn't sure she loved him, she did want him in her life. At least for now. More than that: an engagement is not a marriage. She was under no obligation to marry him, zircon ring or not. So she forgave him. She ignored the feeling of insecurity she felt when thinking of 'all the women' he'd slept with. She ignored his being a bumpkin. She ignored his emotional ineptness. And she did not break off their engagement. Not twenty minutes after Gwen and Tancred had interrupted their argument, Nadia and Robbie – having kissed and cried in each other's arms as Gwen and Tancred looked on, mystified – announced their engagement. Nadia then asked Gwen if she minded the idea of giving up the apartment, so that Nadia and Robbie could begin their life together.

– I don't want to hold it over you, said Nadia, but the lease is in my name, so it's easier if I stay and you go. But you can have as long as you want. Say, three months?

– This is really good timing, said Gwen. I was going to tell you that I'm moving out. Tancred and I are moving in together.

– Really? said Nadia. Were you going to give me a few months' notice?

As this is, Reader, the long-delayed 'Engagement' of our chapter's title and as there may be some dismay at having waited so patiently only to find *this* couple engaged, it's perhaps important to note that Nadia and Robbie had all the makings of a successful couple – successful here meaning long-lasting. Both of them were, to a greater or lesser extent, aware of their own romantic flaws, and more or less aware of the perversity of their situation. Their relationship could not have survived if either of them had sought peace, as opposed to a kind of active stability, achievable only in chaos, a chaos they happily pursued together.

The argument between Nadia and Robbie left its trace in Gwen's mind.

It was upsetting to have to comfort a tearful and distraught Nadia while wondering about the blood on Robbie's chest. It reminded Gwen that one's closest friends are not that much less strange than strangers. It was further proof that Nadia and Robbie were the kind of couple who put their relationship on show. So many of her encounters with them were like episodes in a series devoted to Nadia and Robbie.

Gwen hoped her love for Tancred would not devolve into anything so theatrical.

On the other hand, there was something important about the 'saying out loud.' Nadia expressing herself was courageous. If what she said was true to her feelings, then it was generous, too. If what Nadia said was true, it gave Robbie unobstructed access to her fears and concerns. To be fair, it allowed such access to anyone who happened to be in hailing distance, but the principle was there, and the idea of 'truth' or 'expressing truth' reminded Gwen of Marie d'Auvergne's idea of using one's partner as a compass.

Home from the encounter with Nadia and Robbie, Gwen carried the black box and all three books to the office that faced the lake, her office. There, leaving Tancred to himself for what she assumed would be a few hours, she set about reading the poem again.

To Gwen's dismay, Book One was now only blank pages. You could not have told that the book had been altered. There were no signs of erasure, but the pages that had held the poem were as if virginal. In panic, she turned to Book Two. The first half of this one was blank as well. The earliest translations of the poem and of 'On the Use of the Ring' were gone. The second half of Book Two was as it had been when she'd first looked into it, but now every page she looked at faded from her sight the moment she looked at it. The book was withdrawing from her, and it was doing so deliberately.

The pages of Book Three did not fade as Gwen read them. She was relieved to find that she still had time to read the 'witness-ings' of her foremothers, still had time to write more of her impressions of her grandmother and her mother. For her daughter's sake — for the sake of whoever was to come — Gwen now wrote as truthfully as she could about her experiences with the ring. Having told Tancred that she had difficult work to do, she wrote the whole night long, the dark lake in the window before her growing bluer by degrees.

During that night of reading and writing, Gwen also used the ring to make a second wish. Inspired by Marie d'Auvergne's idea, she touched the ring and said, 'May Tancred always tell me what he really thinks, whenever I ask his opinion.'

Though this wish was made spontaneously, while writing about one of her grandmother's wishes, there was thought behind it. To begin with, knowing that something might be imposed on her for compensation, Gwen wished for something that was not wholly to her advantage. Any number of his opinions might prove painful to her. But Tancred's real thoughts – like Nadia's anger! – would be revealing and, loving him as she did, she wanted to know the real man.

That said, there was a kind of safety valve to her wish: Tancred would speak the truth, but only when she explicitly asked his opinion. Otherwise, he was free to lie, to hide his thoughts and feelings, to keep his private self intact. This point was important to her, because she'd read again (and remembered from a previous reading) two of Marie di Francesca d'Auvergne's dicta: 'No love can survive on a regimen of Truth' and 'Love's armour is deception.'

As in her previous readings, Gwen admired Marie d'Auvergne. She was grateful to have had a foremother so focused on Reason and Truth. But this time, as Gwen read, a hint of dislike crept in, too. It really was odd that Sophie so doted on her mother, odd that she'd managed to write so much about her mother and so little about herself. It was as if Marie had given birth to her own amanuensis. Gwen began to feel sympathy for her foremothers who, in the centuries that followed Marie's death, could not keep themselves from making fun of Marie's words and ideals. Gwen's great-grandmother Alice was among those, of course. But even Gwen's grandmother, Estelle, who had cause to favour the reasonable Marie over her own wildly irrepressible mother, voiced suspicion of Marie's ideas. For instance, about the dicta that Gwen herself admired, her grandmother had written in the margins: 'You could just as easily say, "No truth can survive on a regimen of love" or "Deception's armour is Love." It would be just as meaningful. Just as meaningless.' While Gwen's mother, Helen, had written 'It's not like aphorisms help you make choices.' Here was one of the few instances Gwen had found where her mother and grandmother were, essentially, in agreement. And she understood their caution. But, with a certain defiance, or a defiant embrace of what she thought was Reason, Gwen held the ring and wished for Tancred to speak his mind whenever she explicitly asked to hear it.

The consequences of Gwen's second wish are almost all outside the purview of this book. But Gwen got the first inkling of this wish's effect later that day.

As she closed Book Three and rose from her chair, the sun was rising. It had been years since she'd spent a night awake. Dawn was like an accumulation of chemicals: a slow bright blue light quickening. It was also tiring. Shortly after making her wish, Gwen stopped writing. She made her way to their bedroom, where Tancred had passed out, fully clothed on the bed, his head on a pillow.

He'd been waiting for her.

He looked so handsome and innocent that, tired as she was, she could not keep herself from lying beside him on the bed, happy to sleep beside him, though she, too, was fully dressed. In lying down, however, she woke him.

– Is it morning? he asked.

– Yes, she answered

and kissed him.

– We should get under the covers, she said.

Not understanding the situation, bringing some dream world with him, he asked

– Do you want breakfast? I can make something for us.

– What do you like for breakfast? she asked.

– I like whatever you like, he answered.

– Tell me the truth, said Gwen, what do you truly like for breakfast. What's your favourite?

Without missing a beat, Tancred – momentarily and eerily wide awake – said in a serious voice:

– Peanut butter and ketchup.

He then promptly fell sound asleep.

After a while, so did Gwen, her final thought before losing consciousness being that her second wish had most likely been granted, because no one would confess to a love of peanut butter and ketchup without being compelled to.

The following morning, a Sunday, getting up before Tancred, she woke him and said

– I'm going to make your favourite breakfast. Why don't you stay in bed?

– My favourite breakfast?

– Let's see if I'm right, she said.

And she was at first gratified by the look on his face when she brought him two pieces of white bread on which she'd spread peanut butter and splashes of ketchup.

– How did you know? he asked.

He was not pleasantly surprised. He was puzzled and maybe a little alarmed.

– You told me yourself, she said. Yesterday. Don't you remember?

He did not remember, which Gwen took as proof that he'd been compelled to admit his favourite breakfast. Seeing how disconcerted Tancred seemed, she did not look forward to testing the wish again. She now also worried about what would be taken from her in compensation.

Gwen, talking to her mother while sitting in her office, said

— Mom? What do you think the ring wants from us?

— At some point, said Helen, we've all wondered that. Didn't Marie d'Auvergne say anything about it? If not, she probably didn't have time. None of us has enough time with the books to say everything. Has all the writing disappeared for you yet?

— Almost, said Gwen. The first two are gone, and there's half of the third one left.

— What about the ring?

— It's starting to hurt, said Gwen. I'm going to have to take it off.

— There're all sorts of ideas about the ring, said Helen, but I think most of them boil down to the same thing: we're guardians of something none of us understand anymore, if any of us ever did.

— Do you think the ring is sacred? Like, a sacred object? asked Gwen.

— Sure, why not? answered Helen. That's as likely as anything. I remember liking the poem, so I like the idea it was created for a goddess, and that maybe we're keeping it for her until she returns.

— But I'm not a believer, said Gwen. You'd think the ring would want true believers.

— I don't know about that, said Helen. My gran was a true believer. So was my mother. I wasn't, and you're not. I just don't think it makes a difference. Anyway, why should the divine need your belief in order to use you?

— Did Great-Grandma Alice ever talk to you about the ring?

— No, she never did. No more than your grandmother talked to you about it. I was too young when Granny could have talked to me and by the time I was old enough she'd passed on. Anyway, you'll see. You can only talk about the ring when the ring allows you to.

— The question, Mom, is what do we *get* from all this?

— I really don't think there's an answer, Gwenhwyfar, but, again, I like to think it has something to do with the poem. If it's something created by the divine, it must have traces of divine will and divine mind. Something like the holy grail. But honestly, Gwenhwyfar, I don't think it's our business to know.

— So we just have to accept it?

— Or we're lucky. It's not nothing to be acquainted with the divine.

— Up to now, Mom, this 'acquaintance' just confuses me. I'm constantly worrying the ring is going to take something from me.

— You'll get over it. Once you take the ring off, it mostly moves into the background. I mean, I have regrets. I wish I hadn't interfered in your father's career, for one. But is there such a thing as a life without regrets? Everybody I know has at least some. If I had to do one thing differently, I'd have prepared you for the ring a little better. I should have encouraged you to learn Chinese and ancient Greek.

— You did encourage me. I just didn't want to.

— That's true. But anyway, as I've gotten older, I find it comforting to know that there's something beyond this world — something mysterious that we can't get at.

— I don't know, Mom. I'm just about fed up with the mysterious. Do you really need more mystery?

— Some days, sweetie, you need all the mystery you can get. I live in Bright's Grove, remember? Oh! That reminds me. Morgan and Michael are getting married in August. It's going to be in Toronto and Michael really wants you to go. I gave Michael Tancred's address, so you should be getting an invite any day.

The invitation came the following week:

You are Invited to the Wedding
of
Michael Lynn and Morgan Bruno
(They + He)
Thursday 15 August 2019
Toronto City Hall
11 am

Although Gwen was expecting it, the invitation was still a surprise. It was a surprise because her life had changed so much since the last time she'd seen Michael and Morgan, it felt as if she were being asked to participate in an event long past, though the wedding was a month away.

It wasn't only her life and circumstances that had changed. She was fundamentally different. It was not, as her mother put it, that she'd matured. That, she thought, was an idea that came from outside. It was something that people said about you, a judgment that was not yours to make. What she felt, rather, was awake. She was now more conscious of herself, physically as well as mentally, conscious of the man she loved, conscious of how money works, thoughtful about how it might be used to help others, thankful for her friends. You might almost have said that the *world* had matured, as she'd awakened to it.

The causes of her wakefulness were various. For one thing, she was now more aware of Toronto, in big ways and small. She lived beside the lake, for instance, so that the city and everything in it was north of her. She navigated Toronto from a different starting point. The difference was as simple as the difference between thinking of the lake as south, a point on a compass, and thinking of the lake as home, a point in her soul. Wherever she was, the lake was where she and Tancred lived. Her world had expanded and ramified, including as it now did a place where she felt she belonged.

Then, too, there was Tancred.

It changed the world, knowing you were part of a narrative shared by two, a love story. Well, 'shared by two' but nurtured by hundreds. Gwen was now, naturally, more aware that she was only one in a long line of those who have loved. Being aware of her lineage made her sensitive to Tancred's. His family was like hers, in that he knew more about his mother's people. But Tancred's ignorance about his father played on Gwen's mind. It seemed a shame that her own forefathers were also a sketchy part of the long, secret history that was Book Three. Her fore-fathers were 'those who had been changed.' But though there was no denying her forefathers were significant — her foremothers had all spoken of their beloved or their fathers — they had been less important to the story of the ring.

Unless, of course, her forefathers were the underside of a pattern, the beautiful stitching on the reverse side of an expertly made carpet. Wasn't it possible that all the men her foremothers had loved were the kind of men who would not trouble the ring, as Joseph had been the kind of man who was not troubled by the idea of a virgin birth. A disturbing thought, that the ring had to approve one's choice before granting its wishes.

And speaking of wishes, Gwen's final wish also added to her wakefulness.

When she'd last spoken to her mother, the ring was a bear-able pain. Two days later, it was not. It had become fiery. Gwen made her final wish, took off the ring, and, when she did, the pain vanished. The other thing that vanished was the final legible pages of Book Three. Nor was she able to make an impression in the book, whether she used pen, pencil, or even paint. The words she'd written only days before evaporated, not to be seen again, presumably, until her daughter opened the third book.

When Gwen took off the ring, she felt a withdrawal of the sacred that was just as alarming as her discovery of the ring's existence had been. She put the ring in its place in the box and, of itself, the hinged panel closed and locked, invisible again to any but those who knew it was there. She put the now-blank books in the box and closed it. With the knowledge that she would never again read the words of her foremothers, that what she could remember of the poem was all that was left to her, there came a terrible sadness, a sense of how fleeting the miracu-lous is, of how love passes on.

But what was Gwen's final wish?

It was a wish inspired by one of her foremothers from the nineteenth century, Adele Juttasdóttir Lobdeen, and it was this: 'If he loves me, may he love for who I am.' The difference between Gwen's wish and that of her foremother was significant. Adele Lobdeen had left her beloved no choice but to love her. For Adele, the wish had been 'He must love me for who I am.' Gwen, however, had kept 'compensation' in mind. She felt that, were she to *compel* Tancred to love her, she too would be compelled to something or deformed, as, indeed, Adele Lobdeen had been. Adele had grown physically 'most unappealing' over the course of a month after making this wish, so that, in effect, her husband was the only one likely to love her at all. The marriage was a very happy one, however. Adele adored her husband and 'did not give a fig' about the opinions of others. That said, Adele's story had a final act that stayed with Gwen.

On the death of her husband, Adele Lobdeen was left utterly bereft. According to her daughter, Adele's cries at his burial were as if made by a terrifying animal, and none who heard them were unaffected. At the same time, as soon as her husband died, Adele's physical features changed. They changed back to what they'd been before the ring deformed them. Adele died not long after her husband, the grief being too much to overcome, but her corpse was, according to her daughter, 'strange, but most beautiful.'

With such an unusual tale in mind, Gwen warily anticipated any change in herself, physical or otherwise, that could be taken for compensation. But she did not change. Nor was she, in the days following her final wish, aware of any change in herself that could be attributed to the ring. However, she did discover what she assumed was payment for her *second* wish.

It was July. The summer was 'full,' as one might say of fruit on a tree, and Gwen had just decided to take her two weeks' holiday, when Olivier came for supper. It was not the first time he'd visited. Far from it. He, Nadia and Robbie, Daniel and Fiona, Simone, and Alexander von Würfel were regular visitors – a fact that Gwen found reassuring, worried as she was at times that Tancred spent too much time on his own. Not that there was reason to worry.

Tancred did not want to work because he did not need to. He felt it would have been obscene for him to take a paying job from someone who might need it. Instead, he stayed home, devoting himself to the discipline of Capoeira, to the routine that mastering the piano imposed, and to the writing of a history of the art of pickpocketing that he intended to call A *History of Light Fingers*.

(He'd *intended* to call it that. But now that the woman he loved had lost a finger, he had his doubts.)

You couldn't argue with Tancred's position, but sometimes Gwen wanted to, because she'd begun to question her own working life. Was she taking a job from someone who needed it? If she was going to work, should she not be looking for work in the field that interested her most: pediatrics? Was Tancred's a proper lifestyle when, by fate or accident, one was made shepherd of so much wealth? Nor was the question primarily about Tancred. It was now about her, too.

In any case, Olivier had come to dinner and, before he left, he mentioned that there was to be a celebration of Gordon Thomson's upcoming eightieth birthday and he had volunteered to organize it. Apropos, he asked if it would be possible to have Gordon's birthday in their home. This would likely surprise Gordon, as he'd never seen Tancred's place before, and of course it was beautiful beside the lake in summer.

– If it's too much trouble, he said, I'll rent a –

But Tancred interrupted him at once.

– No, no. It's a good idea, he said. If Gwen's okay with it, let's do it.

But that night in bed Gwen and Tancred both expressed doubts. Tancred was worried about Olivier and saw his involvement in Gordon's birthday party as foreboding. The idea of it left him uneasy. Gwen's trepidation was centred on Simone.

She had come to know and trust Simone, but it seemed risky to have Olivier, who was infatuated with her, organize an event for her husband.

– I don't think Simee knows Ollie's feelings, said Tancred.

– I'm pretty sure she does, answered Gwen. Olivier's around them all the time, doing things for Simee *and* for Gordon. They may not all be sleeping together, but they're intimates.

– Hmm, said Tancred. I trust Simee implicitly. But you can't help wondering if she realizes Ollie has a tendency to dynamite his own relationships.

Simone had invited a number of her and Gordon's friends. She'd also invited her family, for which she apologized. There was no reason for apology, though. Alton, who was one of Gordon's oldest friends, refused the invitation, telling Simone that he would not knowingly be in the same place as Tancred.

Simone's other siblings were unproblematic. Her brother Michael, who lived in an exclusive building called Castle Rose not far from Tancred, and her sister Gretchen were, as far as Simone was concerned, the most likeable of the Azarians. Michael and Gretchen were also kindly disposed to Tancred because, although Tancred was not and had never been Simone's lover, they both believed him to be. Michael liked the idea because he secretly disliked Gordon, his brother-in-law, who reminded him of his father, Robert Azarian. It gave him pleasure to think of Gordon as a cuckold. Gretchen, on the other hand, was sorry for Gordon. But she approved of Simone's taking a lover. She believed all women should be allowed young lovers, given how many men allowed themselves the pleasure. In fact, she was even more admiring of her sister when she was in Tancred's presence, finding him, as she did, extremely attractive.

There was another reason Michael and Gretchen were at ease in Tancred's company: neither of them knew that Tancred had received the bulk of his fortune from their sister, Willow. None of the Azarians knew this, except Simone. Her siblings assumed Tancred was being 'kept' by her. Alton was outraged by the idea, while Gretchen and Michael admired their sister's panache.

None of these things mattered to Gwen, of course. She knew nothing about them. Had she known what the Azarians thought of Tancred, she'd have been upset but also, maybe, a little amused. After all, she herself had wondered about Tancred and Simone's relationship.

No, the thing on her mind on Gordon's eightieth birthday was her home. As she dressed, she had a vivid memory of her mother looking impossibly beautiful, nervously straightening bowls and plates, calling to her father – 'Alun, are you sure there's enough ice?' 'Alun, is there enough rum punch?' – and fussing over her, too, to make sure her daughter's face wasn't dirty. All the while smelling of Chanel No. 5, a bottle of which Gwen and Alun had given her one Christmas, and that she wore on special occasions.

(Gwen had assumed her mother treasured the scent, but, in fact, Helen disliked it. She'd recently confessed that she wore it 'because you and your father gave it to me for Christmas. I couldn't throw it out, but I still have some left, and it's been twenty-something years!')

Gwen's nerves were, of course, part of the recondite geometry of home, but they brought her excitement as well as anxiety, because she *was* home. Tancred was manifestly pleased by her presence, helping when the chef and sous-chefs arrived and set up in the kitchen, when the young men and women arrived dressed in white shirts and black pants to serve the guests, when the barman – or 'mixologist,' as the chef called him – set up a bar at one end of the living room, and when the guests began to arrive, beginning with Simone, Olivier, and Gordon.

Gordon was in a wheelchair pushed by Olivier. Gwen's first impression was of a man who'd only recently learned to be at ease around others. He seemed haughty, as if trying to communicate the idea that, in cases other than his own, a wheelchair might be thought a disadvantage, while in his case, it was more of a mobile throne. On being introduced to Gwen, he paused to look her over, and then held out his hand, which she politely shook. Her second impression, one that followed hard on the first, was of complete vulnerability. The impressions were so different, Gwen wasn't sure which to credit. What settled it was that Gordon seemed to have true affection for Olivier and, clearly, he loved his wife, whose hand he held.

He did not look, physically, as she imagined he would. For one thing, his skin was dark and there was something Indian to his looks, though his name, Gordon Thomson, and his accent suggested an Englishness. He had a bulging tummy, and the bottom half of his face – from his cheekbones to his jaw – was as if widening to hide his neck. His eyes were striking: lids like slits over brown eyes that themselves interrupted the dark ovals – from eyebrows to cheekbones – in which they were set. He was dressed in a mauve suit, a white shirt, and a purple tie with red stripes. His hair was white, as was his beard, a recently trimmed Vandyke.

As if sensing Gwen's ambivalence about Gordon, Tancred put his hand in hers. On seeing this, Gordon Thomson said

– Oh! You're Tancred's girlfriend that Simee was telling me about!

He smiled as he caught Gwen's attention.

Moments later, the place was filled with people, most of whom she did not know – save, of course, for Alex von Würfel, a friend of Gordon's from way back. To Gwen's delight, von Würfel's present for his friend was a framed drawing of an ear, much like one she'd seen in his studio:

And then, all at once, the place was loud and happy: conversations, laughter, a cry of surprise, along with the music that Gordon loved. All Stan Getz: Getz and Gilberto, Getz and Jobim, Getz and Byrd.

As she relaxed, Gwen ventured away from Tancred's orbit, allowing herself to meet some of the people Simone had invited. She had a long conversation with Simone's brother, Michael, about the benefits of veganism. He told her the story of his many addictions, before praising the recuperative power of vegetables. That conversation was followed by a brief one with a woman who'd known Simone since they were children. The woman was visibly disappointed that Gwen did not know the same people she did and, after smiling at Gwen mysteriously, turned away without a word, going off to speak to someone else.

It was a testament to the day itself that Gwen found this snub amusing. It was sunny. The lake was blue. The clouds in the distance were vaporous. As she walked among the guests, she moved through the floral moods of perfume and cologne

– rosewater, citrus, lavender, vanilla, etc. – now sharp, now gone. Then, too, there were the smells from the kitchen: grilled lamb, roast lamb, grilled salmon and asparagus, vegetarian risotto, tarte Tatin ... all the foods Gordon himself wanted. As she navigated the living room, Gwen drank an Apricot Mule – a Moscow Mule shaken with a dash of apricot brandy – because she'd never had one and because the mixologist was, apparently, tired of pouring expensive wines and impossibly rare whiskies.

– There's no challenge, he said archly, to pouring a Penfolds Grange Hermitage or a Château d'Yquem. No challenge at all!

The drink was stronger than Gwen thought it would be and, feeling light-headed from the Mule, she stepped outside and was met by a breeze from the lake, by the smell of cigarette smoke, by the cry of a seagull. She was then surprised when Simone and a guest followed her out.

– Gwen, said Simone, this is Alana.

Looking as out of place as Gwen felt, Alana said

– I think we met at Lisa's reading, didn't we?

– I thought I recognized you, said Gwen.

– Oh! You know each other, said Simone. That's perfect!

She left them to catch up, though they were almost complete strangers.

– Have you known Simone long? asked Gwen.

– Not at all, said Alana. I met her in Muskoka, the same time as I met you.

Gwen looked at her, then, trying not to stare: a sleeveless, black dress that was all loose folds, beneath which a dark top, a beaded necklace, her blond hair falling over half her face in a 'Veronica Lake,' dark, mulberryish lipstick, pale skin, blue eyes, and her demeanour was somewhere among apologetic, defensive, and dryly amused.

– It's so different from Muskoka, isn't it? said Alana. Do you know whose place it is?

– The place? said Gwen. I guess it's mine. I'm still getting used to the idea, because Tancred and I haven't been living together that long. The other thing is, I'm from Bright's Grove, and there were no places like this where I grew up. Did Simone give you the tour? It's really something. I wake up sometimes and I can't believe I live here. It's like I did something wrong.

Alana laughed.

– I get that, she said.

They went, then, together through the apartment, out the front door, and over to that side of the building where Gwen and Tancred lived. After the hubbub of Gordon's birthday party, it was like an oasis of light and quiet.

– It's a mirror image of the other side, said Gwen.

– It's incredibly beautiful, said Alana.

Seeing her home through a stranger's eyes, Gwen was as overwhelmed as she'd been the first time Tancred had shown her their side. Honestly! What had she done to be in this place showing this person around? She'd fallen in love with a man who clearly loved her: that's it. On the other hand, if Tancred's home had been a duplex on Euclid, a first floor on Yarmouth, a place on Runnymede ... whatever, she'd likely have been just as bewildered to find that it was *theirs*: hers and Tancred's.

Ignoring her own dismay, Gwen led Alana through the sun-encompassing rooms, and they chatted quietly – about publishing, about the monograph on von Würfel that Alana was publishing, about how large publishers were changing the way writers wrote, about working in a hospital, about research on dementia, about how they had both come to Toronto to escape from smaller places.

– Isn't it interesting how many different worlds exist side by side? said Gwen.

As if the world were trying to make her case for her, when the two returned to Gordon's celebration, the atmosphere had changed: subtly, but enough to suggest they hadn't come back to the party they'd left. Now, despite the ongoing festivities and the sound of laughter, there was a heaviness. Excusing herself from Alana's company with the promise that she'd try to visit the publishing house where Alana worked, Gwen looked for Tancred. She found him on the balcony looking for her.

– Is everything okay? she asked.

– Yes, said Tancred. I was just wondering where you were. Gordon's about to cut his birthday cake. Is everything okay with you? This must all be a little overwhelming.

– It is, said Gwen, but everything's fine.

There must have been something uncertain in her tone, however, because Tancred said

– Tell me how you *really* feel.

What followed, the *feeling* of it, was different from speaking ancient Greek in bed: not just the circumstances obviously, but the stillness of her mind. It was, as she told him *exactly* what she felt – her dismay, her anxiety, her deep love for him, her trust, her insecurity around people with money, how overwhelmed she still was by their home – as if a part of her were reporting her depths to an authority. She was compelled to tell him. Which is, in the end, how she recognized it as the ring's doing. She had wished to know his thoughts, whenever she asked for them. So now, it seemed, she was bound to tell him her feelings – whatever they might be – when he wanted – a frightening idea to someone as discreet as she was.

Tancred laughed then.

– I don't think anyone's ever been so honest with me. I like it.

He kissed her, entirely expressing his feelings for her. It was the kind of kiss that changes your mind, whatever your mind. It was at this moment, too, that she realized that Tancred smelled of almonds.

– There's nothing to be worried about, he said. All this is just illusion.

Gwen felt two competing impulses: one was to ask Tancred what he was really *thinking*, the other was to make love to him on the spot, the relief of having voiced her true feelings and having them taken in, not judged, was so powerful it was itself aphrodisiac. The timing being wrong, neither of those impulses won out. Instead, they went back to the living room where, as Tancred had suggested, the birthday cake was ready, its eighty candles lit up.

Gordon, who was not supposed to drink, had apparently been drinking. It seemed to Gwen as if the atmosphere was still festive, but now it was festive on the edge of a cliff. Gordon was teetering in his wheelchair, thanking people for coming to his eightieth, then thanking them again, then thanking them again – each time trying but failing to whisper. Simone was unnerved, her smile flagrantly false, while Olivier was discreetly attentive, helping to right Gordon whenever he leaned too far to one side of the wheelchair or the other.

The cake, with its eighty candles, was, Gwen thought, extravagant but impressive. It was a three-feet-high reproduction of Niagara Falls done in sponge cake, spun sugar, and coloured icing. The froth at the bottom of the falls and the *Maid of the Mist* were particularly realistic. The almost manic attention to detail made the cake seem *un*-birthday-like, unless you knew that Gordon, born in Trinidad and raised in England, had become reconciled to Canada when, as a six-year-old, he'd seen the falls for the first time.

But Gordon had not seen the cake before its presentation, and he was overcome by emotion on seeing this symbol of his childhood. Even under normal circumstances he might have been moved to tears. Being drunk, however, he began to weep, repeating when he could catch his breath that he was moved and that he was sorry for crying, but that he was old and knew that he was unworthy of his wife's love. This thought, when it first came up, was affecting, but it was then subverted by Gordon himself when he suddenly suggested that it would be best for all concerned if Olivier made love to his wife.

There was silence and, in the silence, Gordon made the suggestion again, this time adding that, as *he* could not make love to her, because he was impotent, why shouldn't she have someone as young and virile as Olivier. There was again silence, and then someone somewhere laughed. A few people joined in, including Simone, though her laughter was not convincing. But Gordon, as if unaware of how inappropriate his words were, repeated them, now praising Olivier for his youth and good looks. He couldn't blame his wife, he said, for wanting to fuck him. He might have gone on like this, too, but Olivier leaned forward so Gordon could hear.

– Thank you, he said. But it's time to cut the cake.

At which, Gordon stopped crying and, suddenly thoughtful, said

– I know, I know. Life is so short. Please help me with this ...

By which he meant: 'help me cut it.' Which Olivier did, though not before they had all sung 'Happy Birthday' – the most awkward version imaginable – and watched Gordon try to blow out the candles.

Lying in bed later, their home restored to them, Gwen found herself more rattled by what had happened than she thought she should be. Of course it had been unpleasant, but it was easy to forgive a man who'd got drunk and said things he didn't mean. At the end of the evening, Gordon had apologized to her for making a scene. He'd seemed genuinely contrite, and the matter should have ended there.

Turning to Tancred, who'd slipped into bed after brushing his teeth, she asked if he was as disturbed as she was by Gordon's behaviour.

– How disturbed are you? asked Tancred.

– I found it hard to watch, she said. I'm still thinking about it.

– I'm not that upset, said Tancred. Maybe because I thought something like this would happen. Gordon shouldn't be drinking.

— But he collects wines and whiskies!

— It's a habit from when he was young, but he can't drink now. It reacts with his medications. But that's not why I thought something like this would happen. To me, it felt like Gordon was sending Ollie a message. I'm not sure what. It was either 'go' or 'stay,' and I thought there'd be something like that, sooner or later.

— Did he have to humiliate Simee to tell *Ollie* something? Doesn't he care about her?

— I think he does. I think he loves her, but how does anyone know what goes on in someone else's heart?

Gwen was tempted to say, 'You'll always know what goes on in mine,' something to domesticate her inability to hide her feelings from him. But she left his question hanging and put the moment between Gordon, Olivier, and Simone out of her mind, so she could sleep.

It wasn't long, however, before Gwen understood why she'd been upset by Gordon. When, a few days later, she came home from work, Tancred and Olivier were sitting out on the balcony, talking, the noisy city before them. When she'd changed her clothes and got herself a glass of water, she joined them.

— Ollie, she asked, what happened with Gordon and Simone? Was everything okay?

— Tan was just telling me you were embarrassed, he said. I'm sorry.

— Weren't you embarrassed? asked Gwen.

— No, said Olivier. Gordon was only trying to tell me he was uncomfortable.

— To be fair, said Tancred, he was drunk.

— To be truthful, answered Olivier, he was sober. He asked me for a drink. I told him he couldn't drink because of his medication. But he went on about it being his birthday, so I got the bartender to make a virgin whisky sour. He drank three of them and got 'drunk.'

– He did a good job playing drunk, said Gwen.

– He probably thought he *was* drunk, said Olivier. But he didn't surprise Simone at all. I guess he's done this kind of thing before.

– Are you going to stop hanging out with them? asked Tancred.

– I don't know, said Olivier. I don't know how to arrange my thoughts. I know Gordon feels close to me, so I still can't figure out what he was trying to say, unless he just really wants me to have sex with his wife. Which isn't what I want.

– I told you this would be complicated, said Tancred.

Olivier's voice was calm, his demeanour as pleasant as always. But the thing troubling Gwen was not Olivier. His fetishizing of a kind of courtly love and loss was its own special case. Also, as both Tancred and Olivier seemed to accept Gordon's behaviour, she somewhat accepted it, too. What troubled her was 'marriage.' The idea of it had been constantly hovering near consciousness. She'd been thinking about asking Tancred if he wanted to get married. But honestly, the drama she'd seen lately – Simone and Gordon, Robbie and Nadia – had put her off, so that, when she thought about herself and Tancred getting married, when she thought about a wedding, the week wasn't as pleasant as she thought it should have been.

As she, Tancred, and Olivier decided on what to eat – pizza with anchovies, mushrooms, and bacon – the doorbell sounded, and Simone, who'd been let in by the concierge, came out to the balcony.

– Oh, she said, you've got a visitor already.

She kissed them all, Olivier first: on both cheeks, continentally.

– I hope I'm not interrupting, she said. I told John you were expecting me.

– We were just going to order pizza, said Gwen.

– Really? asked Simone. That's a lovely idea. *Or* you could let me order something from The Stone Plough. It's a new Nordic restaurant. The chef did a stage at Noma. She uses whatever's available from her farm. And they sometimes do in-house.

Simone was cheerful, but you could see she was not at ease.

– That sounds great, said Gwen.

At very least, it sounded interesting. But it wasn't anything like the delivery or takeout they'd imagined. Instead, the chef herself and an assistant were coming to cook for them, bringing what they needed: wines, greens, roots, etc.

– I feel like this is the least I can do, said Simone, after Gordon's ridiculous performance.

She looked at Olivier.

– He was drunk, she said. You shouldn't have let him drink whisky sours. It was irresponsible.

Gwen was about to defend Olivier, but he spoke up immediately.

– You're right, he said. But it was his eightieth. I couldn't turn him down.

– Well, what's done is done, said Simone. These little bumps are all part of life and love.

There wasn't anything anyone wanted to add to that. They turned instead to banalities, deciding to eat on the balcony facing the lake. And as they waited for chef Chervil to arrive, the men moved two tables outside while Gwen and Simone set four places.

– Did Tancred tell you I chose all his dishes and silverware? asked Simone. He'd have been just as happy with something from Canadian Tire. He's very funny. You're lucky to find him.

– Do you think it's luck? asked Gwen.

– It's just an expression, said Simone, but if I had to say, I'd probably say yes, it's luck. I tend to agree with Ollie. I believe in chance more than I do in fate. I *could* have married someone other than Gordon. But on the whole I feel lucky to have found my husband.

The two of them were in the kitchen together, while Olivier and Tancred were on the balcony talking. So Gwen allowed herself to ask

– Do you think I should marry Tancred?

– I'm not sure what you're asking me, said Simone. I've been married for forty years. I married a man who is older than me, so I knew the day would come when we wouldn't be able to do things together, and for thirty years that thought never bothered me. When Gordon had his first stroke, everything changed. That was when he was seventy and I was in my fifties. So we had thirty wonderful years together, and if you asked me now if I'd marry him again, I would. If you're asking should *you* marry the man you love, I'd say yes. If you're asking if marriage is always convenient, I'd say no. If you're asking if being married is better than being single, I'd say that depends on the man. If you're asking if you should marry *Tancred* knowing what I know about him, I'd say yes. He's hard to get to know and I can't say I really understand him, but I trust him, and I don't think you'll ever be bored.

Simone was looking directly at Gwen.

– I don't know you, Gwen. I have no way of knowing if you're right for Tancred. And I don't usually give advice about these things. There's no point. Everything I just said to you is based on *my* feelings and *my* experience. Who knows if any of it's appropriate for you.

From all of that, Gwen took mostly Simone's doubt and unhappiness. Some of what she'd said felt as if it were meant to reassure herself. The man she'd married was gone, in a way, but she seemed resigned to it. Why else speak of her thirty years of happiness as if they were now only memory? Gwen thought of asking Simone where Olivier fit into her life. But the point that interested her most was the one Simone made about Tancred: what did she mean Tancred was 'hard to get to know'?

– Are you wondering about Ollie? asked Simone.

Now, how should she answer that?

– I assumed you and Ollie were friends, said Gwen.

– You didn't assume we were more than that?

– No, I didn't, said Gwen.

– You must be one of the few. Everybody seems to think it would be natural to have a young lover 'in my circumstances.' Like it's perfectly natural to have sex with other men because your husband's an invalid. I'm not a young woman. I sometimes wonder if Gordon wants me to sleep with Ollie because *he* wants to. It may be shocking to you, Gwen, but if I knew it would make Gordon happy, I *would* sleep with Ollie. Anyway, I don't need a lover to prove my worth, but I do like to feel desirable. I always have. Is there anything wrong with that? And I certainly don't mind if people assume young men find me desirable. What I mind is anyone who knows me thinking I'd sleep with someone other than my husband. It's disappointing. My family's disappointing.

– You mean Alton? asked Gwen.

– I mean all of them, answered Simone. The thing is that Gordon really likes Ollie. He says he's mortified – mortified! – if he's driven Ollie away. Because he knows Ollie is witty and knowledgeable and good company. So now Gordon wants to hire him as his personal assistant. And I have to ask Ollie if he wants to work for my husband, because it's my fault, apparently, that Gordon drank too much and insulted Ollie in the first place. Now here *you* are asking me if you should get married. It's complicated. The river goes off in many directions. But I thought your generation was against marriage, no?

They might have gone on talking about marriage, the conversation having noticeably raised Simone's spirits. It had also made Gwen that much more sympathetic to Simone's side of the matter. Simone had frankly admitted that she would sleep with Olivier if it would make her husband happy. There could be no starker example, as far as Gwen could tell, of the lengths we go to to deal with the chaos that comes when you love another.

But just as Gwen was going to ask what Gordon had been like as a younger man, the doorbell sounded and chef Atlanta Chervil came in with her sous-chef and a waiter, bringing with them a panoply of kitchen things.

Their meal, impeccably presented, was as far from pizza as Gwen could imagine. To begin with, there were ten courses:

A Broth of Last Season's Preserved Mushrooms and
   Dried Herbs
B.C. Sea Urchin, Carrot Miso, Preserved Rose Tartlet
Lightly Fermented Summer Roots, Herb Emulsion, and
   Chicken Skin
Magdalen Islands Princess Scallop, Ontario Soy Milk,
   and Rapeseed
Dried Celeriac with Vadouvan, Bitter Leaves,and Ox
   Marrow
Cambridge Bay Wild Arctic Char Perfumed, Cabbages,
   and Wild Kelp
Ontario Red Deer Perfumed with Cedar Smoke,
   Preserved Berries, and Grilled Sunchoke
Blue Spruce Granite and Buttermilk
Bartlett Pear with Woodruff and Malt
Plum Ripple, Apple Sour Cream Ice Cream

With each course they were offered wine or, with the cheese, a beer made by chef Chervil herself, called Forest Floor. As well, the chef was on hand to talk them through the dishes she'd made and how they sprang from her background as an artist: her year in Copenhagen, her stage at Noma. It was an informal lesson in postmodern cuisine and, though it should have interested her, Gwen was inattentive. She was distracted by the reddish evening, by a summer breeze that smelled of bread, by Tancred, who held her hand beneath the table, by her own wondering if Simone was about to ask Olivier to work for Gordon. In the end, her impressions of the meal were fleeting: the fermented summer roots, the grilled sunchoke, the unexpected (but pleasing) sourness of the ice cream.

How much had changed since she'd first eaten a meal like this with Simone, Olivier, and Tancred! Rather than being charmed or amazed by the food, she couldn't wait for the meal to end, for the balcony to be restored to itself, to be alone with Tancred. Not because she wanted to make love, but because she longed for a feeling she did not yet take for granted: being at home with him. So, when it was late and the chef and her crew had gone and there were intermittent silences in the conversations and the lake before them had become an oddly textured darkness, Gwen thanked Simone for her generosity and, pleading tiredness, said

— But don't let me break up the party

then kissed Tancred goodnight and went to their side of the eleventh floor and, though she didn't think she was all that sleepy, was asleep before Tancred came in.

The following morning, Gwen rose early. It was a Saturday. She dressed, made herself coffee, and took it with her to the other side, to the balcony overlooking the lake. As soon as she entered this apartment, though, she heard the grand piano being played and discovered Olivier in the living room, dressed as he'd been the night before, playing a piano sonata that she recognized: Beethoven's so-called *Pastorale*, the Fifteenth, her father's favourite for the tympanic bass notes in the Allegro and the playfulness at the end of the Rondo.

Olivier was half hidden in shadow, half revealed in the morning light. He seemed to be lost in the music, but, though he did not look at her, he said

— Simone's upstairs, asleep.

— Is everything all right? asked Gwen.

— Yes, he answered. She was tired. We talked until about an hour ago. She asked me to be Gordon's manservant.

— And you agreed?

— No, said Olivier. I told her my feelings for her would probably become obvious to Gordon, if they weren't obvious already, and that I didn't think that would be good.

— You know, Ollie, I'm sure she knew what you were feeling.

Without interrupting his playing – though he began the sonata again – Olivier said

– I'm sure you're right. I'm not as good at hiding my feelings as I'd like to be.

– I'm so sorry, Gwen said. It must be hard knowing you won't be seeing Simone for a while.

Olivier stopped playing the piano.

– What makes you say that? he asked. We talked about this all night. I'll be working for *her*, not Gordon. Anyway, I'll be seeing her when she wakes up, won't I?

Gwen looked at him to see if he was joking and then, when it was clear he wasn't, she was struck by how a man who was so open could, at the same time, be so closed. It was as if clarity and opacity were in collusion; or like being caught in a Chinese finger trap – the more you struggled to get your fingers out of it, the harder it was to get out of.

To hide her bafflement, she said

– I'm happy for you, Ollie. That's great. Do you want coffee?

August 15, 2019, the day of Michael's wedding to Professor Bruno, was warm, cloudy, and calm. It was a Thursday and so slightly inconvenient for those who worked, like Gwen, but it was otherwise perfect.

Gwen had taken the day off, for a few reasons: for the wedding, first of all, but also to keep her father company while he stayed with them. Then, too, she had invited Michael and Professor Bruno, as well as their guests, to celebrate after the civil ceremony, so she wanted to make sure everything was in place. Finally, Michael and Professor Bruno were arriving at eight in the morning, having chosen to begin their wedding day with Gwen and her father.

To Gwen's surprise, Michael was jittery. The surprise was not the jitters but rather that *Michael* should have them. Michael was one of the most centred and calm people imaginable. But that morning, Gwen found herself having to keep Michael steady. That's not to say that Professor Bruno was calm. He was just as jittery as Michael, so that Alun had to see to him: slipping an early-morning ounce of brandy in the professor's coffee.

As one might expect, the respective jitters of Michael and Professor Bruno had different causes. Professor Bruno wanted to marry Michael. He wanted to make sure that Michael had all the civic privileges attendant on marriage. But Professor Bruno had (for sentimental reasons) decided to wear the suit he'd worn at his first marriage and, no surprise, this brought back memories of his first wedding – which Alun, of course, had attended. In thinking of his first wife, Professor Bruno couldn't help wondering if he was betraying her memory, even if only slightly, and he felt guilt.

– But Barb wanted you to remarry, said Alun.

– That's because she was dying, said Professor Bruno. You can't trust the words of the dying. They've got nothing to lose.

– That's not true, Morgan, Alun answered. Barb always wanted you to be happy.

– Well, you've put your finger right on the spot, Alun! That's why I feel guilty. I didn't feel the same way Barbra did. When we talked about this, I told her that if I died first, I wouldn't want her remarrying. Now here I am marrying again! The very thought of it pains me!

– Morgan, said Alun, you didn't know you'd meet Michael. So you had no idea that it's possible to love again. But anyway, aren't you the one who goes on about love coming from uncertainty?

– Do you think I'm doing the right thing? Tell me honestly, Alun.

– Yes, definitely. I haven't seen you so happy since Barb died. Helen says the same thing.

– I feel guilty about Helen, too! said Professor Bruno. We should have held this in Bright's Grove, so Helen could be with us.

– You're coming to Bright's Grove this weekend! Relax. This is yours and Michael's day. And don't forget: Michael's never been married. If Michael sees you nervous, *they'll* be nervous.

– Yes, yes, said Morgan. Yes, you're right.

But sensible as Alun's words were, Michael was not worried about Professor Bruno's feelings. Michael knew Morgan well and would have been more surprised if he'd been untroubled. What made Michael jittery was the *idea* of marriage. The marriages in Michael's life – beginning with the marriage of their mother and father – had been poisonous. Michael's parents had disliked each other and they had, on the evidence, hated Michael. Then there was the fact that marriage itself is an institution that is, in many ways, hateful, patriarchal, contemptible even. So why marry Morgan at all?

Because Morgan had asked, and Michael had been surprised.

Because Morgan cared about Michael, and Morgan wanted them to live together.

Because although, like most of us, Michael had wide experience of notions of love, Michael was surprised to find that love itself had not been rooted out of their psyche.

Because Michael was overwhelmed by Morgan's kindness.

Because Michael wanted to be there, in a hospital, say, should anything happen to Morgan.

Unlike Professor Bruno, Michael was not comfortable voicing contradictions. So it was more difficult for Michael to deal with nerves. There was only the repeating – either internally or to Gwen – of things related to the schedule: important times, the names of those coming immediately after the ceremony, the names of those who would come to the apartment after five o'clock, when the workday was done.

That said, Michael did manage to convey a few things to Gwen.

– I'm annoyed at myself. I made up my mind months ago. I'm not going to leave Morgan in the lurch. So what's the point of these nerves?

More important to Michael than the idea of 'love for one another' was the knowledge that Morgan loved their company and that they loved his. The difference between 'love for one another' and 'love of company'? Well, to love someone's company was to love their presence while to love them (without their company) was to love an idea. Michael loved their own mother and father but could not stand their company. You could have both, of course. That was the ideal: love in the presence and love in the absence. But if Michael had to choose one, Michael would have chosen the enjoyment of company, the love of one who is there. The only exception to this, in Michael's mind, was God, an absence so strong it made presence superfluous.

In any case, Michael and Professor Bruno shared this love of each other's company.

Nor, Michael suggested, was a wedding a death sentence. Should the daily grind prove too much for them, there would always be a door out. Marriage with Morgan was an adventure in homemaking, but it was a principled one, based on trust – Michael trusted Morgan – and mutual respect.

Another, smaller thing: as with Simone and her husband, there was an age difference between Michael and Professor Bruno, but Michael did not think of it as Simone did. Yes, Morgan was older than Michael by almost twenty years, and this had certain day-to-day implications: his eyes were more watery, the hair on his chin grey and prickly, the smell of him at times more sour, etc. For Michael, saying Morgan was older was much like saying his eyes were brown or that he was six feet tall: obvious and not at all discouraging. If anything, knowing Morgan would likely – *likely* – die first was incentive to cherish him as he was, moment by moment by moment.

Michael wanted to get married, nerves be damned.

Once they were all ready – that is, Gwen, her father, Professor Bruno, Michael, and Tancred – they decided to walk to City Hall: along Queen's Quay and up Bay Street. Michael, slightly taller than Professor Bruno but much slimmer, was dressed in a black tuxedo with a white shirt but no tie. Michael had on glossy, black leather, high-heeled pumps and Michael's hair – greying but still mostly brown – was shoulder-length. Professor Bruno – his hair also shoulder-length but cornstarch-white – was dressed very much like Michael, but he wore a black bow tie and black oxfords.

The sight of the two of them – Michael and Professor Bruno – was a comfort to Gwen. But then so was the walk itself: late summer morning along Bay Street, from the bright lakeshore through the exhaust-filled dark under the expressway, past the glass-fronted buildings of the financial district to the intersection of Queen and Bay where, as always, Gwen felt a joy at being in Toronto: the reddish and gothic 'Old City Hall' on the right, the modernist 'New City Hall' on the left. To be walking here with her father (whose hand she remembered holding the first time she saw the city halls) and Tancred (whose hand she now held) was in itself a kind of consecration.

As they walked across Nathan Philips Square and past Henry Moore's *Archer*, Gwen's memories were displaced by fragments of a poem: 'bronze simplicity ... stark heraldic form ... a force in the bronze churning through the statue.' She couldn't remember where the poem came from. Was it by Gwendolyn MacEwen? Certainly someone she'd read in an English course at some point. But whoever the poet, it suddenly seemed capricious of *Three-Way Piece No. 2: Archer* – the statue's name in the artist's mind – to have allowed itself to be described at all, so imperious did the bronze herald feel this morning.

(It consoled Gwen to think that her home should have such boundless life in the minds of others, its names and landmarks different in different imaginations.)

Once in City Hall, they found the chapel easily enough. It was on the east tower's third floor. The chapel's tall windows let in light. The smell of the place was coffee and cleanser. There were chairs for fifteen guests, but they were five and the ceremony was quickly done, the short service having been written by the two getting married, both for themselves and the officiant.

– I take you, Morgan, for my partner ...

– I take you, Michael, for my lawfully wedded partner ...

– May your love for each other remain an endless, joyous ... *now?*

The officiant was unsure of the wording.

– Yes, said Morgan, an endless joyous now.

And from the witnesses:

– Amen.

It was all very pleasant, but, as they walked out of the chapel, Michael and Professor Bruno happy but visibly relieved, it seemed to Gwen that the lesson was – if weddings have lessons – that 'wedding' and 'marriage' are two distinct things and maybe she didn't need both. Her anxiety was tied to the idea of a moment, a moment of avowal in which you committed to each other. But the idea of being with Tancred, of being married to him, brought her calm, a feeling of rightness.

As they walked back home, Gwen held Tancred back and said

– Do you think we should have a wedding, Tan? Tell me what you're *really* thinking.

Tancred stopped mid-stride and said

– If you want a wedding, I wouldn't object. But it isn't important to me.

Then, surprised by his own words, he added

– I'm sorry. I really don't understand why I'm so ... *direct* with you.

– Don't you find the idea even a little romantic, Tan? Michael and Professor Bruno seem happy.

– Yes, said Tancred, but weddings don't have any real meaning for me. I want to make you happy, and if a wedding's something you want, I'm all for it. But it isn't important to me, that's all.

Gwen's father came back to fetch them.

– Hey, you two youngsters, he said. Keep up!

– I was just telling Tan that I want a big wedding, said Gwen.

– Do you? asked Alun. That's great, but what I really want, Gwenhwyfar, is grandchildren. The rest is just details.

– Dad! cried Gwen.

As if she were fifteen or, as felt truer, as if a fifteen-year-old lurked within, waiting for the presence, voice, or memory of her parents to release her – the truth being that this was not always unpleasant. Now, for instance, Gwen was happy, though she really did not want to talk about grandchildren here, standing at the corner of Bay and Adelaide.

In any case, the idea of a wedding seemed to have been, at least partly, taken off the table, presto. Gwen felt relief and a slightly annoying disappointment. It would almost have been better if she hadn't asked Tancred for his thoughts. Not that this affected her feelings for him in the least. By the time they got to King Street, a short while later, she felt she could not love him more, whatever his thoughts about weddings. And not being able to help herself, she kissed him as they waited for the lights.

Before the guests arrived, Tancred made sure all was ready for them, as Michael and Professor Bruno sat on the balcony over-looking the lake and sipped champagne (Michael) or carbonated apple juice (Professor Bruno), while Gwen and her father spoke together, away from the others, on the balcony facing the city.

– I didn't mean that about you having children, he said. It's what parents are supposed to say, I guess, but I'd be just as happy if you didn't have kids.

Gwen leaned her head against his chest.

– I know, she said.

– Tancred must be very rich, he said, but he seems down-to-earth. I like him.

– Do you really? she asked.

How strange to want your father's approval for a man you would love regardless. But she did, and she was glad when she got it.

– Yes, I really do like him, he said, and I can't wait until your mother meets him. Why don't you two come visit us with Morgan and Michael this weekend?

She looked at her father now, seeing him at last as one in a long line of men on whom the will of the ring had been enacted: before him Raymond, and after him Tancred. There really were few of her foremothers who'd written of this in Book Three. Their silence made sense, though. Their mothers were the ones with missing fingers or toes, or what have you. Their mothers were the ones who'd kept the ring and the books, whose behaviour guided them, consciously or not. Their mothers, finally, were the ones who understood the strangeness of their burden and helped to carry it.

Then, too: by the time her foremothers had grasped what was going on, by the time they realized their mothers' tales were true, most had likely been in the same situation Gwen found herself: bereft of ring and books, so that it was no longer possible to write in Book Three about fathers, lovers, or anything else.

– That's a great idea, Daddy. I'll ask Tan if he can come with me.

Here, Alun exhaled, as if he'd expected a very different answer.

– Thank god, he said. I was afraid you and she might get in the same kind of argument she got into with Estelle. It was hard taking you to visit your grandmother on my own. I never understood what could be so bad that it'd keep your mother from visiting her own mother. And the thing is, you could see they loved each other. Honestly, they were two very strange women, Gwen. I tried hard to convince your mom to come with us, until she flat out told me to mind my own business. Actually, now that I think about it, they both told me to mind my business. And your grandpa was no help at all. He'd just sit around in his nice clothes and smile. He was a lovely man, Raymond. But I used to wonder if there was something wrong with him.

– Did you ever get ... mad at Mom that she always stayed in Bright's Grove? You'd have had a better career if we'd moved to New York, like you wanted, wouldn't you?

– I used to think so, said Alun. I mean, New York's a great city. I could've worked there any time I wanted. On the other hand, New York was frustrating, too. It always felt like I was just on the verge of really getting somewhere, and then something would happen. I'd get sick or miss a meeting with someone who could've helped me or god knows what. I ended up feeling like the city was bad luck to me. I had a lot of friends there. I still do. But I can't say I'd trade your mother for New York.

As she spoke to her father, leaning against him, Gwen wished that she could go back to Book Three and write about this very moment. Because she now saw clearly that, as with Joseph in the Bible, the many men before her father – nameless, many of them – were deeply implicated in the sacred, their lives affected by a rite that they could not know, could not discover, could not be told. Well, no, not quite. The God of the Bible let Joseph in, whereas the ring was implacable in its demand for silence. All her father would know was his wife's refusal to travel.

(Gwen was reminded of Cratinus, Aphrodite's lover – a creation, an illusion. Weren't all her forefathers the creations of her foremothers, the ring's keepers? So, were she and her fore-mothers versions of Aphrodite, goddesses in love, or were they versions of Polyphemus, makers of men?)

Gwen's love and concern for her father were almost over-whelming.

– What's wrong? he asked.

– Nothing, she said. I'm okay. I'm remembering the wedding. Michael and Professor Bruno seem so happy.

– Are you worried you won't be happy?

– No, Dad. I'm not worried about that. I'm just happy for them.

When Gwen and her father returned to the other apartment, Tancred was helping guests put their coats away and directing them to the balcony where they were greeted by Michael and Professor Bruno.

Gwen apologized for his having to serve alone as host. But he enjoyed it, he said, because it was something he very rarely did, and besides, he was only serving as coat check. The bartender had come and the bar was set up in the living room. Not a mixologist this time, but one of Daniel's sons, Jacob, who'd agreed to mix drinks for a small fee — two hundred dollars, which was all Dan and Fiona would allow Tancred to give him.

Gwen helped to put Michael's and Professor Bruno's friends at ease, introducing herself and Tancred, asking how they knew Professor Bruno or how they knew Michael, and wishing all a good time.

An hour passed: happy, uneventful.

Another hour passed: even happier, because the drinks — gin and tonic, mostly — were strong, and because Nadia and Robbie arrived, having been invited by Michael, and because Nadia's open-mouthed wonder at Gwen and Tancred's home was itself a (guilty) pleasure.

— Jesus! Who do you have to kill to get a place like this? asked Robbie.

A third hour passed: happier still, because pizzas arrived, as ordered by Michael.

A fourth hour, a fifth, a sixth ...

Then, at seven o'clock, a toast was made by Professor Bruno's young friend Alfred, who recounted his adventures in southern Ontario with the professor.

— I'll never forget the time I was bitten by dogs, he said.

A further toast was made by Michael's friend Julietta.

— I wish Michael and Morgan all the happiness they deserve.

Then, just like that, as if it had all been a prolonged mirage, the celebration ended. Michael and Professor Bruno, both exhausted, left for their honeymoon after thanking their friends.

The bar — a low table on which the alcohol and ice had rested — was put away. The other guests, most having work the next day, went happily out into the summer evening, much of the evening still left to them.

— Tancred, said Alun, I'm really grateful for what you've done for Morgan and Michael. Thank you.

Rather than shake his hand, Gwen's father hugged Tancred before going up to the guest bedroom, leaving Gwen and Tancred to tidy up.

And so, night.

Having finished cleaning up and washing dishes — part of the daily grind that gives ground to the sacred — Gwen spoke to her mother. They spoke of nothing in particular, once the details of the wedding were gone over. But even there ... Alun had Skyped her already, had told her of everything, including his relief that she and Gwen had no 'mother-daughter issues,' as he called them, and his genuine liking for Tancred.

Then, in a casual tone, as if telling Gwen about something of no great significance, Helen said

— You know, sweetie, the strangest thing happened today. I was so upset about missing Morgan and Michael's wedding, I went for a walk. I went down to the lakeshore and I walked about five kilometres before I looked up. I didn't recognize where I was, but I'd somehow got to Wellington Beach Marine and I had to ask for directions home.

— That's great, said Gwen. You got a good walk.

— Yes, it *was* a good walk. But Wellington Beach is in Camlachie.

And so, the penny dropped for Gwen, as it had for Helen. Almost as if accusing her mother of something, she said

— But you're not allowed to leave Bright's Grove.

— I know, said Helen.

Gwen, of course, was jubilant. The idea that her mother could visit made her inexpressibly happy.

– Don't tell your father, said Helen. I don't know if this really means anything or if Bright's Grove has just grown in my imagination. I'm going to ask your father to go for a walk tomorrow. I'll close my eyes and see how far we get.

Helen said this, but her tone was distinctly cautious. She did not want to jinx her chance for freedom. Besides, there were two issues here. The first was the will of the ring. How far could she go from Bright's Grove? But the second was just as important: what exactly had thirty years confinement done to her? How long would it take for her to psychologically adapt to freedom?

– We'll go for a walk together, said Gwen. Tan and I are coming tomorrow, too.

– Well then, no matter what happens, said Helen, it'll be a good day. I get to meet my granddaughter's father.

It was clear that Gwen was more excited by the possibility of her mother's 'jailbreak' than her mother, but they said their goodbyes, knowing that, whatever happened, they would be seeing each other soon.

As Gwen brushed her teeth, she wondered what became of miracles as they perished. The Red Sea parted, for a time, and then subsided. The loaves and fishes were eaten, eventually. Lazarus returned to earth when it was his time. But each of those things, if they were true, had left their trace in the hearts and souls of men and women who believed, and in the minds of those who did not.

It came to her then that the conjunction of sacred and profane – there where the sacred ended and the profane began – was, of course, symbolized by the ring she'd recently given up. And as she washed her face, she thought of all the other things the ring united: the divine and the human, the real and the imagined, past and present, men and women ...

She was aware, while washing up, of her missing finger, but something her mother had said came back to her and with it came a measure of consolation: 'there are worse things than to be acquainted with the sacred.' Which suggested, at least, that the price of the acquaintance might be justified.

The bedroom was cool, so she wore one of Tancred's T-shirts – something black that said 'One Punch Man' on it and had a drawing of a bald man in a yellow jumpsuit and red cape.

– What is this? she asked him.

– Something Japanese, he answered. Ollie gave it to me, but it looks better on you.

They cuddled then and kissed, and she said

– You don't mind if we don't make love, do you? I want to get up early tomorrow.

He said no, he didn't mind, and it was in the way he said it that she felt, not for the first time since wishing for Tancred to love her for who she was, that perhaps the cost of her wish was that she was obliged to love him for who *he* was, too. A vaguely troubling thought. She could, if she tried, think up unpleasant scenarios. What if he was a murderer or still a thief?

As she thought this, a dream she'd had came back to her:

... she was walking up the steps at King and Atlantic. She was clearly in Liberty Village. She looked up and saw the words 'Goodlife Fitness' above her. As she looked up, she saw Tancred at the top of the steps, coming down ...

The dream had been disturbing because, for some reason, Tancred had become angry. It should have disturbed her still, but now even this vision of him angry seemed, somehow, endearing.

It occurred to her, as she looked out the window at the squares of light in the office buildings, that there was, perhaps, a danger to her 'May he love me for who I am,' a drawback she hadn't fully considered: to love another's flaws is, at least to some extent, to enable them, isn't it? What incentive was there to deal with one's imperfections, to become better, if one were loved regardless? This thought did not trouble her for long, though, because it was accompanied by its own balm, a counter-thought: to love one who is flawed is not to love the flaw, nor is it to give up the right to point flaws out. It implied, rather, that it was possible for certain kinds of judgment to begin and end with love.

Really, there was no doubt about it. She was obliged to love Tancred for who he was.

She moved her body closer to his, took his hand, and held it on her breast. She drifted then, the city before her, the darkness around her, and, in little time or much time or some time, fell asleep in the arms of a man with whom she was unafraid.

Quincunx 3
Berlin, 2020–21

A Note on the Text

Ring, a novel of Toronto and southern Ontario, was written and edited in Berlin Schöneberg, where the author lived during the pandemic, 2020–21. The novel was influenced by a number of books read before or during its writing:

The Complete Poems of Anna Akhmatova (tr. Judith Hemschemeyer, Zephyr Press, 2000)

Sämtliche Gedichte, Gottfried Benn (Klett-Cotta, 1998)

Hecale, Callimachus (tr. C. A. Trypanis, et al., Harvard University Press, 1973)

Early Greek Philosophy (tr. Daniel Graham, Cambridge University Press, 2010)

Parmenides, Martin Heidegger (tr. Schuwer and Rojcewicz, Indiana University Press, 1998)

Playing by the Greek's Rules, Sarah Morgan (Harlequin, 2015)

Chroniques de l'étrange, Pu Songling (tr. André Lévy, Editions Philippe Picquier, 2005)

Safe Harbour: A Novel, Danielle Steel (Corgi Books, 2003)

The menus in Chapter 1 and Chapter 5 were created for the novel by Ben Spiegel.

The drawings in Chapter 1 and Chapter 5 are by Linda Watson.

The poems in Chapter 1 are by Lisa Robertson (from the book Cinema of the Present) and Roo Borson ('Painted Garden, Part II' from Cardinal in the Eastern White Cedar).

In Chapter 1, the poem by John Skennen is by Lea Crawford.

In Chapter 2, Professor Bruno quotes from Gwendolyn MacEwen's 'Dark Pines Under Water.'

In Chapter 2, the translations from – or, rather, into – ancient Greek are by Ben Akrig.

In Chapter 3, the divine words engraved in the ring are adapted from a song by Christian Bök.

In Chapter 3, the poem 'Ring' was edited by Kim Maltman and Roo Borson.

In Chapter 4, the little finger belongs to Michael Brennan.

In Chapter 5, the lines about Henry Moore's *Archer* are from Dennis Lee's *Civil Elegies*.

Gravenhurst exists, perhaps.

About the Author

André Alexis was born in Trinidad and grew up in Canada. His most recent novel, *Days by Moonlight*, won the Rogers Writers' Trust Fiction Prize. *Fifteen Dogs* won the 2015 Scotiabank Giller Prize, CBC Canada Reads, and the Rogers Writers' Trust Fiction Prize. His other books include *Asylum, Pastoral, The Hidden Keys*, and *The Night Piece: Collected Stories*. He is the recipient of a Windham Campbell Prize.

Typeset in Albertan, Gotham, Futura, and Parfumerie.

Printed at the Coach House on bpNichol Lane in Toronto, Ontario, on Zephyr Antique Laid paper, which was manufactured, acid-free, in Saint-Jérôme, Quebec, from second-growth forests. This book was printed with vegetable-based ink on a 1973 Heidelberg KORD offset litho press. Its pages were folded on a Baumfolder, gathered by hand, bound on a Sulby Auto-Minabinda, and trimmed on a Polar single-knife cutter.

Coach House is on the traditional territory of many nations, including the Mississaugas of the Credit, the Anishnabeg, the Chippewa, the Haudenosaunee, and the Wendat peoples, and is now home to many diverse First Nations, Inuit, and Métis peoples. We acknowledge that Toronto is covered by Treaty 13 with the Mississaugas of the Credit. We are grateful to live and work on this land.

Edited by Alana Wilcox
Cover design by Ingrid Paulson
Interior design by Crystal Sikma

Coach House Books
80 bpNichol Lane
Toronto, ON M5S 3J4
Canada

416 979 2217
800 367 6360

mail@chbooks.com
www.chbooks.com